The game

T

just beginning.

USE ME

K. Knight xo

USA Today bestselling author

Kimberly Knight

COPYRIGHT

USE ME

Print Editions

Published by Knight Publishing & Design, LLC

Cover art © by Okay Creations

Book Formatted by Cristiane Saavedra

*To **Jeremy Roenick**: If by chance you ever read this book, I hope you don't mind your role. You're one of the bests to me and I still remember your 500th goal while you played with one of the best hockey teams. Thank you.*

PROLOGUE

Rhys

Fourteen Years Old

High school sucks.

Actually, being a freshman sucks. My parents had always told me that high school would be the best years of my life, but I didn't know when it would turn into the best years of my life because right now, I hated it.

I stood at my locker, getting my books for fifth period, when I saw *him*. He was walking through the double doors at the end of the hall, and he wasn't alone. He was never alone. I didn't know why people wanted to be his friend. Maybe it was because everyone feared him.

I did.

The jerk was a senior, and all he did was terrorize freshmen. We played varsity hockey together, and in practice he could (*and would*) get away with slamming me against the boards all he wanted. He'd talk shit every day at practice too. It didn't matter who we were or if we'd never done anything to him. He got pleasure from being an asshole to everyone, and I seemed to get the brunt of it, especially after Coach made me starter last game and not him.

I was tired of being pushed around, spit on, tripped. So, every day after practice, I used my dad's weights in the garage hoping I could bulk up and kick *his* ass. All I wanted was for him to leave me alone so

I could laugh with my friends in the halls and on campus. Be a normal high school student. I didn't want to have to run in fear because some jackass thought using me as a punching bag was an extracurricular activity.

And sadly, we still had months until he graduated.

I stuffed my books into my backpack that I needed for the rest of the school day and for homework, hoping to make my escape before *he* saw me. Just as I exited the doors on the opposite side of the hall, I heard *him.*

"Hey, faggot!"

I didn't stop.

"Cole!" he shouted behind me. "Aww, the baby is running home to his mommy."

The group of boys he was with laughed behind me, but I didn't turn around or stop. Maybe if he thought I didn't hear him, he'd leave me alone.

I heard footsteps running in the snow, and before I realized it, my backpack crashed to the ground. I spun around to pick it up, trying not to look at him, but anger got the best of me. I glared. At that moment, I was finally going to stand up to the asshole. I didn't care if he and his friends kicked my ass. I was done. But before I could utter a word, I stopped.

He was holding a knife.

I looked down at my backpack on the ground and noticed the straps had been cut. *That was how the bag fell off my shoulders.* As I started to stand, he pushed me and I fell on the ground. The snow I was sitting on started to soak through my jeans.

He kicked snow at my face. "You think you're some big, badass hockey player that can come to my school and take my position, faggot? You ain't shit. You better hope I don't see you off campus because you won't be able to walk once I'm done kicking your ass. Watch your back. I'm getting my start back one way or another." He kicked snow at me one final time before he and his minions walked away.

The laughing continued as the group of boys walked through the door I had tried to escape through. I couldn't wait to get home. I was going to lift double the amount of weights so I could bulk up faster. He'd regret bullying me one day.

One day when I kicked his fucking ass.

CHAPTER ONE

Ashtyn

Present Day

"I'm Ashtyn Valor. Thank you for watching. Have a good night, Chicago."

I gave a slight nod as I smiled warmly and drew a heart on the paper next to me as though I had something important to write while I waited for the signal that we were no longer broadcasting.

"And we're clear." People started to move as the live broadcast ended.

My news studio was a little different from your standard local news station. Typically, newsrooms had the same anchors report the five, six and ten o'clock news, but we only had a five o'clock and a ten o'clock broadcast, and each time slot had a different anchor.

After I received my master's degree in journalism, I'd worked my way up until I was the one who reported the news each night. Ideally, I wanted to report the evening news and have the five o'clock slot, but for the last two years I'd worked the nightly news at ten. It gave me enough time to get housework and errands done before I had to report in at four in the afternoons, and it also worked well with my boyfriend's schedule. Corey was an Air Traffic Controller at O'Hare and worked the night shift, though I worked Monday through Friday and his schedule changed all the time. It didn't matter. We made it work.

"See you tomorrow," I said to Mitch, my fellow co-anchor, as I removed my mic.

"Have a good night," Mitch replied. I stood and started to leave the room.

"Your weekly flowers arrived." Abby, the closest friend I had at the station, grinned as we passed each other. We were the complete opposite in the looks department but had the same personality. I had blonde hair, she was a brunette. I had green eyes, she had brown. I was also four inches taller than she was.

"If only they were from my actual boyfriend," I muttered and continued to walk toward my desk. I'd been getting these flowers from a secret admirer for at least a year now. I loved getting them because it brightened up my workspace. I just wished they were from my boyfriend of ten months.

The red roses came into view as I got closer to my desk. Each time they had a note with them from a secret admirer. The first one had read:

Dear Ms. Valor,
You looked beautiful tonight.
-SA

The notes had slowly progressed:

Dear Ashtyn,
You're the most beautiful woman in the world.
-SA

And the one last week was borderline creepy:

Dear Ashtyn,
You're the one I'm thinking about when someone asks me what's on my mind.
-SA

I pulled out the small card that was sticking out of tonight's bouquet.

> Dear Ashtyn,
> Do you think about me as much as I think about you?
> - SA

I assumed SA stood for secret admirer. *Made sense to me.* I took this week's card, threw it in the trash, and then grabbed my purse and left to go home.

A few days later, Corey was finally going to meet my best friend, Jaime.

Jaime and I had been friends since high school, and given our crazy lives, we'd rarely seen each other since I started dating Corey. It was hard to get together because I worked late nights and spent my weekends with Corey when he wasn't working. But tonight, we were *finally* having a double date.

The weather was starting to get a little chilly at night, so I dressed in jeans, a black and pink floral halter blouse, and heels. My long blonde hair was pulled up into a high ponytail, and I put on dangly silver earrings and a necklace set.

I stepped out of my room, ready to go, and saw Corey sitting on my couch watching TV. "Ready?"

He sighed and grabbed the remote, turning off the television. "I guess."

I stopped walking toward the door. "You don't want to go?"

"I just don't see why we need to have dinner with your friends."

I balked, staring into his hazel eyes. "What do you mean?"

"I'm happy with it just being us."

"I haven't seen my friend in months."

"That's why I agreed to go in the first place." He smoothed back his blond hair and grabbed his black jacket, shrugging it on.

"What's wrong with my friends?" Every time I suggested we do something with my friends, he conveniently had to work.

"Nothing is wrong with them. I just don't understand why you want to hang out with them."

"You're kidding, right?"

"Why would I be kidding?" He yanked the door open. "I'd just rather stay home and watch the game."

During baseball season, it was hard to get Corey away from the TV because the Cubs weren't all that bad nowadays. I thought that would end when the season was over, but then hockey started. Hockey seemed to be a whole new level of addiction for him. Granted, we lived in Chicago and hockey was huge in this town, but Corey never missed a game.

I didn't have a problem with sports. In fact, I had to know the basics for work. What I had a problem with was that it was Corey's priority and I wasn't. On Saturdays when the Cubs had day games, Corey would take me out to dinner. Those were the times I longed for. Now he was being a jerk about meeting my friends for dinner.

"Fine. Forget it." I turned on my heel and started to walk back to my bedroom to change. I was a few steps away when he spoke.

"No, wait. I'm sorry. I'll go. Are you wearing that though?"

What. The. Hell? I slowly turned around to face him. "Yes."

"Don't you think it shows too much skin?"

My brows furrowed. "I'm wearing jeans."

"I mean your shoulders."

"Are you kidding me?"

"I just don't want people staring at what's mine."

I laughed sarcastically. "They're shoulders!"

Corey's face started to redden, and then he took a deep breath. "Fine, but grab a jacket."

"Whatever," I hissed as I grabbed my leather jacket. I was already planning on it anyway since the weather was crisp.

We didn't speak as he drove us to the restaurant. I'd never heard of someone not wanting to get to know their significant other's friends. Maybe after they'd met them and didn't get along, but not beforehand. However, when we strolled into the restaurant, I put a smile on my face. As soon as I saw Jaime, we rushed to each other and hugged.

"How are you?" I pulled back and looked at her slim body. "You look amazing!"

"Thank you." Jaime beamed, her hazel eyes glistening from the white decorative lights that hung around the trim of the room. She brushed her blonde hair behind her shoulder. "You too."

I turned to her husband. He had short, black hair and crystal blue eyes that looked almost exotic. Jaime did *good* scoring him. I gave him a hug. "It's good to see you, Chase."

"You too, Ashtyn," he said.

"Corey, this is my best friend, Jaime, and her husband, Chase. Guys, this is Corey."

All three shook hands with each other. We waited a few more minutes to be sat at a table. Corey and Chase talked about sports while Jaime and I caught up about anything and everything. The food was delicious and everything was going okay until the bill came.

"Since it was Ashtyn's idea to have a date night, it's only fitting she pays, right?" Corey laughed.

I glared at him, but then quickly smiled and agreed so I didn't cause a stink. Chase tried to offer to pay, but I waved him off. Corey was right. It *was* my idea, and I was okay with paying because I made enough to not have to depend on a man.

"I'm Ashtyn Valor. Thank you for watching. Have a good night, Chicago."

Another week was in the books at work, and another flower delivery arrived on Monday.

Ashtyn,
When you smile, it lights up my TV.
-SA

When I arrived home that Friday, I was surprised to find Corey there. We didn't live together, and tonight I thought he had to work, so I wasn't expecting him for a few more hours.

"Hey," I greeted, throwing my keys in the dish on the table by the front door.

"Hey," he replied back, not moving from where he sat on the couch.

"I thought you had to work tonight?" I asked, kicking off my heels.

He rubbed the back of his neck and sat up. "We need to talk."

My stomach dropped. The dreaded four words that should never form a sentence. I didn't move as I stared at him waiting for him to continue.

"Fuck," he sighed. "This is hard, and I don't want you to freak out."

I still didn't move. I couldn't move. My heart had started to beat uncontrollably, and I was thinking the worst. Did he get fired? Did he want to break-up? Did he cheat on me? Was he sick? The questions swarmed around, but I couldn't get them out of my mouth as my feet stayed planted across the room from him.

"Sit down." Corey patted the cushion next to him.

I shook my head. "Just tell me."

He took another deep breath and turned his head away from me, looking out the fifteenth-story window of my condo. "I've been thinking about this a lot lately. It's time."

"Time for what?" I wasn't sure why I asked the question. My gut was telling me the answer already.

"Can you sit down, please?"

I crossed my arms over my chest. "Can you just spit it out?"

Corey groaned. "I saw your Pinterest board. You left it open the other day."

I blinked, not understanding why Pinterest had anything to do with this. "And?"

"We want different things." He shrugged.

"Different things? Like I want to make homemade biscuits with almond flour, and you want to make them with all-purpose flour?" I asked sarcastically.

He blinked. "What?"

"I don't understand how my recipe board or my do-it-yourself Board have anything to do with wanting different things in life."

"That's not what I saw."

"What did you see then?"

"You had a folder or whatever about our imaginary wedding."

My heart stopped. I couldn't believe this was happening. Every single woman who wanted to get married had a wedding board. Granted mine was a secret, and I wasn't engaged, but I had pinned stuff here and there. I wasn't necessarily planning my wedding with Corey. I was just pinning ideas for when the time came. I never expected Corey to see it.

"I'm confused," I finally admitted.

"Are you going to make me spell it out?"

"Why is having a wedding board an issue?" We never spoke about getting married. I'd just assumed we were headed down that path since we'd been together for almost eleven months.

"It's an issue because I don't want to get married."

My chest clenched. "To me?"

"Ever," he stated matter-of-factly.

"So you want to break up?" I whispered.

Corey stood and took a step toward me. I stepped back, and he sighed. "Ash, I don't want to hurt you, but I think that's best. We've had a good thing going for a few months, but we want different things with our futures."

"I thought you loved me." A tear slid down my cheek.

"It was nice while it lasted." He took another step, not confirming he *once* told me he did.

I took another step back. "While it lasted?"

He grinned. "You think you're the only one I'm seeing?"

"What?" I shrieked.

"There are others, Ashtyn."

"You told me you loved me."

"I told you what you wanted to hear."

More tears spilled from my eyes. "This isn't a game."

"Isn't it though?"

"You're thirty-seven. Wasn't fucking around what your twenties were for?"

"We can go round and round about this. I'm sorry, but I'm moving on."

"Get out!" I yelled and went to the door. I swung it open. "Get. Out!"

He grinned at me as he walked to the door. "I'll call you tomorrow so I can come get my things."

"You'll be lucky if I don't burn them," I hissed.

"Not your style, baby."

"Who are you right now?" This wasn't the guy I'd been dating for the past several months. It was as though I'd been dating a psychopath.

He stopped and turned back around as I stood in the door frame of my condo. "Don't you get it? I faked everything with you because you're hot."

And then he left.

I watched as the door clicked and then I crumpled to the wood floor, more tears sliding down my face as my heart broke in my chest. How was this happening? Why was this happening? A part of me felt as though it was my fault. I'd waited so long to try and settle down. My twenties were for me and my career, and I'd hoped my thirties were for me to start a family.

I was wrong.

Given that it was close to midnight, I crawled in the shower and cried some more. My tears mixed with the soap and water as they all went down the drain and out of my life.

Just like Corey.

After my self-loathing, I threw on my pajamas and cried myself to sleep.

When I woke the next morning, my green eyes were puffy, red, and swollen from all the salty tears and heartache I'd endured the night before. I still couldn't believe that Corey had broken up with me, or that he'd told me he was just using me because I was good looking.

I fucking hated him.

While my coffee dripped into my mug, I went to the front door and grabbed the morning paper. Even though today was Saturday and I wasn't working, I still had to keep up with everything going on in the world. I had to live and breathe news. As I glanced at the front page, a part of me expected to see a headline that read:

Breaking News: Ashtyn Valor and Corey Pritchett have called it quits.

But, of course, breakups didn't make the morning news unless you were famous and I wasn't. Except in Chicago, I guess, but I was just a local news anchor. In fact, I never spoke much about my dating life in public. I even went to last year's Chicago/Midwest Emmy Awards alone because he had to work. Or at least that was what he'd told me. Now after everything he said to me, he was probably with another woman.

After my second cup of coffee, my phone buzzed with a text from Corey:

Corey: I was called in to cover for someone this morning. I'll come over around eight to get my things.

I didn't text him back.

Instead, I changed into workout clothes, went down to the gym in my building, and ran for thirty minutes straight trying to run my anger out.

At 7:48 that evening, I was showered, dressed in my nicest pair of jeans that Corey always said my ass looked great in, and a black sweater that hung off my shoulder. I wanted him to think I was okay when, in reality, I wasn't sure if I ever would be. I loved Corey …

Or at least I thought I had.

Could I fall out of love that quickly? It was easier to think so given how angry I was, but at the same time, my heart still hurt.

At 7:55, I went in search of wine. I thought that maybe Corey had drunk the rest at some point, but sitting on my counter was half a bottle. I took out a glass and poured myself a full glass of the burgundy liquid.

At 7:58, I finished the glass and poured myself the remaining wine, this time sipping it as I browsed the internet, staying current with the world news.

At 8:09, there was a knock at my door. Corey still had a key, and I expected him to come in on his own like he always had. I needed to remember to get it from him.

I walked to the door, the wine making me dizzy for a split second, and opened the door to see his handsome face. I mean, his douche of a face. I needed to keep telling myself that he was an asshole. God, I loved his face though. I loved the way his short beard would tickle me between my legs. How I would tug on his blonde hair, moaning as I came. And how his hazel eyes would sparkle in the morning light when he smiled his dimpled smile every Saturday morning.

No! You stop that right now, Ashtyn! I scolded myself inwardly.

"Hi," he greeted as though nothing had happened the night before.

"Hi?" I narrowed my eyes. "You think I'm happy to see you?"

"I texted you."

"I don't give a fuck."

"Let me get my things, and I'll be on my way."

"Give me my key first."

He dug into his pocket and pulled his keys out. After he took one off the ring, he handed it to me. I tested it in the lock to make sure it was the correct key, and then I reached down and picked up the box I had packed for him. I shoved it into his chest. "Here you go. Goodbye."

I started to shut the door, but he stopped me. "One last fuck for the road?"

A snort escaped my chest. "Yeah, I'll give you one last fuck." I swung my leg back and then forward, hitting him square in the balls. "Fuck you!"

His eyes widened before he dropped the box of his belongings. Some of the contents fell out, so I shoved them out of the way and finally slammed the door. I don't know how long he groaned outside my door, but at 8:34 I left to go to the liquor store for more wine.

The air seeped into the denim of my jeans. I definitely needed more wine. Enough to numb the pain and the cold. It was late October and at least in the low fifties. And as luck would have it, it was raining. I had no idea the sky had mimicked my crying heart as if it too were heartbroken. It was only fitting that I had left my umbrella in my condo. I was too upset and hurt to care, so I started to walk down the city street in search of the closest liquor store. I walked along the buildings trying to stay under the eaves and out of the rain until I came upon a bar that was a few blocks away from my condo. Since the bar was closer than the liquor store, I changed my mind and decided to go there instead.

What I didn't know was that decision was going to change my life.

CHAPTER Two

Rhys

I stared as Bridgette moaned, her hips rocking and her dark brown hair cascading down her back. She had a nice back. Hell, she had a nice ass.

I was going to miss that ass.

She moaned again, her back arching as some dude's dick thrust up into her. It wasn't my cock, and I wasn't the one making her moan. Nope, some guy was in *my* bed, fucking *my* girlfriend as I stood in the doorway of *my* bedroom. Whenever I'd seen this scenario play out on TV or in movies, there was a thought in my head that told me I'd go nuclear and murder the dude if it ever happened to me. However, as I stared at the live porn in front of me, I wasn't mad or angry. I was—amused.

Should I clap when they finish?

Should I whistle?

Should I pay them for the show?

I should do all three.

Before I could do anything—like stop watching—Bridgette screamed. A scream I knew so well. A scream that meant she'd come. The guy thrust some more and then grunted his release.

I started to clap. "And Female Performer of the Year goes to … Bridgette Walters."

She turned around, scrambling off the rod that was lodged inside her, bringing the sheet up to cover herself. Covering a body that I'd seen naked every day for the past two years. "Rhys," she gasped. "You're home early."

Yes, I was home early. The game I was covering was canceled due to the ice not being suitable for playing conditions. It was a rare situation. We didn't have all the details, but it had to do with a concert that was held the night before. In my time, I'd only heard of it happening once, and that was a pre-season game in Arizona. After my crew and I went live and told the public that the game would be rescheduled between the Chicago Blackhawks and San Jose Sharks, I went home.

I chuckled and looked over at the dude as he covered his junk with *my* pillow. "Should I nominate you for Male Performer of the Year?"

"What are you talking about?" Bridgette asked.

"I mean I've never seen live porn before," I chuckled and waved my index finger between the two of them, "but that performance was pretty good. I'm sure you two could win something at the porn awards in Vegas."

"Porn awards?" she snorted.

"I should go," the dude said.

"Nah, man. Stay. Eat my food. Use my shower. Hell, you want to take some of my money 'cause you've already taken my girlfriend in *my* bed?" I was bitter. Maybe I wasn't fully amused at the situation.

He stared at me, not responding. Did that mean he knew Bridgette had a boyfriend? Did he know this was my condo? Ah, who the fuck cared? She wasn't my girlfriend any longer.

I turned to leave but then turned back around to say my final goodbye to Bridgette. "Get your shit and get the fuck out. If you're here when I get back, I'm calling the cops."

I grabbed my keys from the dining room table where I'd thrown them just moments ago. I'd been a sports anchor and reporter for a local network for eight years. My job was to cover the Blackhawks, and I loved it. Sports were my life growing up, and since I didn't get a chance to play in the National Hockey League because I was never drafted, I decided I wanted to talk sports for a living. I obtained my journalism degree and made it my passion, my *life.* My job was to do pre and postgame shows as well as intermission coverage. It was early in the season, and while I typically wouldn't be home until the wee hours of the morning, tonight I decided to take my work home and study the stats. However, that wasn't what I'd checked off on my to-do list.

Find out my girlfriend is a cheating whore – Check.

Realize my mother was right when she told me I needed to keep an extra set of sheets in the hall closet – Check, though I didn't think she'd meant for this specific reason.

Decide to drink my dinner tonight – Double check.

I walked out of my condo, choosing to forget about work and whores, and walked a few blocks in the rain until I came upon a bar I frequented a few times a week. Bridgette would usually come with me, and we'd party with each of our friends, dance a little by our table if the mood felt right, and drink beers until closing, but tonight would be different.

Tonight I needed more than beer.

I walked into the dry bar, my body instantly warming, and walked straight to the wood bar top. It was slightly early for a Saturday night, so I was able to get a seat at the bar. A seat I wasn't going to leave until last call.

The bartender caught my eye and walked over to me. "Your usual?"

I smiled. "Not tonight, Tommy. Tonight I need something strong. Let me get a seven and seven on the rocks."

Tommy nodded slightly then turned to make my drink as I got my phone out of my pocket and started to delete all the pictures of Bridgette and me. *Fuck that bitch.* After deleting a few, the bartender slid my drink in front of me and I handed him my credit card. "Keep it open."

He bobbed his head again and then left to help other customers. I returned to my phone deleting picture after picture between sips of my whiskey drink. Then out of nowhere, a hand grasped my arm, startling me.

"This is my boyfriend, sorry."

I looked up from the hand touching me, and into the green eyes of a woman I recognized: Ashtyn Valor from one of Chicago's nightly news stations. You couldn't live in Chicago and have a dick and not know who Ashtyn Valor was. I was certain people watched her nightly news broadcast just to see her in her tight dresses. She was gorgeous. And she was touching me.

Did she say I was her boyfriend?

Her smoky green eyes widened, begging me to play along. "Yeah," I agreed as I stood and draped my arm over her slender shoulder.

The mystery man blinked and stared at my arm for a few moments and then back to Ashtyn. "You're dating Rhys Cole?" He asked the question as though he couldn't believe that two news people would be dating. "Really?"

Ashtyn looked up at me and smiled. "Really."

I grinned down at her. "It's been what …?" I trailed off trying to think of a timeframe that would be believable given we weren't dating and had never been in the public eye together before. Granted who really cared about the love life of the local news people? I didn't. Though, as I stared down into her dark green eyes with exotic black flecks, I instantly cared who she was really dating. Maybe she was married? But if she were, she could have just flashed her ring to this dude. However, we were acting as though we were a couple so that meant she wasn't. *Right?*

Ashtyn answered for me. "Four months tomorrow."

"Right," I agreed, my smile widening at just the thought. *Bridgette who?*

Ashtyn and I both turned our heads to look back at the dude with short, light-brown hair, though I noticed Ashtyn didn't want to make eye contact with him. "My mistake."

He left, and Ashtyn's body instantly relaxed under my arm that was still around her. "Thank you," she breathed.

I sat back down on the barstool, turning my body to face her. "Dudes hit on you often?" I mean, I assumed they did. Look at her. Straight blonde hair, stunning green eyes, slim shoulders that I was certain led to a flat belly. Her breasts were just big enough for my hand to cup and I wasn't too sure about her ass, but the way the denim was hugging her thighs made me hard. If I were single—wait, I *was* single—I could hit on her, and I wouldn't mind getting to know Ashtyn Valor.

"No." She gave a tight smile. "I'm not usually alone in a bar on a Saturday night. Or any night for that matter."

"Neither am I." I laughed. "What's the special occasion?"

She reached for her wine glass and finished it off. "Broke up with the real boyfriend."

"Ouch." I grabbed my chest as though I'd been wounded. "I'm not sure I like that you're insinuating I'm your fake boyfriend."

Ashtyn laughed. "Well … I mean …"

I smiled. "I know. You just want to use me."

She grinned. "Sorry about that, but thank you. I wasn't ready to talk to some random guy."

"Like me," I deadpanned.

"Luckily I know who you are."

I nodded. "Just like I know who you are too."

"The price we pay for being on TV."

"We're famous in these parts," I joked.

"If you say so."

We both laughed. "Let me buy you another drink. At least to keep up my front as your boyfriend."

Ashtyn turned to look at her empty glass. "Sure. One more."

I raised my arm and motioned for the bartender. As Tommy poured her drink, I said to Ashtyn, "If it makes you feel any better, I just broke up with my girlfriend too."

"I'm sorry," she replied and reached for her glass.

I took a sip of my whiskey drink. "Did you walk in on him cheating on you too?"

Ashtyn choked on the dark red liquid. "What? You walked in on your girlfriend screwing another guy?"

I nodded and took another sip of my drink, finishing it off. "In *my* fucking bed."

Her eyes widened. "Wow."

"I know." I flagged Tommy again. I was the one who needed another round this time. "I'll be sleeping on the couch tonight until I can buy new sheets tomorrow."

"You don't have a spare set?"

"I'm a guy. I only need one set."

"Clearly you need two."

I laughed and nudged her shoulder with my hand. "Okay, Mom. You were right."

Ashtyn let out a loud laugh. "She sounds smart."

"I'll make sure to tell her that Ashtyn Valor thinks she's smart. She'll die."

"Oh please. You're just as *famous* as me. She won't care."

"You have to have more Emmys than I do." There were various Emmys to be won for Ashtyn: Outstanding Coverage of a Breaking News Story, Outstanding Continuing Coverage of a News Story, Outstanding Feature Story, Outstanding Investigative Journalism, and Outstanding Business and Economic Reporting.

"We're going to compare them?"

"Only one way to find out who's better."

She chuckled. "I have five."

I smiled. "So do I."

Her grin widened. "Then we're in the same boat."

We took a few more sips of our drinks and then I asked, "You want to talk about it?"

She scrunched her eyebrows. "You want to talk about why I was dumped?"

"Honestly, I'm curious as to why some fuck nut would ever do such a thing. You're fucking gorgeous."

Pink tinted her cheeks as she swirled her finger around the lip of her glass. "I think the wine is getting to my head because I could have sworn you were just hitting on me."

I took a swallow of my drink. "What if I was?"

"Are you?"

I shrugged. "We're both single, Ashtyn."

"Newly single," she clarified. "I'm not looking for another *real* boyfriend."

I smiled. "And I'm not looking for another *real* girlfriend."

"How long were you with her?"

I sighed. I wasn't necessarily heartbroken, but shit happens. "Two years."

"And you want to jump into," she waved her handed between us, "whatever this might be."

"Let's be real here. It's different for girls than it is guys. We don't think with the same head."

"But I'm a girl, and I can't just place a Band-Aid over my heart."

I took another sip. "Why not? To get over someone you need to get under someone else, or whatever the saying is."

"I'm not drunk enough for this conversation." She laughed.

I smirked. "We can fix that." I raised my arm again to flag over Tommy. "Two shots of Fireball."

Ashtyn snorted. "Wow."

"Look, Ashtyn. I'm just messing around with you, but if you did want to go back to your place, I'd be all for it."

She stared at me for a beat. "I can't."

"You can't or you won't?"

Ashtyn sighed. "Both."

"Okay, well," I slid her a shot glass of the cinnamon whiskey, "here's to new friends." We clinked the glasses together and then downed the fiery goodness.

We fell into a brief silence before she spoke again. "We were together a little less than a year."

I nodded. "Sucks, huh?"

She sighed. "Yeah, but can I ask you something?"

"Of course."

"Do you want to get married?"

"To you?" I laughed.

"No, in general."

The answer was on the tip of my tongue, but there was something deep inside me that wanted to elaborate. It was a crazy feeling. I didn't know much of anything about Ashtyn except for what she did for a living. I knew she was at the Emmy Awards for the past few years, but our paths had never crossed. Now we were both nursing our heartaches with booze and apparently talking about marriage.

"Yes," I simply answered.

"My ex didn't. Actually, that's what he had started to say when he was breaking up with me, but then he let me know I wasn't the only one he was seeing." Her cell phone buzzed against the wood top and we both stared at her phone. It was lying face down, so she couldn't tell who had texted her.

"His ears are burning," I said, assuming it was her ex.

Ashtyn looked up to meet my gaze. "Should I read it?"

I thought for a moment. "Why did you come to this fine establishment?" I waved my arm behind me to indicate the dimly lit, brick-walled bar.

"To forget."

"Me too," I agreed. "So put your phone away and help me forget."

Her lips slowly spread into a grin. "I have a better idea."

"Oh?"

She grabbed the phone off the bar, pulled up the camera mode, flipped the view to take a selfie and said, "Lean over."

I did without hesitation, a huge grin on my face. Just before Ashtyn was about to snap the picture, I leaned in farther and placed a kiss on her bare shoulder where her sweater had slipped down. Just as my lips met her soft skin, I heard the click of the shutter. She didn't say anything as she slowly turned her head to look at me.

"Sorry. Take another."

I wasn't sorry. In fact, I'd do it again, but instead, we posed for the picture, both with huge smiles, and then the shutter clicked again. I watched as Ashtyn clicked the Facebook app on her phone to post the picture. "Oh, let me friend you." I grabbed my phone, searched her name on Facebook, and sent the request.

"I think the asshole's still my friend."

"And the bitch is still mine, so make sure you tag me." I smirked.

"That's the plan."

After she posted the picture, I held my finger down on the image on Facebook and saved it to my camera roll. I wanted to ask her to send me the other, but I didn't. Instead, I asked, "Want another drink?"

"I better not or I'll be over the edge and slurring my words."

"You haven't forgotten," I pointed out.

She stared into my eyes. "Then help me forget."

CHAPTER THREE

Ashtyn

I was trying to play it cool.

I was a thirty-three-year-old adult who'd just had her heart broken, and now I was talking to one of the most breathtaking men I'd ever laid eyes on. Granted if I'd known this was going to happen, I wouldn't have drunk half a bottle of wine at my house. The wine and cinnamon whiskey were helping me forget, but I was on the breaking point. If I stood, I might not be able to walk straight. I could picture the headline now:

Breaking News: Ashtyn Valor got naked wasted with Rhys Cole last night.

Even though I'd just posted the picture of us on Facebook, I wasn't ready for the entire world to know that we were fake boyfriend and girlfriend. I just wanted one person to know. I wanted Corey to see the picture and regret ever breaking my heart.

Rhys didn't seem heartbroken about his breakup, and he *was* trying to get naked wasted with me. Friends with benefits? I'd heard once that there was no such thing as friends with benefits because there would always be one person who wanted more. I didn't want more. I'd just broken up with Corey, and I never thought in a million years that I would have met a new guy tonight, but I wanted to get naked wasted with him. I mean, what woman with a pulse wouldn't?

Rhys had a jock vibe about him. His finger-length dark brown hair was enticing me to run my fingers through it, and the way his electric blue eyes were staring into my green ones, made me want to open up and tell him all my secrets. And when he would smile his crooked smile that made his dimples show, I wanted to crawl into his lap and touch his smooth face as I kissed him senseless.

"You haven't forgotten," he said.

I, in fact, hadn't forgotten Corey. I knew I wouldn't in just a few hours, but as I stared into Rhys blue eyes, the words slipped from my mouth. "Then help me forget."

He smirked, leaned forward, and before I realized it, his lips were attached to mine. I could taste the whiskey as his tongue parted my lips. I didn't hesitate. I couldn't. Kissing Corey had turned into sweet little hello or goodbye kisses. No tongue unless we were having sex and then it didn't last because we'd get straight to the point. But the way Rhys was kissing me was completely different. It wasn't innocent. It was hot, passionate and fiery. Just like the Fireball whiskey we'd consumed not too long ago. The whiskey had warmed my insides, and so was the way Rhys was using his tongue to help me forget. His hand cupped the back of my nape, and I wanted to thread my hands through his dark brown hair, but I resisted. We were in public, and both locally in the limelight.

"Well?" he asked after I pulled back.

"I'm getting there."

Then as though we hadn't kissed, Rhys changed the subject, and we talked about work. He told me how his game was canceled tonight for a fluke ice issue, and I told him about the nightly news, my goals, and everything that my buzzed mouth wanted to spill. Being in my line of work, I had to stay up on everything, so when Rhys talked about the current season for the Blackhawks and how he thought they'd fair, I was able to follow along, especially since my dad and brothers were hardcore fans and Corey never missed a game.

"Bridgette hated sports."

I blinked at his confession. "Don't get me wrong, but how can a guy who has a career in the sports industry date a woman that hates sports?"

He shrugged. "The sex was great."

I chuckled. "Apparently you weren't giving it to her enough."

He tsked. "Bustin' my balls already, Ashtyn? That's a low blow."

"Not sure I have room to talk. My ex is probably already screwing one of his other women."

"You're probably right."

Rhys's words stung. I'd have to be blacked out drunk for them not to hurt or for me to forget. "Who's your favorite player?" I asked, changing the subject.

"In general or that play for the Hawks?"

"Both?"

He grinned as though he was a kid about to talk about his hero. "Well, my all-time favorite has to be Gretzky. There's no kid who grew up in the eighties and nineties, who loved hockey, and didn't think they were going to be just like Wayne."

"My dad and brothers talked about him all the time when I was a kid."

"Yeah, he was one of the greats."

"And who's your favorite all-time Blackhawk?"

"Well, when I was about ten-years-old, I thought I was going to turn pro. That was my dream because I'd been playing since I was five, and at ten I thought I was hot shit. Gretzky was in his prime, but I didn't get to watch him play every game because he was never a Hawk and back then we only got to watch local sports. But the one guy who stuck out to me that year was Jeremy Roenick. He helped the Blackhawks reach the Stanley Cup Finals that season and scored over a hundred points in three of his eight seasons. I also liked him because he was rough and strong and fought his way past his opponents to drive the net. I wanted to be just like him."

"Did you play in the NHL?"

"Nope." He shook his head. "I was never drafted. I used to be pissed because that was my dream, but now I don't get beat up for a living."

"They do fight a lot, huh?" I chuckled. I knew fighting was technically okay in hockey, I'd just never seen one before. But Rhys was making me want to watch a game.

"Yeah, they do."

"Have you ever met this Roenick guy?"

Rhys frowned a little. "Nah. He was traded way before I decided to become a sportscaster."

"He has to play for visiting teams though, right?"

"He retired back in '09, and I never got the chance."

"Last call," the bartender said to Rhys.

Rhys turned to me. "Want one more?"

I smiled. "I'm good. I should head home." I hadn't realized how late it was. Now, all of a sudden, it was two in the morning.

"I'll walk you."

"Thanks."

Rhys paid the tab, including my first glass of wine, while I shrugged on my leather jacket. After he put his coat on, we stepped out into the fall air. It had stopped raining.

"Sucks your game was canceled tonight."

"Yeah, but if it hadn't been," he said as we began to walk in the direction of my condo, "I wouldn't have walked in on my cheating girlfriend, and I wouldn't have met you."

I could feel the heat hit my cheeks. "This is true, but I wish we would have met under different circumstances."

"I don't," he stated. "Then I wouldn't have gotten to be your fake boyfriend for a few hours."

I laughed. "Thank you again for that."

"Anytime, Cupcake."

"Cupcake?" I laughed.

"Yeah."

"Why cupcake?"

"Because I want to lick and eat you." I tripped over the imaginary bump in the sidewalk, stumbling slightly in my heels. "You okay there?"

"First time walking in heels," I joked. Then I looked up and realized we were at my building. "This is me."

Rhys looked at the building and then across the street before looking back at me. "No shit?"

"Yeah." I nodded.

"I live in that building." He pointed to the one across the street.

"Really?"

"Crazy, huh?"

"Yeah. Maybe I'll see you around sometime then?"

He stepped forward, and as his hands went to cup my face, he whispered, "I'd like that." Then his lips were on mine, and instantly my body heated. His tongue was again demanding, and hell if I didn't want to invite him in for *coffee* that would lead to sex.

I couldn't.

That wasn't me.

But I *could* kiss him. And he was a *good* kisser.

I wanted to kiss him until the sun rose. Then that thought led to me thinking about him licking me like I was icing on a cupcake, and that just made my panties dampen between my legs.

"Give me your phone," Rhys said when we pulled apart. I reached into my purse and then handed it to him. He hit the screen a few times. "Use me sometime."

"Use you?"

"Whenever you need to forget him, call me. You can use me anytime."

I looked at the screen when he handed it back, realizing he'd programed his number. "Thank you again for everything and also for trying to help me forget."

"Anytime, Cupcake. You're going to make some guy really happy one day."

He kissed me one last time before walking across the street.

The following morning—or should I say, afternoon—I woke up to notice my phone had blown up with a ton of notifications on Facebook and a text from Jaime:

Saw the picture of you and Rhys Cole. Does Corey know you were out with another guy last night?

I didn't have the energy to text her back, so I opened up Facebook and read all of the comments people were saying on the photo I'd posted the night before of Rhys and me. When I got to his, I smiled as I read it:

Use me anytime ;)

There was reply after reply from my confused friends, all of them questioning how I'd "used" him. There wasn't, however, anything from Corey. I hadn't expected him to comment, but that also meant I wouldn't know if he saw the picture or not. I decided right then and there that I was going to unfriend him, not caring anymore if he'd seen the picture.

Fuck it.

Instead of texting Jaime back, I sent one to Rhys before crawling out of bed:

If sportscasting doesn't work out for you, you'd make great money as being a fake boyfriend. Thank you for letting me use you.

I didn't tell him who it was because I thought my message would do that for me. Then I typed in Corey's name and unfriended his ass followed by deleting every picture we'd ever taken with each other.

After using the bathroom, my phone buzzed:

Rhys: I only want to be your fake boyfriend though.

I smiled as I walked to my door to get the Sunday paper and typed a reply:

I can live with that.

Rhys: Use me anytime, Cupcake :P

I laughed, making my way to get a cup of coffee as I read his last message. Again, the thought of Rhys licking me like I was icing on a cupcake made my belly dip, but I needed some time so that my heart could heal before I moved on to the next guy.

Fake or not.

After my first cup of coffee I texted Jaime back:

Corey and I broke up. I'm sure he doesn't care I was with Rhys.

I just hoped he did.

My phone started to ring, and Jaime's name flashed on the screen. I rolled my eyes and took a deep breath before answering. I didn't feel like explaining the last twenty-four hours, but she was my best friend, and I knew it was only a matter of time.

"Hello?"

"What do you mean Corey broke up with you?"

I groaned and told her what had happened except the part where he stated he was cheating the entire time.

"I'm sorry about you and Corey, but I kinda saw this coming."

"How?"

"Because he's a total ass and only cares about himself."

"You barely know him," I corrected.

"That's exactly my point. He didn't want to come over for my Christmas party, so you came alone. And he conveniently had to work when we had the barbecue in July."

"Because he did have to work," I stressed.

"He *conveniently* had to work, Ash."

I sighed. "You're right. He was sleeping with other women while he was with me."

"I'm going to kill him."

"It's fine."

"Is it?"

I was silent for a moment while I looked out at the sun shining. "Nothing wine can't fix." *And Rhys if I give him a call.*

"I'm sorry. I love you, but I'm glad you two broke up. There's someone better for you. Speaking of, tell me about this picture with Rhys Cole you posted last night."

I smiled at the memory. "I went to Judy's for a drink, and he was sitting next to me at the bar."

"You two looked very cozy."

"We were just drinking buddies for the night." My grin widened thinking about Rhys and how he came to my rescue.

"Is he just as hot in person?"

"Jaime!" I chastised, still smiling.

"What? I just want to know."

I paused for a moment, still grinning like a fool. "Hotter."

"If you weren't heartbroken over Corey, I'd give you a hard time about not getting with Rhys."

"It wasn't like that." I didn't want to tell her about the kisses because I *was* heartbroken about Corey. It was nice to get to know Rhys, but now talking about Corey and what had happened, and with no alcohol running through my veins, my heart was hurting again. Even if he was a cheating asshole, my heart just needed a break and time to heal.

"Right. Sorry. So, what can I do?"

I shrugged even though she couldn't see me. "Nothing. I mean, I just need time."

I knew it was going to be hard. The last several months my free time was spent with Corey. And now there was no Corey. My heart felt as though it was cracking in my chest. Was Rhys right? Would I meet a guy and be happy—*finally*? I wasn't getting any younger.

"You want to go to dinner tonight?" That way I could get a drink or two. I'd have to stop at a liquor store after work tomorrow.

"Sure. Name the time and the place, and I'll be there to help you get drunk."

And that was why Jaime was my best friend. She got me.

CHAPTER FOUR

Rhys

When I got home, Bridgette was gone. Thank the fucking Lord! Was I thankful though? Even in my buzzed state of mine, I realized my place was silent. There was no chick drama show on the TV, no loud cackling, no Food Network BS that made me hungry, and there was no sex for me tonight.

I would have went home with Ashtyn though. Fuck, I would have.

Kissing her was not enough for me. I wanted more. When I told her to use me, I was serious. We could both use each other to forget about our exes. But did I want mindless sex to get over Bridgette?

Yes, I did.

I wanted all the sex so I could erase the image of Bridgette riding some guy's dick in my bed. *I need to burn my sheets.* I had no idea how long her cheating had been going on because I worked crazy hours when there were games. Most hockey games were at night, and one or two nights a week were home games, so I wouldn't get home until the bars were closed. When we played on the west coast, I was home a few hours earlier. I loved it.

I didn't, however, love coming home to see my girlfriend cheating on me.

After taking a shower, I stripped my bed of the nasty sheets, stuffed them in the trash and then lay on my bed with a blanket from my couch. I was going to sleep on the couch, but why would I do that when the mattress was okay? *Was* the mattress okay? I checked for cum stains but didn't see any. Even if there was, I wouldn't know if it was mine or not. Fuck it. I was getting a new mattress too. I decided to sleep on the couch.

The blanket I draped over me smelled like Bridgette. Everything smelled like Bridgette: vanilla and shit. I'd given her a key a year or so ago, and she'd moved in. I hadn't asked her to, but one day her toothbrush was at my place, and the next her entire closet.

Shit.

That thought made me realize I didn't get her key back and she didn't leave it. I unlocked my phone to text her, but there was a notification from Facebook that I was tagged in a photo on my lock screen. It caused me to forget what I was doing. I smiled because I knew exactly what photo it was. After swiping the notification, I unlocked my phone, and the moment the picture graced my screen, my grin widened. There was comment after comment about how awesome it was that two young newscasters from different stations were together. I didn't know why people thought it was weird. I didn't. Maybe people were tripping out because these were our friends and word hadn't gotten around that we were both single? If they only knew that my lips had tasted hers …

I left a comment that she would only know the meaning of:

Use me anytime ;)

I'd be her fake boyfriend any day or night.

The sound of my front door made me jolt awake.

I'd forgotten I'd fallen asleep on the couch until my head turned to the sound of heels walking into the room. "What are you doing here?" I groaned.

Bridgette closed the door behind her. "I was hoping we could talk."

"What is there to talk about?" I stood and went to start a cup of coffee.

"I'm sorry."

I laughed. "Sorry? Let me guess, you fell?"

"What?" Bridgette asked coming up behind me. She sat on the bar stool while I prepared the Keurig.

"You fell on his dick?"

She sighed and repeated, "I'm sorry."

She didn't answer my question, but I knew the answer. I turned around and crossed my arms over my chest. "Sorry? How long has it been going on?"

"Does it matter?"

I stared into her brown eyes, not replying. Did it matter? Did I want her back? Obviously, she was here to talk which meant she wanted to get back together. Did I want that? Could I trust her again?

"Why?" I finally asked.

Bridgette averted her eyes. "I don't really have an answer. It just happened."

"How many times?"

"Just a few."

"Here? In my bed?"

"Yes," she whispered. "But I cleaned up afterward."

The Keurig gargled behind me indicating my coffee was almost made. "Just go," I hissed and turned around to get my coffee.

"Baby—"

I snapped. "Nothing you will say will ever make this situation okay, Bridgette. It's over. Get the fuck out!"

I went to the fridge to grab the creamer as she slid off the barstool. "You know I was only with you so I could meet hockey players. Right?"

I rose from the fridge. "I thought you hated sports?"

Bridgette smirked. "I do, but that doesn't mean I don't want to get with any. Do you know how much money they make?"

I did.

"Have fun meeting them now." I slammed the door of the fridge.

"Take care, Bridge, and leave your fucking key on the island."

There wasn't enough caffeine in the world to make this day any better.

The following Friday, the Hawks had a game against the Nashville Predators. I hadn't heard anything from Bridgette again, and I hadn't heard anything from Ashtyn other than the morning after we met. Granted it was just a text, but at least I had her number now. I spent all of my time at work, going over stats for upcoming games, not wanting to go home to an empty condo. If I knew Ashtyn's condo number, I'd go over there. I was sure I could figure it out, maybe even text her for it, but I wasn't going to chase after her. She was going through shit too, and time would tell what was meant to happen.

A few nights during the week, I'd caught her broadcast and each time talked myself out of contacting her. I told her to use me, not the other way around. If she didn't want to get together, then I was sure there was someone else for me. That didn't stop me from thinking about her at night while I jerked off.

"News is on in the break room," Kenny informed me, sliding into his desk chair that was in the cubicle across from me. He was shorter than me by a few inches, had shaggy brown hair and brown eyes. Kenny had been my best friend since the moment we'd both started at the station, and he was like my right hand man.

"And?"

"Your girl's lookin' hot tonight."

"My girl?" I eyed him curiously.

"Ashtyn Valor."

A smile spread on my face. "She's not my girl."

"Everyone's seen the picture, and you told me it was the night you caught Bridgette cheating. It adds up."

I threw my pen down on the pad of paper and leaned back, turning my head to look at him. "There's nothing to add up. I haven't talked to her since that night."

"But you want to," he pressed, smirking.

"What are we, in high school?"

Kenny chuckled. "All I'm sayin' is that if I had the number for Ashtyn Valor, I'd be all over that—and under that."

"And this is why you're single."

"Why do you say that?"

"You think she'd give you the time of day if she heard you talk like that?"

"I wouldn't know. *You* would know," he emphasized and leaned forward. His dark brown eyes brightened as though he was amused and wanted to know more.

"I've been busy," I lied. I was working as much as possible, but I did it for an escape.

"Go check out the TV in the break room, and if you come back and tell me you don't want to hit that, then I'll drop it."

I didn't need to go to the break room. I knew I wanted to get with Ashtyn. I was still thinking about her soft lips and how I wanted to feel them on more than just my lips. "Nah, man. I just need to find someone else to warm my bed. Tomorrow night. Judy's." I motioned between him and me. "We're gonna get laid."

Since my breakup with Bridgette, I'd turned my condo back into a bachelor pad. There were no more flowers or fringy shit in sight in my entire place, and I bought new sheets, new pillows and a new comforter for my bed. I didn't buy a new mattress. Instead, I vacuumed the shit out of it and hoped that worked. I also had my TV only on ESPN because if I had to see one more yelling match between middle-aged women who were supposed to be rich and classy, I'd lose my ever-loving mind.

As I got ready to head out with the guys, a memory of mine and Bridgette's one year anniversary entered my mind.

"Damn," I whistled. "Baby, that dress. God, that dress."

"You like?" Bridgette twirled around, and my eyes instantly went to

her ass that was covered by a short—very short—red dress.

"Yeah, I do, but so will all the other guys in this town." I couldn't move as I continued to stare. I knew what she looked like naked, but this dress was something else. It hugged every curve of her body.

"I don't care. I'm with you, and this is our one year anniversary. I wanted to look nice."

"I'm not sure I can make it through dinner. Let's just stay in and order pizza."

"You promised me a special dinner."

I'd made reservations at the Signature Room on the ninety-fifth floor of the John Hancock Building. I'd seen pictures of the view from way up there, and I thought it would be perfect. Plus, I could actually afford it now.

She bent to do something. I wasn't sure what because the moment she did, her skirt exposed her bare pussy. "I think I love you." I said the words before they registered in my head.

"You love me?"

Did I? I loved seeing her in that dress. I would also love seeing her out of that dress. And I fucking loved pussy, and I had just caught a glimpse of Bridgette's. But since my mouth had a mind of its own, I went with it.

"Yeah. I love you," I lied.

"I love you too," Bridgette squealed.

That night had cost me a pretty penny. I should have known that Bridgette was a gold digger. She'd ordered the lobster and multiple cocktails. When we got back to my place that night, she was too tired to celebrate our anniversary, and therefore, she passed out while I jerked off in the shower.

I chased the memory away with thoughts of Ashtyn. I could still feel her lips on mine. I could remember the way the wine tasted on her tongue, and how she had parted her mouth to let me deepen the kiss despite how our evening went earlier. If I was being honest with myself, I'd been thinking about that kiss for the last week. I wanted more, but again, the ball was in her court. Women needed time and all that shit.

My phone buzzed with a text from Kenny:

I'm here. Let's go.

I grabbed my keys instead of texting him back, and left to meet him downstairs so we could walk across the street to the bar.

Judy's was your typical bar where people loved to unwind on a Friday or Saturday night. It had a rustic sports bar feel to it, but they only served alcohol. You couldn't get food, but you could catch any sports game playing because they had TVs hung throughout that made sure to have something on it. The games were muted while music played, but I didn't need to hear other broadcasters telling me what I already knew from watching.

The weather was starting to get colder at night, but I didn't want to carry a jacket while I let loose, and I wanted to let loose. Working long hours was starting to get to me. Journalism wasn't what it was cracked up to be, but when you had to live and breathe your profession, it became a part of you. I still needed at least one night a week to let off some steam.

"Hey," I greeted Kenny as I came out of the double doors of my building. He was dressed similarly to me in jeans and a button-down shirt.

"It's about time. I'm freezing my balls off."

I laughed. "You could have waited inside the doors, jackass."

"Whatever. Clark and Jett are meeting us there."

We started walking, and I glanced up at Ashtyn's building wondering what floor she was on and if she was home. God, this woman had me all twisted up inside. I definitely needed to get laid tonight.

Whenever I went out drinking with the guys, Kenny parked his car in my guest parking spot because it was easier than finding a place on the street. Plus, nine out of ten times he'd crash on my couch or, if he was going to get laid, he'd go to her place. Clark and Jett lived in the same part of town and usually took an Uber together. Jett was my co-anchor, and Kenny and Clark were our news writers who made sure the stats were correct before Jett and I told all of Chicago. It was cool having friends you worked with. I didn't have to field questions the entire night about the Blackhawks because they already knew what was up. We could just hang and have a nice night of getting drunk.

We made it the few blocks to Judy's and then bee-lined it straight for the bar where Jett and Clark were waiting for us. Jett was built like a hockey player because he used to be one. He was one hell of a fighter. He'd go round and round with them, and most of the time helmets would fly off, and his finger-length black hair would flop around. But it was the determination in his blue eyes that most men feared when going toe to toe with him. He'd had plenty of concussions over the years, but the one he got in his last game was enough to give him post-concussion syndrome. He never returned to the ice as a pro.

Clark was the opposite. He hadn't played pro, and he hadn't played in college either. He got into sports journalism for the same reason I did. He loved the game. His dark hair was always spiked in a way that looked like he just rolled out of bed, and when we'd joke with him that he rolled out of bed with a woman, he'd smile his crooked smile, and his azure eyes would shine deviously. He was a ladies man because he looked like the boy next door with his sweaters and shit, but I knew the truth. He'd let the women borrow some sugar in exchange for some *sugar*.

"Did you order us a round?" I asked them.

Jett chuckled. "Nope."

"Asshole." I raised my hand to get Tommy's attention.

He came over. "The usual or seven and seven?"

While a seven and seven sounded delicious, I needed to pace myself. "The usual." Tommy grabbed a pint glass and started to pour me a Miller Lite from the tap.

Kenny nudged me. "Your girl's here."

I turned my head in the direction he was facing and smiled when I saw her ass moving to the beat of the song playing in the background.

My girl was here all right.

CHAPTER FIVE

Ashtyn

Dear Ashtyn,
Just when I thought I knew all about you, you surprised me.
I read this quote and thought of you:
Wine is bottled poetry. - Robert Luis Stevenson
-SA

After the weekend I'd had, it was nice to get my weekly roses. It felt good to know someone admired me, except this note made the hairs on the back of my neck stand up. *"Just when I thought I knew all about you, you surprised me."* What did that mean? The thought of some random person sending me flowers each week was now starting to feel weird, though I was sure actors, models, and authors received gifts from fans all the time. *Didn't mean anything, right?*

The week passed, and you'd think that each day would get easier, but I caught myself thinking about the one-time Corey told me he loved me.

The warm wind whipped through my blonde hair as Corey held my hand, leading me to Navy Pier for dinner. I was starting to feel things for him. I loved spending time with him, and I looked forward to Saturday morning when I could wake up next to him. I knew I loved him. I wanted to tell him, but I was waiting for him to tell me first because I wasn't sure how he felt. We'd only been dating for five months, but I knew we could last forever. I could envision myself walking down the aisle in a white dress I'd pinned on Pinterest with all of our friends and family there. I wanted that. I wanted that with Corey.

"Where are we going to dinner?"

"Riva Crab House."

I smiled. Crab was one of my favorite things to eat.

We had a view of the water as we ate, and afterward, we decided to take a walk to the end of the pier. "I had my prom there." I pointed to the glass windows that housed a giant ballroom at the end of the pier.

"Me too." Corey chuckled. We went to different high schools, and were four years apart, but I knew it was a common location for proms. "I was Prom King."

"You were not." I slapped his arm playfully and chuckled.

"I was."

"Why have you never told me that?"

"That was nineteen years ago."

"You make us sound so old." I groaned. I wasn't far behind him in age, but it had been fifteen years since my senior prom. Just then there was a loud boom, and when I looked up, glittery silver showered the sky. After some time I said, "I love fireworks. They're so beautiful." I looked over to see Corey watching me.

"So are you, Ashtyn."

"You don't have to woo me. I'm already yours." I leaned into him, still looking up at the show.

Corey wrapped his arm around my waist and chuckled. "I'm not trying to woo you. I'm stating facts."

I looked at him. "Well, thank you."

He smiled. "And, I love you."

How was I so stupid? Everything had seemed perfect that night. Granted, Corey never uttered those three words again, and I should have taken that as a sign, but I never expected him to be such a good actor.

Saturday morning as I read the morning newspaper, my phone buzzed next to me.

Jamie: Girl's night tonight?

Usually, I'd spend my Saturday evenings with Corey like we had the night we went to see the fireworks, but now I was free in a sense, and I needed my friends to keep my mind off my breakup.

Me: Judy's?

Jamie: I'll meet you at your place at nine.

At nine o'clock sharp, there was a knock on my door. When I opened it, Jaime and our friends Kylie and Colleen were standing there with huge smiles on their faces. *The more the merrier.* Now I could answer their burning questions and be done with it.

When the four of us got together, we looked like we'd stepped out of an episode of *Sex and the City*. Kylie had her dark brown hair up in a high ponytail, her bangs perfect across her forehead. Her brown eyes sparkled as she held up a bottle of Patrón. Colleen's red hair was cut into a pixie cut, and her petite frame was opposite of her big green eyes, but they worked for her face. And Jaime had her blonde hair loosely curled.

"We brought tequila!" Jaime squealed, and Kylie thrust the bottle toward me. It was then I noticed Colleen had a bag of limes, chips, and salsa.

"We're having girl's night here?" I thought we were going to the bar.

All three of them moved around me and into my condo. "It's the pre-party," Kylie confirmed.

"This way we only need to have one or two drinks at Judy's."

"Or for you three to stall and quiz me about Corey," I commented, following them to the open kitchen.

Jaime grinned. "We also want to know about Rhys." Even though I'd told her all there was to know already about Rhys, a week had passed and apparently, she thought we were more of a thing. We weren't. I hadn't heard from him since.

"Rhys?" I questioned, sliding onto a barstool while they got to work with the shots and snacks.

"We haven't heard from you since your breakup," Kylie stated.

That was true. I hadn't responded to their texts either. The Sunday after my breakup, I'd stayed home all day. I didn't want to talk to people, and I was still confused about the whole situation. One minute I was getting my heart broken, and then the next I was kissing a new guy. A guy I hadn't heard from and was probably using me to get in my pants, but I wasn't the type to have a booty call on speed dial. Though the thought of it being Rhys did things deep in my belly.

"Basically, I spent almost a year of my life dating a guy for nothing."

Jaime came over to me with a shot of the tequila. "But how are you really feeling?"

"Alcohol has been my new best friend this week." Most night after I got home from work, I would drink a glass of wine and then take a hot shower before drinking another glass before bed. It was the only way for me to sleep because every time I tried to do it without any wine, I would crawl into my king-sized bed and reach my hand over into the cold, empty space and then cry before I'd get up in search of wine.

"Well, here's some more." Jaime handed me the shot, and I snatched a lime from the counter in front of me where Kylie was cutting slices.

"But really," Colleen said, opening the tortilla chips, "you're moving onto Rhys Cole?"

"Just because I took one picture with a fellow anchor doesn't mean I'm dating the guy."

Jaime sat next to me with a shot of Patrón in front of her. "It wasn't because you took a picture. It was because we'd never seen you smile like that before. You were fucking glowing, and you'd *just* broken up with Corey."

"I wasn't glowing," I muttered. "It was from all the wine. And maybe the shot of Fireball." *And because he'd kissed my bare shoulder and caused goosebumps to rise on my skin.* I left that part out. I also left out the part where we'd kissed—three times. I downed my shot. "Let's just drop it. I don't want to talk about boys."

"That's the whole point of a girl's night." Kylie laughed.

"Well, let's talk about all of your love lives."

"We're all married." Colleen laughed. "We have boring pre-scheduled sex."

I sighed. "I'm not having sex anymore. Or getting married for that matter."

"I'm sure Rhys Cole would be up for sex. He told you to use him, so fucking use him." Jaime slid her shot to me.

"He didn't mean for me to use him like that," I lied. "He meant he'd be my fake boyfriend if I needed rescuing from some guy again."

Kylie poured me another shot and handed it to me. I noticed I was the only one to take a shot, and now I was the only one getting another. "Fine. So tonight you find a guy to go home with and have hot sex. It won't kill you to have a little fun. Just remember we get to go home to snoring and farting, but you can go home and have hot stranger sex."

"Hot stranger sex?"

Colleen sighed. "Sex where you give up control and just feel. You don't need to worry about how your boobs look while you lie on your back, or if your belly is sticking out some. You just go have sweaty sex and be done with it."

Maybe the girls were on to something. And maybe Rhys was right. Maybe I needed to get under someone to forget about Corey. It was worth a try. "I'm not getting any by having you three grill me. Let's get this show on the road."

Two more shots later, chips and salsa in our bellies, we were out the door and walking to Judy's. I was still two shots ahead of them, and I was feeling it. Corey who? Why shouldn't I try to meet someone else? I could have stayed home, eaten an entire gallon of ice cream and drunk an entire bottle of wine, but I wouldn't have been happy, so I chose to go out with my friends and seriously consider this stranger sex thing.

"Hi," I greeted the bartender as my girls and I maneuvered between people. It was the same guy from a week ago.

"What will it be?"

"Four red wines. House is fine." Girl's night wasn't about drinking for taste.

"No," Jaime cut it. "Four shots of Patrón and ..." she thought for a moment. "Four seven and sevens." I smiled, remembering that was what Rhys was drinking the other night. It wasn't a drink I'd normally order, but tasting it on Rhys's lips wasn't bad. Jaime turned to me after the bartender moved away to make our drinks. "No wine tonight. You don't have to work tomorrow, you have no boyfriend tying you down, and the girls and I are Ubering home. You can let loose. The looser you are—"

"Are you done?" I laughed. "I wasn't going to object, *Mom.*" We were already doing tequila shots. One more, and a seven and seven, was going to put me over the edge and I *was* going to let loose. I knew it. I also knew I needed that to actually go through with stranger sex.

"Good. Now down your shot and let's grab a table." Jamie handed her credit card to the bartender and told him to keep it open. The four of us clinked our glasses together and then downed the agave goodness.

We made it to a high top table diagonal from the bar. If we had been ten or fifteen minutes longer, the bar would have been packed. After eleven was when things really heated up. I knew that much about going to the bars. In fact, I wasn't sure if it was the alcohol flowing through my veins or what, but the music seemed to get louder even though there were more bodies in the small space.

The song switched to *Strip That Down* by Liam Payne, and it was as though my hips had a mind of their own. I slid off the stool and started swaying to the beat next to the table. Kylie joined me, and before I knew it, all of us were singing and laughing as the music continued to play from the speakers above. I was letting loose, not caring if anyone was watching or if anyone knew or recognized me. It wasn't as though I was a huge celebrity in this town, but sometimes I was recognized by older people who watched the news before bed. That was part of the gig.

Colleen nudged her head, indicating for me to look behind me.

My heart stopped as I saw the man I'd met a week ago. Rhys was leaning against the bar, a pint of beer in his hand and a huge you're-making-me-hard-by-dancing-like-that grin on his face. I smiled back and then turned back to my friends as the song switched. I could no longer focus on the words that were being sung or even the beat because my thoughts were solely on the man behind me. Was he going to come dance with me? Was he hard like I assumed he was? Did he get back together with his girlfriend? Did he come here a lot or just on Saturdays? Would sex with him be considered stranger sex?

It didn't take long for me to get at least one of my answers.

Make that two.

Before I knew it, a hard—and I mean *hard*—body was pressed against my backside. All of my friend's eyes widened, and I smiled, feeling busted. I didn't know why. Rhys and I weren't a thing, but it felt as though I was keeping a secret from them. Of course, the only secret was the three kisses that had meant nothing.

Rhys stepped around me and stuck out his hand, introducing himself to the girls. Then he turned back around and whispered into my ear, "We should take this back to my place."

I was lucky that alcohol made me red because I was certain I was blushing. Rhys, in such a short amount of time, seemed to have a way of making my heart smile even when I was sad and lonely. Maybe he was the key to making my heart whole again? Even if we were just fake boyfriend and girlfriend. His words were like a drug that had an instant effect on my body, and laughing with this man seemed to be a way for me to heal.

I didn't respond. I couldn't. I mean, I wanted to say yes, but I was with my friends. Then my gaze darted past Rhys, and I saw three other guys walking toward us.

"Ladies," one of the guys said with a nod.

Rhys remembered my friend's names as he introduced them and myself to Kenny, Jett, and Clark. I recognized Jett as Rhys's co-anchor, but the others weren't sports broadcasters. Rhys mentioned they were journalists for his station, so I assumed they helped get stats and other sports-related things.

"Another round?" Rhys asked twirling his finger around to all of us.

"Are you buying?" Kylie asked.

Rhys smiled as the ladies and I returned to our seats. "Of course."

"I'm okay," I stated. "If I have another, you'll have to carry me home."

"Not like I'm not going that way, Cupcake." Rhys winked and then left to the bar. His friends followed.

Once they were out of earshot, all three of my friends hissed, "Cupcake?"

I shrugged. "He wants to lick and eat me."

They were speechless as their mouths hung open.

I shrugged again. "He was joking."

"He wasn't joking," Jaime whispered, low. "If you don't get with him, we aren't friends anymore," she continued.

I laughed. "You'll disown me as a friend for not spreading my legs for a guy?"

"No," she corrected. "For not spreading your legs for *that* guy."

I followed the way her finger was pointing toward the bar. The guys were grabbing our drinks, two each, and then they started to make their way over to us. "I'll see what happens."

"And we want details," Colleen stated.

A lot could happen in an hour, but it was what could happen after last call that excited me.

CHAPTER SIX

Rhys

"I knew something was going on with you and Ashtyn Valor," Kenny whisper-yelled as we stepped up to the bar.

"Nothing's going on." *Yet.* Having more than my lips and hands touch Ashtyn made me crave her even more. There was no doubt that she could feel how hard I was as my dick rubbed against her ass while we danced. I couldn't help it. I needed to be near her, and I didn't give a fuck. I wanted her to know—no, I *needed* her to know that I still wanted her.

"You said you wanted to get laid tonight. Why not with Ashtyn?"

I didn't look over at Kenny as he spoke. Instead, I watched Ashtyn. Yes, I wanted to get laid tonight. "She just broke up with her boyfriend. I don't want to be her rebound." Well, maybe I did. I told her to use me for sex, except a part of me knew that once I had all of her, I wouldn't be able to get my fill with only one time.

"Dude," Jett cut in. "There's nothing wrong with a little bump N' grind between adults."

My gaze moved to his, and I started to laugh. "Who are you? R. Kelly?"

He narrowed his dark eyes at me. "Don't compare me to that child—"

I cut him off. "You're the one quoting his song."

Jett reached around me to grab two of the drinks Tommy had placed in front of us. "No, I'm telling you to fuck her brains out."

"Who's tab?" Tommy asked.

"Mine," I replied and grabbed the last two seven and sevens. Each of us had two drinks. When we got back to the small table, I placed the drink in front of Ashtyn. "Tommy said this is what you ladies are drinking. I hope it's okay."

Jaime spoke before Ashtyn could. "It's perfect. I actually think that we," she moved her finger around to indicate everyone except Ashtyn and me, "should go pick a song on the jukebox."

"Good idea," Kenny replied and slapped me on the back as I watched the six of them leave.

It wasn't the first time Ashtyn and I had been alone in this very bar, but it was the first time that we had an audience watching our every move. As I stood next to her, both of us sipping our drinks, my gaze fell on the group at the back of the bar. Each one would take turns looking at us, and once they'd realize we were watching them instead of talking to each other, they'd turn around quickly as though they'd been caught. They were. We knew what was up.

"Our friends are weird." I looked down at Ashtyn as I stood next to her.

"So weird," she agreed and took a sip of her drink.

I turned my body fully to her. "How've you been?" Yes, I asked that question even though ten minutes ago my dick was trying to get frisky with her.

Ashtyn's smoky green eyes peered up at me. "Hanging in there. You?"

"Good," I lied. I mean, I was good, but I wasn't great. I was trying to focus all my time on work so I didn't have to think about anything else. I didn't even care about Bridgette anymore. The more time that passed after our breakup, the more I realized I'd never loved her. I loved her as a person, and I loved spending time with her and having sex with her, but I wasn't *in* love with her. If I had been, I would have asked her to marry me, and the thought of marriage never entered my mind.

"How's work?"

I stared at her for a moment before I spoke, "Are we really going to make small talk?"

She blinked. "What do you mean?"

We could talk about work, weather, our favorite colors and shit, but time was ticking before our friends would come back, so I just went for it. I leaned down and rested my elbows on the table next to her as I whispered, "I mean that our friends over there are obviously wanting us to talk about more than the weather. And I'll be honest with you, Ashtyn, I've been thinking about you a lot. Thinking about other places your mouth could kiss my body." I told her the fucking truth in hopes she felt the same way.

"We're both single," I continued, "and in two more minutes our friends will come back and keep dropping hints that we need to go back to my place. So, Ashtyn, Cupcake, let me pay my tab and let's get the fuck out of here."

Her gaze moved quickly to our friends and then back to me. She shrugged with a smirk. "Okay."

I grinned. "Put your jacket on and meet me at the bar." I strode to the wood top and motioned to Tommy that I needed to sign the credit card bill in a fucking hurry. We didn't need to tell our friends goodbye or goodnight or whatever. Once they turned and saw us gone, they would know we went back to my place. Kenny would need to crash at Jett's or Clark's or in his fucking car in my guest parking spot. I didn't care. I scribbled my name on the credit card bill, grabbed her hand and then we were out of the bar in a flash.

"My place or yours?" she asked.

"Well, I do have new sheets I need to christen." I smirked and tugged her hand so we could cross the street.

"I can't wait."

"Yeah?" I asked.

"Since we're being honest with each other, I've thought about you this past week."

"You don't know how happy that makes me."

We made it to my building in record time, but the elevator didn't descend fast enough. I was excited, my heart beating a little fast as I pushed the up button with my free hand repeatedly until it finally arrived. When it did, Ashtyn went in first, still holding my hand. As the door closed, my mouth met hers, and all memories of our earlier kisses came floating back. Her lips were soft, sweet and a little demanding. She was like that first sip of single malt whiskey after a long day: sweet, smooth and refreshing. I went with it, backing her against the wall, moving my hips into her again. If the elevator didn't hurry, I was going to strip her of her jeans and silky shirt and do all the things I'd been dreaming about for the past week with her body.

When we finally arrived on my floor, I stepped away from her warm body and directed her, still hand in hand to my front door. Before I could find my keys, I was pushing her up against the wall next to my door, kissing her again. I couldn't get enough. At the same time, I was trying to find my keys in my pocket, but it was hard.

And so was I.

Finally, I got the door open, and we were moving inside. At that moment, I had no idea where my bedroom was. I didn't care. Ashtyn was in my condo, my hands were all over her body, and my lips were still tasting her. We started to strip our clothes, leaving a trail from the front door to the living room. I was two seconds away from leaning her over the back of the couch and having my way with her, but she spoke against my mouth.

"Where's your bedroom?"

"You can only fuck in a bed, Cupcake?"

She pulled her head away from me. "No, but I thought you'd want to get rid of her memory."

I did. And since we'd started this relationship—*or whatever you wanted to call it,* with us ending other relationships, she was right. I needed new memories to go with the new sheets. I wanted to smell Ashtyn on my pillow and not the laundry detergent I used.

I led her to my bedroom, both of us partially undressed. "Turn around," I instructed.

Ashtyn turned, and I moved to her, brushing her blonde hair to the side, and then I ran my finger down her spine until it met the clasp of her bra. Her head fell forward, and under my touch I felt her skin rise, responding to my trace on her skin. I moved forward, kissing down her back where my finger had left a trail. I was right, my lips loved more of her body than just her lips, and by the way Ashtyn moaned, I knew she did too. Instead of stopping at the clasp again, I continued my path. My lips slowly descended as I bent behind her and wrapped my arms around to the button of her jeans. The nickel button slide through the slit and I pulled her zipper down, my lips never leaving her skin until I got to the waistband of her jeans. I shimmied her pants down until she was standing in front of me in only her black bra and matching panties.

"He's fucking crazy," I breathed, looking at the way Ashtyn filled out her panties.

"Who?" she asked, looking over her shoulder.

My gaze met hers. "Fuck nut."

She smiled. "I agree."

My hands went to the cotton on her hips, and I slid it down her legs until she stepped out of her panties. I tossed them behind me and then unclasped her bra and threw it in the same direction.

"Turn around," I whispered. My heart was pounding, anticipating the sight I was about to take in. When she turned and looked down at me, my dick strained against the zipper of my own jeans.

"Why am I the only one naked?"

That was a good question.

I brought my lips to hers again. We kissed as I worked on undoing my jeans. We kissed while I tugged them down my legs. And we kissed while I stepped out of my boxers. Once we were both completely naked, our mouths stayed fused as I pushed her back until she hit the end of my bed. Then, as she scooted to the center of my king-sized bed, I crawled on top of her.

I trailed kisses from her mouth, down her neck, across her breasts, not stopping my journey until my tongue took its first taste of her pussy. She was sweet, almost like the whiskey I'd been drinking that night, and the moans coming from Ashtyn's throat told me I was on the right path. I spread her more, my tongue going as deep as it possibly could. I added my finger as I circled her clit with my tongue until she moaned and clenched her thighs together as she came.

No words were spoken as I slowly ran my hands along her smooth, ivory skin from her calf up to her breast. My lips returned to hers, my hard cock pressed into her side and my hand pinching her nipple. I didn't know how long I could hold out, but I was waiting for Ashtyn's breathing to return to normal. Granted, I was still working her body instead of letting her rest. I couldn't help it.

A warm hand wrapped around my dick causing me to break our lips apart. She started to stroke me with her soft hand and I really couldn't let it continue because I was on the brink of coming as it was. Instead, I reached into the nightstand and grabbed a condom. As I rose up on my heels to sheath myself, Ashtyn's hand fell away from me, and she spread her legs, welcoming me to enter her.

I didn't waste any more time as I sank into her causing her legs to wrap around my waist. My lips were on hers again like I needed them to breathe. For all I knew, I did.

My hips rocked into Ashtyn as our bodies moved in sync with each other. Her pussy tightened at times causing me to growl low in my throat. Fuck, she felt good. So fucking good. I didn't want to stop in fear that this would be the only time we'd spend together, but I needed to come. I broke our kiss, thrusting faster, my balls slapping between her legs. Ashtyn's back arched as she grabbed her tits. The sight of her playing with herself caused me to groan my release at the same time Ashtyn shattered under me, her pussy milking me until the last drop.

After I cleaned up, I expected to walk back into the room where I'd see Ashtyn putting her clothes back on. Instead, she lay in my bed, her blonde hair fanned across my pillow. The sight of her put an instant smile on my face.

"You know fake boyfriends and girlfriends stay over for the night, right?" I asked, moving toward the bed. I didn't want her to leave. I crawled under the covers, bringing her naked body flush with mine.

"Oh yeah?"

I kissed her bare shoulder. "Yeah."

"Then you better turn off the light so we can get some sleep."

I smiled and did just that.

CHAPTER SEVEN

Ashtyn

Breaking News: Ashtyn Valor and Rhys Cole got naked wasted last night!

Okay, maybe I was the only one wasted, but I remembered everything.

The way he kissed practically every inch of me.

The way he licked me between my legs.

The way he drove into me, causing my back to arch and me to come undone.

I was buzzed for sure which made me loosen up and agree to go home with him. And I didn't regret it.

As I woke, I faintly smelled coffee. I hadn't woken up to that smell since I lived at home with my parents. Never once had Corey made me a cup of coffee or brought me breakfast in bed. I was always the one awake first. In fact, none of my previous boyfriends woke up before me. Was Rhys making me coffee or just for himself?

I crawled out of the warm bed, grabbed my clothes, and went to the connecting bathroom to freshen up the best I could. After getting dressed, I finger-combed my long blonde hair and took a swig of mouthwash before finding my way to the kitchen.

Coming out of the bedroom, I stopped at a table at the end of the hall. It sat between both bedrooms. One was the master bedroom, and the other was an office. Just like my place. The skinny, wood table had pictures of Rhys standing with who I assumed were hockey players because they were all autographed to him. I smiled as I looked at each one, and then turned and walked down the hall in the direction the coffee smell was coming from. It didn't take me long to find it because the moment I cleared the hall, the kitchen was to my right. Rhys was sitting at a breakfast bar, with his back to the living room. The sports paper and a cup of coffee were in front of him.

"You read the paper too?" It might be a weird question to ask, but I meant it in the sense that he wasn't getting his news from the internet.

"Only for the stuff I missed the night before. Usually, I get it all on my phone or the computer."

"Me too." I smiled.

Rhys slid off the brown stool, his eyes roaming my body. "Sit. I'll make you a cup of coffee."

It wasn't coffee in bed, but the fact that Rhys was going to make it for me made it that much better. As he put a pod in the Keurig, I grabbed the front page of the paper and started to skim it. Corey never understood why I actually bought and read the newspaper when the news was always at our fingertips, but it was because everything I needed to know was right there in black and white. Granted, just like Rhys, I too read a lot online, but there was just something about reading the morning newspaper while sipping coffee that made me feel like our lives weren't consumed with social media and notification alerts.

"How do you take it?"

I looked up to meet his blue eyes. "Cream and one packet of stevia."

I'd expected him to tell me he didn't have stevia and I'd have to drink real sugar, but he didn't. He smiled and turned to do just that I assumed. He placed the mug in front of me and then sat beside me on his stool.

"What do you want to do today?"

The mug of hot java stopped at my lips. "With you?"

He smiled that smile that made his dimples appear. "Yeah. We *are* fake boyfriend and girlfriend after all. Plus, I'm assuming we both have today off."

"How do you know I don't have plans?"

"Do you?"

I shook my head. "No, but I thought we were both just letting off sexual frustration and heartbreak last night?"

Rhys turned his body toward me, his knees pressing against the side of my thigh. "We did, but that doesn't mean it needs to stop there."

"I'm not ready to date," I confessed.

"I'm not either," he admitted. "I just thought we could spend the day together and not have to sit alone while we think about our exes."

Rhys was right. I would go home, and even though I unfriended Corey, I'd go to his page and see if he posted a picture with someone else. After a few seconds, I asked, "What do you have in mind?"

"Well, looking at the weather report it seems this might be our last day to have decent temperatures. Before we know it, it will be snowing and shit. So, how about we take a boat ride on Lake Michigan?"

"Friends take boat rides on Lake Michigan together—alone?"

He smiled again. "Maybe, but so do fake boyfriends and girlfriends."

"This feels like it will be a real date."

Rhys grabbed my hand, running his thumb along the back. "It's just two people who don't want to be alone, out on a boat and getting to know each other. I even promise not to kiss you—much."

I grinned at him. "Much?"

He shrugged and released my hand then reached over to grab his coffee. Before he took a sip, he smirked. "What can I say, you taste amazing."

My cheeks heated at his words. I grabbed my coffee to take some time to think about what he was proposing. The two times I'd spent with him, I enjoyed it. Granted the last time was sex, and I'd definitely enjoyed that. I didn't want to go home and stalk Corey like I knew I would, but going on this non-date with Rhys felt like it would be a real date. Was I ready to take that step?

I turned my head toward him and smiled. "Okay, but we buy our own lunches."

"Deal."

After we drank our coffee, Rhys walked me to my condo so I could get ready. I expected him to only walk me to the front door of the building, but he surprised me and walked me all the way to my door. He didn't kiss me, and the moment he walked away I realized that I wanted him to. I was so confused. My brain was telling me that it was only a one-night thing and that we'd got what we wanted and he'd be long gone. My body was telling me I wanted it to be more. And maybe I would get more since he wanted to spend the day together.

I'd been on tours on Lake Michigan many times. There was even talk about someone building a private, floating island in the middle of the lake. Paradise would be just a short boat trip away, and I wanted to experience everything I'd read about from the sundecks to the pools, to the cabanas, to the spa, and to the restaurants. I was going to pitch that I should cover that story when the island opened.

I dressed in jeans, a purple sweater, and my dark grey Chuck Taylors. When I got downstairs, there was a black Mazda SUV parked in the loading zone with Rhys leaning against it. As I walked to him, a smile graced each of our faces.

"Cupcake," he greeted, taking a step away from the car.

I laughed. "Still calling me that after last night?"

"You're telling me that you've only eaten one cupcake in your entire life?"

"No." I snorted.

I stopped just before him, and he stepped forward, almost coming nose to nose with me. "Exactly. Now that I've had a taste, I'm not stopping at just one time."

"Is that right?" I chuckled again although my belly dipped at the thought.

He stepped back and opened the passenger side door for me. I slid in. "Well, at least I hope I'll have more. Cupcakes are fucking delicious."

My face started to hurt from the wide smile I had spread across it. It was clear to me that Rhys had licked his fair share of icing off *cupcakes* before, and honestly, I wasn't going to tell him he couldn't.

Rhys drove us to Navy Pier. I realized I hadn't been there since the night Corey told me he loved me. Now I was making new memories. We locked my purse in the truck so I wouldn't have to carry it out on the water. After he closed the trunk door, I noticed the Blackhawks sticker on the window.

"I didn't peg you as a bumper sticker kinda guy."

"Have to represent the boys."

We exited the parking garage and came upon a building in front of the carousel. "We're going on a booze cruise?"

Rhys smirked. "Nothing wrong with a little day drinking."

I wasn't opposed to day drinking. If I were at home stalking Corey on Facebook, I'd probably have a glass of wine in front of me. "Sounds fun."

I insisted I pay my way. This wasn't a date. At least I kept telling myself that. Rhys hadn't kissed me once today. No good morning kiss. No goodbye kiss. No you-just-showered-and-smell-fucking-awesome kiss. He hadn't even held my hand. So we weren't on a date. Just two friends going out for lunch on a booze cruise.

After we paid, we boarded a multi-level blue and white boat. It was more than just a boat. It was huge, and I figured it could hold at least one thousand people. We were instructed we could do whatever we wanted for the two hours we were out on the lake. There were games on the upper deck, a buffet on the middle level and a couple of open bars throughout. Since we hadn't eaten breakfast, Rhys and I sat at a table for two against the window after filling our plates with salad to start. We each ordered a cocktail, and then enjoyed the view as we chartered away from the city.

"That building right there," Rhys pointed to the Aon Grand Ballroom, "is where I first got laid."

I choked on my bite of lettuce. "In the ballroom?"

"Junior prom with Natalie Westwood."

"I had my prom there too, but I was too busy dancing."

"Then you did prom all wrong, Cupcake."

I laughed, and then we made small talk as we ate another round of lunch from the buffet. Afterward, Rhys led me to the upper deck where people were drinking, laughing and playing games like shuffleboard and life-sized Jenga.

"Want to play anything?"

I grinned. "Of course."

We grabbed another cocktail each. Since the only game I really knew how to play was Jenga, we decided to wait until the current game ended. I hadn't played in at least twenty years, and the last time I'd played wasn't on a rocky boat. As we waited for the other team to put the pieces in place after their game ended, Rhys left to get us another drink. He didn't ask. He just did it. I could deny it all I wanted, but this felt like a date.

We played with the other couple: two versus two, taking turns strategically taking a wooden block out of a layer and placing it on top of the tower. The closer we got from removing each bottom layer, the more my anxiety kicked in. I didn't want to be *that* person: the loser who caused the high tower to fall.

"Do you do this often?" I asked Rhys.

"Jenga?"

"The booze cruise." It was essentially a bar on the water with games.

"Never have, but always wanted to. What about you?"

I smiled. "Same." I had to admit that playing games while drinking on a boat with the Chicago skyline in the background was fun.

That was, of course, until *she* came up to us.

"Rhys." It wasn't a question. She knew it was him. I could tell in her tone before either one of us turned to look at her.

Rhys turned first, and then I followed. He didn't say anything for a few moments as though he was taking time to gather his thoughts. He stared directly into her brown eyes. I, on the other hand, gave her a once over. I wasn't sure if this was his ex or not, but it didn't seem like he was excited to see her. She had long brown hair, doe eyes, and a slender body. Her boobs were trying to overspill from the top of her halter top.

"Bridgette," Rhys finally clipped.

His ex. Rhys found *this* attractive? As I stared at her, I envisioned how Rhys must have seen her in his bed with another man.

She smiled. "I wasn't expecting to see you here."

"And?" he clipped.

As I stood awkwardly, I wondered if I should introduce myself. Should I pretend to be his girlfriend just like he'd bailed me out? I had no idea what to do because I wasn't sure if he still harbored feelings for her. They had just broken up like Corey and I had, and if he were to come out of nowhere, I'd want Rhys to be my fake boyfriend again.

Bridgette's gaze moved over to me, and she glared. I took that as my cue to move closer to Rhys and slip my arm into the crook of his. I felt Rhys's gaze move to look down at my arm. I didn't look at him. Instead, I smirked at Bridgette.

"Can we talk?" she asked.

"I hate to be rude," I smiled and then looked up into Rhys's blue eyes, "but I think they have *cupcakes* at the buffet and we didn't have dessert yet."

Rhys furrowed his brows, and then he smirked. "Cupcakes?"

"Cupcakes," I confirmed.

Rhys took my hand, and we didn't say another word to Bridgette, though we hollered quickly to our Jenga opponents that they'd won.

As we made our way to the second level, we didn't go to the dessert table. I wanted to make sure Rhys knew what I meant by cupcakes, so I led him to the women's bathroom. It was a single bathroom, and thankfully it was empty. I turned and locked the door, then stared at his handsome face and wondered how many times this bathroom had been used for this exact thing.

"There's cupcakes here?" Rhys asked, looking around the small room that had a nautical themed décor.

I stepped forward, removing my sweater as I did. "Only the ones you crave."

"Those are the best ones." Rhys licked his lips as he watched me place my sweater on the sink's counter.

We both looked at the door as the knob jiggled and I held my breath, worried someone was going to walk in and catch us. "We better hurry."

"Not like they can kick us off the boat. We're in the middle of the lake."

"True."

Rhys bent and tugged my jeans down to my ankles, bringing my panties with them. I expected him to spread me open as best he could from that angle, even hook my leg over his shoulder so he had a better angle to lick, but instead, he picked me up and placed me onto the edge of the counter next to my sweater. He removed my Chucks and then my jeans, leaving me in only my black laced bra.

"Once again I'm more naked than you," I stated.

"Seeing as we only have a short amount of time before someone breaks down the door, I'm going to need to taste your cupcake later."

I watched as he took his wallet out of his back pocket, pulled a condom out and then tossed his wallet onto the counter as he stuck the foil between his teeth.

"I see you came prepared."

He smirked. "It's like an American Express. You should never leave home without it."

I chuckled as he undid his own jeans, slid them and his boxers a little down his hips and then sheathed himself. The doorknob jiggled again. This time we didn't look to see if someone was going to walk in. Instead, I spread my legs, inviting Rhys to step forward and into me. He did just that, not checking to see if I was ready. I was. Just the thought of being with him again was enough to make me wet.

I was aching to feel his lips on mine again—craving it even. "Kiss me," I whispered.

His azure eyes met mine, and at the same time his lips descended upon mine, he quickened his pace. We kissed, my arms going around his neck and my back moving against the mirror behind me.

"Thank you," he mumbled against my mouth.

"For what?"

He pulled his head back, still thrusting into me. "For letting me use you."

I didn't need for him to explain. It was a weird line, but at the same time it fit perfectly with what I was trying to do for him. We were using sex as a way to take his mind off of his ex upstairs. His ex that was still on the same boat. Maybe even his ex who was trying to use this very bathroom. It didn't matter.

What mattered was I wanted this man to be happy. When I was with him, he made me happy, so I felt I needed to do the same in return. We were there for each other to chase away the darkness that held us hostage because the pain was too fresh and raw to deal with it alone.

And I had to admit, I was enjoying the chase.

CHAPTER EIGHT

Rhys

"We'll see you back here Thursday for Pregame Live before the Blackhawks take on the St. Louis Blues. Have a great rest of your night." I stacked the papers in front of me as I waited for the all clear. The Blackhawks had just beat the Minnesota Wilds in overtime, and I was exhausted.

"And we're out."

Unlike what I assumed was Ashtyn's daily broadcast, mine was only when there was a game. I was on TV anywhere from thirty minutes to an hour each pre and post-game, two or three times a week. Jett and I would discuss the Blackhawks and either the game coming up or the game that had just ended, plus what to expect in the next game. There were interviews with the game broadcasters and players from the game and, of course, hours spent in the newsroom because our jobs were more than just going live.

Look at me thinking about Ashtyn as if we're dating. We're not. Apparently, we're just fucking, and I'm okay with that.

Sure we had spent twenty-four hours together, but we'd only fucked a few times, and the time on the boat was out of the blue. I'd needed it, though. I'd needed to get lost in the moment and forget the bitch who was trying to cause shit between Ashtyn and me for no reason. When I'd turned at my name, I almost thought my eyes were playing a trick on me. I never in a million years would have ever thought I'd run into Bridgette on a boat in the middle of Lake Michigan. As I stared into her brown eyes, I'd felt trapped. Or at least I thought I was. I was also mentally preparing myself for a catfight. However, Ashtyn dragged me down to the restroom using the nickname I had for her.

I fucking loved cupcakes.

As I grabbed my stuff from my desk, I reached for my phone from my pocket to send a text to Ashtyn. I'd been thinking about her for the past few days since our night and day together, but I wanted to let her come to me. However, the more I waited, the more I thought that maybe she was doing the same. If I wanted to continue whatever we had going on, then I needed to at least communicate and show her I was still interested. She was more than likely on her way home, and I wanted to see how her day had been. I wasn't able to catch her broadcast today, and the nightly news seemed to be my new favorite show these past two weeks.

As I pulled up the text for Ashtyn, I received one from Bridgette instead.

I miss you, baby. Call me.

I stared at the words on the screen. When was this girl going to give it a rest? That's what I got for dating someone ten years younger than I was.

"We still on for poker Friday?" Kenny asked, walking up to me. Every week the guys would come over to my place and bring beer and chips, and I would order a few deep dish pizzas. Since hockey games were on different days each week, poker was on various days that fit with our schedule. This week we were having it on a Friday night.

"Of course."

"That Ashtyn?" Kenny nudged his head toward my phone.

"Bridgette," I corrected.

He groaned. "What does that bitch want?"

We started to exit the building. "My connections."

"She really thinks that after she told you straight up that she was only with you to meet hockey players you'd take her back?"

I shrugged. "She's trippin'."

"For reals. I never liked her. Sure she was nice to look at when she'd dance with her tits practically falling out at Judy's, but I never knew what you actually saw in her. She wasn't all upstairs either."

"You waited long enough to tell me. What would have happened if I proposed to her?"

"I knew you weren't that stupid."

Luckily, I wasn't. Kenny and I made it to our cars, and then each drove away. When I got home, I half expected Bridgette to be waiting for me. *With my luck, she made another copy of my key.* But when I opened the door, it was dark and quiet inside my condo. Peaceful even.

I turned on the TV to ESPN, trying to make the room feel less quiet and lonely, before making my way to the shower. Before I stepped in, I sent the text to Ashtyn that I'd wanted to send an hour before.

How was your night? I missed your broadcast, but I'm sure you were awesome.

Before I hit send, I thought about adding a winking smiley face. I didn't. Instead, I sent the text then got into the shower. When I got out, there was a reply from Ashtyn.

Just another day reporting the news. I heard the Blackhawks won, so that means you had a good night too?

I smiled as I texted back.

They did. And I did. Are you home?

I silently prayed she'd invite me over as I slipped on my boxers. She replied:

I am. Are you?

Me: Yes. Want to come over?

I figured I'd at least ask her since she didn't ask me first.

Ashtyn: I'm already in bed.

I could work with that.

Me: All right. So … what are you wearing?

A guy had to try. The dots danced across my screen as I ran to my living room, shut off the TV, and then crawled into my bed. It helped that the sheets still smelled like Ashtyn too. I could really get into this if she went along with my idea.

Ashtyn: Should my response be nothing?

I laughed.

Me: That would help with the visual I'm painting of you right now.

Ashtyn: Okay, then I'm naked.

I wasn't sure if she was telling the truth, but I went with it.

Me: In bed?

Ashtyn: Yes.

Me: Tickle your stomach.

Ashtyn: Tickle my stomach?

Me: Just go with it. Run your fingertips lightly across your belly and then up to your nipple.

Ashtyn: What are you doing while I pinch and rub my boob?

I didn't tell her to caress her tit. She just went with it. All part of the plan. If she wasn't really naked, I was certain she would be by the time I was done.

Me: What do you want me to do?

I watched the bubbles dance again. They'd start, then stop, then start again. Finally, I got a reply.

Are you naked?

Me: I am.

I lied, but quickly stripped off my boxers and threw them onto the floor to rectify the situation.

Ashtyn: Then I want you to pinch your nipple too.

I laughed.

Me: How did you know I liked my nipples pinched?

That wasn't necessarily true. It had never happened before, but I decided to go with it.

Ashtyn: Because it feels good. Does it feel good to you?

Yep. We were totally going to do this. Ashtyn was on board.

Me: Yeah, Cupcake. Does it make you wet?

I was instantly at full mast when my brain thought about Ashtyn wet.

Ashtyn: Soaked.

I groaned and rubbed my hand over the tip of my hard dick a few times before I texted back.

Me: Send me a picture of your tits.

The three dots dance again on my screen as I held my phone with one hand and slowly stroked my cock with the other. Then they stopped, and I held my breath and waited.

And waited.

And waited.

And waited.

Finally, my phone rang, and Ashtyn's name appeared on the screen.

"Cupcake."

"I'm not sending you a picture of me naked."

Maybe she didn't trust me yet. I'd win her over eventually. "You're face doesn't need to be in it."

"I know." There was a slight pause before she asked, "Are you hard?"

"Yes." I resumed stroking myself slowly, not wanting to rush whatever was about to happen.

She moaned into the phone.

"Are you touching yourself?" I asked.

"Yes."

"Where?" I needed to make sure my visual in my head was correct.

"Between my legs. I can feel how wet I am through my panties."

Oh, Jesus. Ashtyn wasn't naked as she'd said in the earlier text, but that didn't matter. What mattered was she *was* touching herself. "Fuck, Ashtyn. Keep going."

She moaned again. "I'm touching myself, pretending you're here with me."

"I can be there in three minutes," I stated and waited for the okay.

Instead, she said, "Tell me what you would do to me if you were here."

Okay … "For starters, if I walked in on you touching yourself, your panties soaked, I would let you play with yourself while I watched."

"Yeah?" She breathed heavy into the phone, and I knew she was really touching herself.

"Yeah. Can you do that for me? Pretend that I'm there."

"Mmm hmm."

"Slowly I would walk to the bed then start kissing you. My tongue slipping into your mouth. You'd mimic with your fingers the way my tongue swirled around yours."

"Yes," she moaned.

I continued to stroke myself, still not rushing anything. "After a minute or so, I'd slowly lick down your neck to your nipples, making sure they were just as hard as I was."

"I'd like that."

"Are you making your nipples hard, Cupcake?"

"Yes," she breathed.

"Play with your clit again."

She moaned again, and I knew her hand went straight between her legs. Fuck, I wished it was my own.

"I'd begin to kiss you lower and lower until I reached your hand that was against your pussy. I'd move it away and replace it with my tongue. Can you feel me?"

"Yeah," she panted.

"While I'm working your clit with my mouth, I'd reach around to your thigh and slowly run my hand up to cup your ass, bringing your pussy closer to my face." I had no idea what I was saying because if my face were between her thighs, there would be no room for me to tilt her hips. However, I'd press my face against her and go to town feasting on her *cupcake.*

"You're good at licking icing." She gave a slight chuckle that turned into another moan. Fuck I loved that sound.

"Yeah, baby. Your cupcake is like being on a high that never goes away. You ready for me to be inside you?"

"Yes," she moaned. "God, yes."

"Then I'd ease into you, stretching you with my dick until I was buried deep inside you."

She let out another whimper, and I knew her fingers were inside her as she envisioned they were my cock.

"Does that feel good?" I asked, starting to glide my hand faster up and down my shaft. Pre-cum had already coated my hand, helping it move easily as I stroked.

"So good."

We were both panting into the phone, and I was getting closer and closer to coming from just hearing her heavy breathing through the receiver. The thought of her bringing herself to the edge, pretending it was me, made me fucking hornier. God, the sounds she was making into my ear were going to stay with me forever. I knew that every time I jerked off from now on, I'd think of this moment, hear her breaths, her moans, her pants.

"Can you still feel me inside you?"

"Yeah," she panted again. "I think I'm going to come."

"Fuck," I groaned, "me too, baby." We both continued to breathe heavily for a few more moments, and just as I was about to come, I asked, "Are you ready?"

She didn't respond with actual words. Instead, she moaned over and over, her gasps short as though she was thirsty for air. Then I heard her come. There was a slight pause in her breathing and I pictured the face she made that I'd seen twice before as she came. I followed, my own cum shooting out in ropes across my stomach.

We were silent other than both of our breathing trying to return to normal.

"Did you finish?" she asked after a few seconds.

"Yeah, Cupcake."

"I wish you were here."

"Do you?"

"Yes."

I reached for a tissue on my nightstand to clean up. "Are you just saying that or inviting me over?"

She paused for a moment. "I am able to have multiple orgasms."

"Fuck yeah you can, Cupcake."

Ashtyn chuckled in my ear. "I'll let my doorman know you're coming."

"I'll be there in three."

There was an extra pep in my step as I strolled into the studio the following day. I would say it was because I got laid, but when I was with Bridgette, our sex life wasn't bad at all. I'd told Ashtyn that my sex life with Bridgette was awesome, and in the beginning, it *had* been amazing, but that died down over the two years. Was that how relationships worked? I'd had plenty of girlfriends over the last thirty-three years of my life, and I always thought my sex life was awesome. There was no way I could be bored while I drove into a woman, but being with Ashtyn was different.

"Someone's happy this morning." Kenny leaned against my desk, his arms crossed. Jett and Clark looked up and agreed with a nod each.

"Looking forward to taking all of y'alls money on Friday."

"Yeah, we'll see about that." I expected Kenny to walk off and get to work, but he didn't. Instead, he said, "But seriously. You and Ashtyn see each other last night?"

I leaned back in my chair. "Why are you so hung up on my relationship with Ashtyn?"

Kenny shrugged. "I actually like the girl you're finally dating, and I'm hoping she has a single friend or two."

"Or three," Clark said in agreement. Jett nodded and took a sip of his coffee.

I chuckled without sound. "First off, we're not dating. Secondly, I have no idea if she has single friends." The three women Ashtyn was with at Judy's on Saturday all had wedding rings on.

"Well, find out."

"I know you need my help getting laid—"

"Fuck you!"

All of us laughed. "I don't even know when I'm seeing her again. We aren't dating, and have no future plans to see each other."

Of course, I was going to try and rectify that situation, but I knew I needed to play it slow. We both weren't looking for a relationship, and I didn't want to come off as the guy who was using her for sex, even though I'd told her to use me. That was what I wanted the night we met, but now I genuinely liked everything there was about Ashtyn Valor. On some level, I wanted to get to know her better. I wanted to be that person she called when she needed to forget, and I wanted her to be that person when I did too.

Especially since Bridgette wasn't leaving me alone.

CHAPTER NINE

Ashtyn

Each day of work, we'd start with a meeting to discuss the upcoming broadcasts and assign each reporter to a story or stories to cover. While they were in the field, the news anchors usually did promo videos for their upcoming broadcast that night, followed by a lunch/dinner before getting ready to go on air. I didn't miss being in the field, especially in the dead of winter, but there was one story I was hoping to cover.

"Are you sure you want to go back into the field again?" Leonard, my boss and the news director, asked.

I nodded, a smile spread across my face as we sat around the newsroom table for our daily meeting. "Yes."

"Who wouldn't want to cover the floating island?" Mitch asked sarcastically. "I'm jealous Ashtyn mentioned it first."

"Yep, I call dibs." I laughed. While we were a successful station and we had news reporters that covered the stories in the field, there had been exceptions. This was one that I hoped would get me out of the newsroom to actually report the news instead of only reading it. However, it wasn't even close to being open yet. We still had to get through winter, but I saw a blog post this morning that they were making progress and I wanted to claim the story first. I wanted to get in contact with them and schedule a pre-launch interview, hoping I'd get to use the entire island for the day.

"All right. You got it." Leonard nodded and wrote on his legal pad. "Anything else?" Everyone looked at each other as we shook our heads. "See you back here at nine."

After my promo videos, I was craving a pumpkin spice latte and wanted it before we had to go live. "Hey. Want to go to Starbucks with me?" I asked Abby as I walked up to her desk.

"Can you bring it back? I'm waiting for a call back on a story I want us to break tonight."

"Sure." I smiled. "What do you want?"

"Grande pumpkin spice latte, please."

"Got it." She tried to give me money, but I waved her off. "My treat."

After shrugging on my coat, I left to walk down the block to the nearest Starbucks. The sun had just set, and even though it was dusk, I could make out *his* car sitting at the light. I didn't need to look in the window. I just knew. I knew by the feeling in my chest that the red Mustang idling two cars ahead was Corey. The closer I got, the more I prayed that the light would turn green.

But, of course, it didn't.

My heart started to beat faster, and my pace started to slow as I walked by the car. I tried with all my might to not turn my head and look, but of course, I turned my head, this time praying that he wouldn't turn to look at me.

No such luck.

Our gazes locked, my feet faltered, and my breath caught. I didn't stop, though. Instead, I turned my head quickly as though he was just another person in a car. Was this how my life would be now? I either needed to move or move on. That was why whatever I had with Rhys was good. I saved him from his ex, and he could save me from mine.

My legs moved again, and I quickly went inside Starbucks and pulled out my phone to text Rhys while I waited in line to order.

Me: Just saw fuck nut.

I loved the nickname Rhys had chosen for Corey. It fit perfectly. It also put a smile on my face as I typed the words and waited for his reply. I didn't know if he'd reply right away, but I hoped so. I needed the distraction.

I ordered the coffees, and before my name was called, I received a text back.

Rhys: Where?

Me: He was at the light when I walked to get coffee on my break.

Rhys: Did he say anything to you?

Me: No. I kept walking.

Rhys: Where are you now?

Me: Waiting for my coffee.

My phone rang instead of a text. It was Rhys.

"Hey," I answered.

"You okay?"

"Well, now I know how you felt on the boat." Though his encounter was worse than mine. I wouldn't even know what I would do if I came face to face with Corey. Like actually face to face and not twenty or thirty feet between us. I'd probably slap him.

Rhys chuckled in my ear. "Are you saying you want me to meet you for a quickie in the restroom?"

I smiled. If I didn't have work, I'd take him up on it. Being with Rhys was like a mini getaway from all my worries. I'd say it was like a stress reliever, but it was more. It was as though we were meant to meet that night at Judy's, meant to be each other's escape.

"I would, but I have to anchor the news and all that."

"Tonight after my poker game then."

"You play poker?"

"Try to every week. Sometimes work gets in the way."

"With your friends I met the other night?"

"Yep, and two other guys."

"What time does it end?"

"When it does." I heard him laugh again.

"So, you want me to sit and wait by the phone for you?"

"Yeah, and naked."

I snorted my laughter. "Right. Keep dreaming."

"But seriously, I'll text you when they leave, and if you're still awake, I'll come over."

"Okay." I nodded even though he couldn't see me. The barista called my name, indicating my drinks were ready. I stepped forward. "Can I get a carrier?" I asked the barista. She nodded.

"I'll call you tonight," Rhys stated.

"Okay, don't forget to watch my newscast. Ratings and shit."

Rhys laughed again into my ear. "I'm already on that channel."

We hung up, and I grabbed the light brown carrier and turned around, right into a hard body. The hot coffee fell backward and down the front of my grey, wool coat.

"I'm so sorry," I muttered, looking down to see the beige liquid pooling on the floor.

"I should be the one to say sorry," the guy stated. "I didn't get any on me."

I looked up and into his brown eyes. "Yeah, but I think I ran into you. I'm really sorry."

"Don't be. Let me buy you two more."

I smiled and looked down at the mess. "That's okay. Really. It was my fault."

"Well, at least let me get your coat dry cleaned for you."

A Starbucks employee with a mop came up to the spill. "We're already making you two more." The man and I stepped away so she could clean it up.

"See. No harm." I took a napkin the guy was handing me. "Thank you."

"You're Ashtyn Valor, right?"

I smiled slightly and nodded as I tried to soak up the coffee from my coat. "I am."

"You're even more beautiful in person."

My entire body flamed with embarrassment. Compliments just had that effect on me. "Thank you."

"Seriously, let me get your coat cleaned for you."

"It's really not a problem."

"Then let me at least buy you dinner."

I glanced up and really looked at this guy. He wasn't bad looking at all. He had short, light-brown hair and a nice smile. That was all I could see without making him take off his coat.

"Unless you have a boyfriend."

I hesitated a moment. Corey and I had broken up, and Rhys and I were just … screwing. "I don't."

"Then let me take you to dinner." I opened my mouth again to protest that spilled coffee didn't equal dinner. Instead, he continued, "This is how it works, right?"

"What's that?"

"In those romance movies. The guy and the girl have a chance encounter, and it leads to them falling in love."

My eyes widened in surprise at his romance movie reference. Men usually didn't watch love stories unless they were forced by women in their lives, and then they usually liked them, but more than likely they'd never admit it. Was this guy saying he liked romance movies? I did, especially when my favorite romance novel was turned into a movie.

"I'm kidding. But seriously, I would like to take you to dinner." He stuck out his hand. "I'm Philip."

I took his hand. "It's nice to meet you."

The barista called my name again, and after I grabbed the carrier, I slowly turned around. I was about to tell him no thank you, but he said, "Everyone's gotta eat."

I paused another moment and thought about what was actually happening. He was right, and maybe those people who made up hopeless romantic stories really did know what they were talking about. Maybe this was how I was to meet the next person I was supposed to date. And by Philip's knowledge, fall in love.

"Sure. Let me give you my number. I really need to head back to the studio."

"Right." He smiled and dug into his pocket for his phone. "You do the nightly news." I nodded and then rattled off my direct line at the studio as he saved it into his phone. "I'll call you to set it up, and sorry again about the coffee."

"It really wasn't your fault."

I opened the door and headed back to work. On the way back, I realized Philip looked familiar to me. I couldn't place where I knew him from, but I had a feeling I'd seen him before.

My phone buzzed, waking me up. I grabbed it from the nightstand, squinting to read the screen.

Rhys: You awake, Cupcake?

I smiled and texted back.

No.

Rhys: Are you naked?

I laughed, remembering how that question just the other night had turned into so much more.

Me: No.

Rhys: Do you want to be?

Me: What did you have in mind?

Rhys: I'll be there in three minutes and show you.

I chuckled to myself. It took him longer than three minutes to walk across the street last time.

Me: I'll be waiting.

Six minutes later, there was a knock on the door. I walked to it wearing only a long T-shirt with no pants, no panties, and no bra. If I weren't worried a neighbor might walk by when I opened the door, I would answer it naked.

"Cupcake," Rhys greeted and stepped forward.

I stepped back, pulling on his shirt to bring him inside. He shut the door behind him, but we didn't move.

"You still thinking about him?"

"No." It was true, but only because I was sleeping. The entire evening, I'd thought about what Corey must have thought when he saw me. Or at least a part of me hoped that seeing me had tripped him up too.

"Because you were sleeping?"

I laughed. Seemed Rhys knew me better than I thought he did. "Maybe."

"You really want to do this?"

I bit my lip. "Well … I'm not wearing any panties."

Rhys's blue eyes dropped to look down as though he could see through my sleep shirt. Before I knew it, he was lifting me in the air and my legs went around his waist as he carried me to my bedroom. No more words were spoken until he set me on the bed and we both started to strip ourselves of our clothes.

"On all fours."

I smiled and turned, moving to be on my hands and knees. There was no foreplay. No needing to make sure the other was ready. All systems were a go as I spread my legs a little and waited for the bed to dip behind me.

"I kinda love having you across the street from me."

I chuckled. "It is coming in handy, huh?"

The bed dipped, and Rhys grabbed a palm full of my butt cheek. "So handy." He ran his fingers along the slit of my pussy. "You sure you weren't having naughty dreams about me?"

I shook my head.

"So you're always wet?"

"Only when it comes to you." That was true. In the past, I'd always need at least kissing and rubbing to turn me on, but thinking of Rhys and hearing how cocky he was, made me ready.

He groaned. "Christ. Don't tell me that or I'll be waiting at your doorstep every night."

"Will you just fuck me already?"

Rhys groaned his response and then I heard him rip open a condom wrapper. It didn't take him long before he grabbed my hips and slammed into me. I cried out as he filled me, enjoying the ride and the pleasure building inside me with each drive of his shaft. We were no longer having stranger sex, but I didn't care. I wasn't embarrassed by anything that was happening right now. All I was thinking about was how good Rhys's cock felt as it hit the spot that made me moan.

"Hearing you moan is enough to make me come," Rhys grunted, still thrusting into me.

"Close," I panted.

He reached around with one hand, kneading my breast and then pinched my nipple. It sent a spark of electricity down my spine, straight to my toes, where a cool sensation started to build from my feet up. It was weird because even though my body was hot and there was a light sheen across my skin, the cool sensation was the spark I needed before coming apart. Rhys grunted a few more times and then he stilled, spilling into the condom.

Rhys leaned forward and placed a kiss in the middle of my back and then slid out. He went to the bathroom, and a few seconds later returned and reached for his boxers.

"Wait," I said.

He looked up at me.

"Do you want to stay the night?"

Rhys stared at me as I lay with the sheet draped across me. "Only if you sleep naked."

I smiled and lifted the covers to show him I was still without clothes. He threw his boxers back on the floor and grinned as he climbed in behind me.

I didn't know what was happening between us, but if it was only friends with benefits, I was *definitely* loving the benefits.

The next morning, I woke to the sun shining through the blinds and a warm hand caressing my inner thigh. I also thought I smelled coffee.

"Did you have coffee without me?" I mumbled, looking over at Rhys.

He rolled over toward the nightstand. "You mean this coffee?"

I sat up, smiling. "Yes."

Rhys handed me the warm cup of heaven. "Is this the way to your heart?"

I paused, my hand halting the mug at my mouth. "Are you after it?"

It was Rhys's turn to take a moment to respond. "I love what we're doing, Cupcake, but I don't think we're both ready for that."

I nodded and took a sip of the java before responding. "I agree. So, are we doing a don't ask/don't tell situation?"

"Meaning?"

I shrugged. "Are we going to date other people?"

"Do you want to?"

"I'm not sure." I took another sip of my coffee, and so did Rhys. "But I was asked out last night."

"You were?"

I told Rhys about Philip. If he did call, would I go?

"While I don't want what we have going on to end, I think maybe you should go out with this guy. He could be what you're looking for."

The thought of not continuing whatever it was that we had together made me sad. "If he even calls."

"No guy in his right mind would pass up the chance to go out with you."

Except Corey. I wasn't enough for him. "We'll see. I'm not even sure I want to date yet." He nodded his understanding and then I asked, "Want to go to breakfast?"

"I would love that, but I have brunch with my folks before I need to head in for tonight's game."

"Oh!" I perked up. "What did your mom say about us hanging out?"

Rhys laughed. "Haven't told her."

"She didn't see our picture?"

"She doesn't use Facebook."

"So she doesn't know you're sleeping with Ashtyn Valor?" I teased.

He laughed. "No, and I have no plans to tell my mother who I'm sleeping with."

I smiled. "I'm going to jump in the shower. Want to join me? You know, save water and all that?"

"I will never turn that offer down."

CHAPTER TEN

Rhys

Ashtyn went to get the shower ready while I finished my cup of coffee. I was on my final sip when she started to sing, her voice carrying into her bedroom. It was some rap song I couldn't remember the name of, but hearing her stumble through the words made me smile. Everything about this woman made me smile.

Except when she told me she was asked out on a date.

I tried to play it cool, but on the inside, I was jealous. I wanted to be the one to take her on a real date. Sure we went on a booze cruise, but I wanted to take her to dinner and then take her back to my place. My blood started to boil at the thought that she might go home with this dude. Fuck. I thought that she wasn't ready to date. I thought I wasn't either, but now …

Fuck.

Fuck.

Fuck.

The only chance I had was that the date would suck and she'd come running back to me.

Running back to use me.

Use me to forget about every other guy in her life.

Now though, I wasn't using her. Who was Bridgette again? Maybe I needed to go on a date?

My phone on the nightstand buzzed with a text. I grabbed it and groaned deep in my throat. And now I *remembered* who Bridgette was.

Bridgette: I made a mistake. I'm sorry. Please call me.

I didn't respond. Instead, I drank the last sip of my coffee and joined Ashtyn. Saving water had turned into something so much more.

I spotted my parents at the packed restaurant where we had brunch once a month. It was our thing. They lived in my childhood home, forty-five minutes away and with my schedule during hockey season, I saw them less and less, but we made sure to meet at least once a month. Plus, my sister, Romi, and her husband, Shane, always came, too.

Mom saw me first. She stood, moving past my father, and engulfed me in a hug. "It's good to see you, sweetie."

"You too, Mom." We broke apart, and I hugged my father. "Dad." People say I looked like my dad, and I could see it. We both had the same facial features, but I had the color of my Mom's hair—or at least before she started turning grey.

The three of us sat down at the wood table of the rustic breakfast joint and while we waited for the waitress so we could order, I asked, "Where's Romi and Shane?"

"She wasn't feeling well, so they aren't coming," Mom stated.

I shrugged. It was probably better they didn't come because my mother always asked when I was getting married when I was around them. My mother wanted to have a slew of grandchildren, and apparently, that entailed me getting married in her eyes. However, she never did ask me in front of Bridgette, and she had never asked me when I was going to propose to Bridgette.

"Where's your girlfriend?" Dad asked. It had never struck me until now that they never referred to her by her name.

"We broke up." I took a sip of my water that was already on the table.

"Oh, thank heaven," my mother breathed.

I smiled. "You're glad I'm single?"

"I'm glad you finally saw you could do better."

"Like Ashtyn Valor?" I asked, knowing full well that my mother would be happy if I were dating Ashtyn.

Mom's blue eyes grew wide. "Yes. Are you dating her?"

I shook my head. "No, but I'm friends with her."

Mother leaned forward, resting her elbow on the table and her chin in the palm of her hand. "What's she like?"

My mother always watched Ashtyn's broadcast, saying that the other anchors bugged her. Maybe it was the class Ashtyn brought to the news or how her smile made you feel as though she was generally happy about the story she was reporting. I was always captivated when I saw the airing of her broadcast when I was at my parents' place for dinner because Ashtyn was hot. Plain and simple. I'd wait until after the news was over to drive home just so I could watch her.

And now I was sleeping with her.

"She's everything you've imagined her to be and then some."

"So you *are* dating her?" Dad asked.

I smiled, thinking about this morning … and last night. "No. We're really just friends. She actually lives across the street from me."

Dad eyed me curiously as though he knew what I really meant.

"Can I meet her?" Mom asked.

I nodded. "I'm sure she wouldn't mind."

"When?"

That was a good question because if Ashtyn had her date soon, then there was a chance all of this would go away. "Well, I need a date for the Emmys now."

Every year the News & Documentary Emmy Award was present by the National Academy of Television Arts & Science. It was typically held in the fall, but Chicago and the Midwest were having the ceremony in early December.

"I'll buy my dress this week."

Dad shook his head. I figured he was annoyed because he knew my mother's true motives. It wasn't because she wanted to meet Ashtyn. It was because she wanted to meet any women she could set me up with.

"Can we stop talking about his love life now and start talking about the Hawk's season? You think they're going to bring home the cup this year?"

Bridgette: *Can we talk?*

I stared at my phone as I sat at my desk going over the stats for tonight's game. If I didn't respond, the texts would keep coming.

Me: I'm busy.

Of course, she texted back right away.

Bridgette: Can I come over after the game?

I snorted.

Me: No.

Bridgette: Please! I want to talk.

Me: There's nothing to talk about. Please stop texting me.

I threw my phone in my desk drawer and got ready for my broadcast.

I was exhausted. The game had gone into overtime, and I wanted to do nothing but crawl into bed.

Crawl into bed with Ashtyn.

This was not how friends with benefits worked, was it? I didn't care. I texted Ashtyn before driving away from the studio.

Me: You awake, Cupcake?

By the time I arrived home, Ashtyn had texted me a few times.

Ashtyn: Yes.

Ashtyn: I'm at Judy's with Jaime.

Ashtyn: Come join us for a drink.

I didn't text her back. Instead, I made my way down the few blocks to Judy's. Once I entered the warm bar, I saw Ashtyn laughing with her friend, and it instantly put a smile on my face. Was this what pussy whipped was like? Fuck it. Ashtyn's pussy was like heroin to me. I knew I'd heard that quote somewhere before, but now I got it. It was more than just sex. I craved her.

I walked up behind Ashtyn and whispered into her ear, "Cupcake."

Ashtyn turned, a smile on her lips. "You made it."

I slid onto the stool next to her. "I did. It's nice to see you again, Jaime."

Jaime grinned. "You too."

"You're not drinking?" Ashtyn asked.

"Nah, I'm beat."

"Tell me about it." Ashtyn nodded. "I took a nap on the couch after lunch."

"Something you two want to fill me in on?"

We both turned to look at Jaime, but Ashtyn spoke. "You already know. Stop acting like you haven't grilled me this entire night."

I chuckled. "You're talking about me, Cupcake?" Her eyes widened as she looked over at me. "I'm flattered."

"Well, that's my cue to leave," Jaime said sarcastically.

"No," Ashtyn protested. "Stay for another drink."

Jaime slid off her stool. "Your man is tired, and I need to get home to my babies. Chase is probably up to his ears in shit."

"Your man." I liked the sound of that.

"Okay, we'll wait with you until your Uber gets here."

"No, you guys stay."

"It's fine. We'll wait with you."

Jaime pulled her phone out, and I assumed she was requesting a ride. "They'll be here in two minutes."

Ashtyn and I stood. "You need to pay your tab?" I asked.

Ashtyn shook her head. "No. We didn't leave it open."

The girls walked in front of me, and after they hugged and Jaime got into her ride, Ashtyn and I started to walk toward our condos.

"I watched the game," she confessed.

I grinned. "Yeah?"

"I even saw you on the postgame show, but I couldn't hear anything. We were already at the bar."

"I'm sure sports talk isn't your thing."

"Well, I can make it my thing. I want to go to a game."

I perked up. "I can make that happen."

"You can?"

"I have connections." I chuckled. They were also known as buying tickets. I usually got a discount, though. Sometimes I'd score a few free ones, but it wasn't like I could ever use them.

"But you wouldn't be able to go, huh?"

I shook my head, and just as I was about to say that she was right, I felt eyes on me. I looked to my left and saw Bridgette standing at the entrance to my building, staring at us. "Fuck," I hissed. Bridgette's gaze met mine and then she was walking across the street toward us. I didn't even know if she looked for cars before she stepped out. She just made a beeline.

"You've got to be fucking shitting me."

"What?" Ashtyn asked.

"Bridgette."

Ashtyn turned just as Bridgette started to yell, "So you *are* fucking her?"

"Excuse me?" Ashtyn hissed.

I stepped forward, blocking Bridgette. "Go home, Bridgette."

"Don't tell me what to do!"

"Let's just go." Ashtyn tugged on my arm.

"Shut the fuck up, bitch!" Bridgette hissed.

So many thoughts were running through my head, but before I could do anything, Ashtyn moved to stand next to me. "It's kind of hilarious watching you try to fit your entire vocabulary into one sentence. Sometimes it's better to keep your mouth shut and give the impression that you're stupid rather than open it and remove all doubt."

Bridgette was speechless.

I was shocked.

In a nutshell, Ashtyn had called Bridgette stupid, but yet, she did it with the class Ashtyn was known for. And that was why my mother admired this woman. That was why I did too.

I grabbed Ashtyn's hand and walked into her building while Bridgette stood on the sidewalk dumbstruck.

CHAPTER ELEVEN

Ashtyn

Last night was … *different.*

After I told Bridgette off, we walked into my building and up to my place. I'd expected Rhys to be all over me. That was our thing. When we had a run in with our exes, we had sex with each other. But he didn't even try. Instead, we snuggled in my bed and fell asleep. And I was okay with that.

Now for the second morning in a row, I woke to the smell of coffee. "I'm going to get used to this." I grinned and rolled over to face Rhys.

He reached for my mug to hand it to me. "That's what I'm hoping for."

I stared at him, my hand reaching up to take the coffee from him. "I thought—"

"I'm kidding, Cupcake. I know what this is, but I'm not going to just leave. We are friends, right?"

I smiled and took the cup. "Of course, but …" I hesitated. Did I really want to ask what was on the tip of my tongue? Bring *her* up again. Or even tell him that I was starting to feel as though I might want to date again, and if Philip called, I'd go out with him.

"But what?"

I smiled tightly still not sure, but I went with it. "But are you going to get back with Bridgette?"

"Fuck no!"

"Last night was the second time we've seen her while we were together. I'm not sure she'll ever give up."

"She's fucking crazy."

"Should I be worried?"

Rhys scrunched his eyebrows. "Meaning she might hurt you?"

"Well, she seemed pretty angry last night, and now she knows I only live right across the street."

Rhys draped his free arm around me. "She's twenty-three, and she just threw away the best guy she will ever be with."

I snorted. "Cocky much?"

"You keep coming back." He winked.

This was true. Rhys was a great guy. So great that if he asked me out on a real date, I'd go with him. I was curious if we could work, but he told me he didn't want a serious relationship right now, so maybe I should just date and have fun? Marriage and kids could wait. Women were starting to have their first child in their early forties now. I could do that. So if Philip called, I was going to go out to dinner with him.

There was nothing wrong with dinner.

Ashtyn,
The rose is red. The violet is blue.
Sugar is sweet. And so are you.
-SA

I wanted to get an update from the developer of the floating island because the last I'd heard, they still hadn't announced a completion date. Just as I was sending the email, my desk phone rang.

"Ashtyn Valor," I greeted.

The man cleared his throat. "Hey … it's Philip."

My breath caught before I responded. He was calling to ask me out, and now I wasn't sure if I wanted to go. I didn't want to stop what Rhys and I were doing. What if Philip was the one I was meant to be with, and Rhys was just the one to get me over Corey? I hated thinking of Rhys as the rebound. He was more than that.

Dinner. I could do dinner.

"Hi, how are you?"

"I'd be better if you finally agree to have dinner with me."

I hesitated for a beat, but then just went for it. "I'm free on Saturday."

"Saturday it is."

"Perfect. Where were you thinking?"

"Ever been to the Signature Room?"

I hadn't but had always wanted to go. The restaurant was on the ninety-fifth floor of the John Hancock Building. "I haven't, but I heard the view is amazing."

"And the food."

"Okay. I'll meet you there."

"Aren't I supposed to pick you up?"

I wasn't letting a stranger know my address. Maybe it would be different if he didn't know who I was or if I weren't on TV, but I had to take precautions when I could, and that was why I gave Philip my office number.

"Maybe on the third date," I teased.

"Oh, so there will be two more dates?"

I chuckled. "If date one goes well."

"No pressure."

"None at all," I affirmed.

Watching Rhys talk about hockey was like staring at a pair of shoes in a store window. They were beautiful and exciting, but you couldn't touch them.

I wanted to touch him.

A feeling of sadness fell over me as I watched his broadcast while I lay in bed. Why couldn't Rhys be the one who wanted to take me out? I'd even settle for another date on a booze cruise. But he wasn't ready, so I fell asleep with Rhys talking in the background about shots on goal and power plays.

I hadn't seen Rhys all week. I knew he was busy, and so was I, but for the past four weeks we'd at least seen each other—well, went back to my place. However, it seemed as though once I told him I had a date, he stopped talking to me. The day after Philip called me, I'd texted Rhys with the news. Maybe that was my mistake, but I thought we were only friends with benefits. I didn't expect him to stop talking to me.

Me: So ... I have a date on Saturday.

Thirty minutes later, he texted me back.

Rhys: I have a game.

Me: He's taking me to The Signature Room. Have you been before?

There was another lapse in time between texts. This time only five minutes.

Rhys: Once. Took Bridgette there for our anniversary last year.

I stared at his reply. Even though I was going with another guy to the restaurant, I was instantly jealous as I read the words.

Me: Do you recommend anything? I've never been.

Rhys: Well, since you're going with another dude, get the center cut.

I smiled as I texted back.

Me: Is that the most expensive thing on the menu?

Rhys: Well, the seafood tower is, I think. But I don't think you can eat that by yourself.

We'd texted a few more times, and then it stopped, and I hadn't heard from him since.

For my date with Philip, I dressed in a sophisticated rosebud print, maxi length, crepe fabric dress with long sleeves and frilled details. Given that it was winter and snowing outside, I paired it with knee-high black boots, a black belt around my middle to give the dress more of a waist, and my wool coat I had dry cleaned after the coffee was spilled on it.

Before I called for an Uber, I tousled my hair that I loosely curled to give it a little more volume, and then I shrugged on my coat. The car pulled up a few seconds after I made it downstairs, and I slid inside. Without thinking, I looked over at Rhys's building. A slight pain squeezed my heart as I realized I was really going out on a date with another man. I envisioned him running outside, opening the car door and pulling me out to tell me he didn't want me to go. However, I knew he wasn't home because he told me he had a game tonight.

What if I never saw Rhys again? If things worked out with Philip, could I walk away from the man who made me laugh? The one who made me coffee each morning we were together? The one who I could be comfortable with and not care how my ass looked as he took me from behind?

The car pulled up to the skyscraper, and right away, I saw Philip standing outside in the freezing cold. When he saw that I was getting out of the car, he rushed to it and held out his hand.

"Thank you." I smiled as he helped me out. "I hope you weren't waiting long."

Philip smiled as he gestured for me to start walking. "Not at all."

We walked into the building and right into the waiting elevator. Philip pressed the button for the ninety-fifth floor.

"I see the coffee came out of your coat okay."

I nodded. "See? I told you it was no big deal." It really wasn't. My coat was dark grey, and after it was dry cleaned, there was no evidence of the spilled coffee.

"You're right. K & K Cleaners does an excellent job."

"How—" Before I could ask how he knew which dry cleaners I

went to, the elevator door opened.

After checking our coats at the coat check, we were seated at a table against the window. Philip ordered the braised short ribs to start and a bottle of the most expensive merlot on the menu. I wasn't sure if it was meant to impress me or if he really did like that wine.

"How did you know I go to K & K Cleaners?" There were several dry cleaners in Chicago.

He continued reading the menu as though he didn't hear me.

"Philip?"

"Oh … What was that?"

I repeated my question. "How do you know I go to K & K Cleaners?"

"I don't. Just a lucky guess because it's by your studio, right?"

I let out the breath I was holding. "Right."

We both returned to our menus, and once I figured out what I was going to have for dinner, I asked, "What is it you do for work?"

"I'm a nuclear engineer."

"Wow, that's amazing."

"Yeah, it's not boring at all to play with radioactive materials and get paid for it."

"I bet." The waiter came over and poured us each a glass of the burgundy merlot and then I ordered the center cut for my meal. The moment the words came out of my mouth, I couldn't wait to tell Rhys. He'd be proud of me. I took a sip of my wine.

"You know, you look very familiar to me, but I'm not sure from where."

"Judy's," he stated against the lip of his wine glass.

I balked. "Judy's?" The only people I'd met at Judy's were Rhys and then his friends the next time I'd been there. When I was with Jaime the other night, we didn't talk to anyone except when Rhys showed up.

"Do you have a boyfriend?" he asked, changing the subject instead of clarifying when I'd met him at Judy's.

I furrowed my brows. "If I had a boyfriend, then I wouldn't be out on a date with you."

He nodded and took another sip of his wine. "So you and Rhys broke up?"

My breath caught. "Rhys? I'm not dating Rhys."

Philip chuckled without sound. "You two told me you were dating for four months about a month ago. So you broke up or …"

I stared at him as realization dawned on me. He was the guy who'd caused me to actually meet Rhys. The one I wanted to leave me alone when I was trying to drown my sorrows because of Corey. I hadn't got a good look of the guy because I didn't want to make eye-contact with someone I was lying to. But he did look familiar and now confirmed it.

Before I could answer his question, he asked another, "Or are you just sleeping with him?"

I started to stand to leave, but he grabbed my hand. "I'm only trying to figure out if I have competition. That night I did, and Rhys won. I'm not mad."

After a few moments of hesitation, I swallowed and sat back down. "Rhys and I are only friends. That night I didn't want to be bothered because I'd actually broken up with my boyfriend."

"Corey."

The hairs on the back of my neck stood. "How do you know about Corey?"

Philip grinned. "I Facebook stalked you after we met."

"My profile is private," I stated. I'd made sure of that because I didn't want random people to friend or follow me. I did, however, have a business page, but I'd never shared anything personal on it.

"Not your profile pictures."

"Oh," I breathed as once again Philip stated facts. *Facts about me and my life.* But I'd deleted all pictures of Corey after we broke up. Or at least I thought I had.

"I'm sorry, I didn't mean to scare you. I just wanted to make sure I wasn't going to be in some sort of love triangle."

I took a deep breath before responding. "No, you're not." I meant it because after this date, I was never going out with this guy again. Something seemed off about the entire conversation and him.

"Good. Let's enjoy ourselves then." Philip looked out at the Chicago skyline, and I did as well. We were silent for a few minutes as I watched the snow fall from the sky and disappear many stories below.

My phone buzzed in my clutch that was sitting on the table. I was silently praying the waiter would bring our dinner, but a fake emergency text could work. Normally, I wouldn't bother to see who it was, but I needed any excuse to get out of here.

Jaime: How's your date going?

"Everything okay?"

"I think so. I'm just going to use the restroom and give my friend a call back to make sure."

"No problem," Philip said and reached for the bottle of wine to refill our glasses.

I grabbed my clutch and stood. Just as I was about to turn the corner to ask the hostess where the restroom was, I looked back at Philip and saw what appeared to be him slipping something into my drink.

My body went cold, and my heart started to race. Was he drugging me? How was this happening? Of course, I wouldn't have slept with him tonight, but I'd mentioned to him that if things went well with this date, then there would be more. How could there be more if he drugged me? I would never go out with this guy again, especially if I woke up tomorrow and didn't remember anything.

I hurried to the coat check instead of the restroom, gave the attendant my ticket and turned to the elevators to leave. I wasn't going to tell Philip goodbye, and I wasn't staying for the meal. If I were to go back into the dining room, I was sure I'd cause a scene, and I couldn't have that floating around on the internet. Instead, I pressed the button for the elevator over and over until it came. Then I did the same with the lobby level button until I was on the ground floor. I hadn't even used the app to call Uber. Instead, I hailed a cab and got the fuck out of there.

CHAPTER TWELVE

Rhys

As soon as my broadcast was over, I went home. I wasn't in the best mood. The Blackhawks had lost, and Ashtyn was out on a date.

When Ashtyn mentioned that she'd agreed to go out with that guy, I told her I would be working. That was partially true because the Hawks had an early game and I'd be home at a decent hour. I hadn't even heard from her since she texted me she had a date, and that just caused me to be even more in a bad mood. My horrible mood lasted all week.

While she and I were friends with benefits, I wanted more with her. However, I might have waited too long to make my move. I thought I was giving her time to figure out what she wanted or who for that matter, so I never pressed her to be more. And then when she mentioned some guy wanted to take her out, I just let it happen.

I fucking let it happen.

Now as I pulled into my parking space in my garage, Ashtyn was out with this guy, and I was left to wonder if she was having a good time. Of course, I wasn't going to be that crazy guy and text her or call her. If she ended up liking the dude, then she and I were only meant to be each other's rebound.

Instead of going up to my condo, I decided to go to Judy's. I needed a drink and not one where I was drinking alone. If anything, I could talk to Tommy. Bartenders did that sort of shit, and Tommy and I had some sort of friendship since I'd been frequenting Judy's for the past several years.

When I made it to the bar, I strolled right up to the wood top, took a seat and ordered a seven and seven. It wasn't a beer night. I needed the extra alcohol content whiskey would provide. I needed to forget. It was crazy how I felt as though I was in the same bar, trying to forget some woman. Though this time, I was actually upset about it. Upset that Ashtyn's lips might touch this guy. Her mouth might touch other parts of him, or he might get a taste of her. The whole situation made me angry. In hindsight, I should have just told her I wanted her date to be with me and only me.

"Bad game for the Blackhawks." Tommy set my drink in front of me. I handed my credit card to him. He stuck it in the cup by the register, knowing I was keeping my tab open.

"Sure was," I agreed.

"You think they're going all the way this season?"

I shrugged then took a sip of my drink. For once I didn't want to talk about hockey. In fact, I didn't want to talk about anything which was weird because I didn't want to be home alone either. I just wanted the alcohol to get into my system and put me at ease. "They have a good chance."

He nodded and went to help another patron while I gulped a few sips trying to better my mood. I was at the bottom of my glass when someone stood next to me. I turned and my day got worse.

"You've got to be fucking shitting me!" I groaned through gritted teeth.

"Just hear me out."

I stood, anger flooding my blood. Today was not the day. "There's nothing to talk about, Bridgette. Just fucking leave me alone. It's over."

"We have a problem here?" Tommy asked, standing directly behind the bar from us.

"If you don't leave, I will have Tommy call the cops," I warned. A part of me wanted that to happen, but the other part could never do this to her. I just wanted her to leave me alone so I could move on. Move on to who was the question.

"The cops don't need to get involved," Bridgette pleaded. "I just saw you were alone and figured you broke up with Ashtyn."

"Apparently they do because you won't leave me alone." I didn't bother to correct her about Ashtyn. There was no point.

"Because I love you and I want to make us work."

"You love me so much that you had to fuck another guy in my bed?"

I saw Tommy out of the corner of my eye reach for the phone that was behind the bar. I shook my head slightly in his direction, and he set the handset back down.

"I made a mistake," Bridgette whined. "Please."

"Also you straight up told me that you were only with me so you could meet a hockey player. You think I'm stupid enough to take you back?"

"I lied about that. I wanted to hurt you because—"

"Because you got caught and you were the one heartbroken?"

"I'm sorry. I made a mistake."

I stepped closer to her and got within inches of her body. My blood was on fire. I was done. So done. "I don't give a fuck, and if I see your face one more time, even by a random accident, I will get a restraining order so fucking fast."

A tear slid down her cheek. "You won't give me another chance?"

"No. Now please leave. We're done. You made that choice when you thought it would be okay for some other dude's dick to be inside you." What was funny was that was the best thing Bridgette could have done for me. I didn't know it then, but looking back, she was just there going through the motions of life with me.

Bridgette stared at me for a moment, and then she stormed off and out of the bar. Hopefully out of my life forever.

"Hawks lost, and you have girl problems? Let me get you another."

I chuckled without sound as I watched Tommy grab the whiskey bottle. I sat back down and ran my hand through my finger-length hair. "I'm not even sure how it could get any worse."

Then as if life was laughing at me, *he* walked in laughing with his friends. Flashbacks of being a freshman entered my mind. He moved closer, and even though it had been almost twenty years since I'd seen him, I could pick out Corey Fucking Pritchett in a lineup. He still had that cocky smirk that showed his fucking dimple I wanted to stick a cigarette in. Though now, I was bigger and stronger. I wasn't the toughest guy around, but looking at him walk in the door, I could tell that I was finally bigger than him. Except he wasn't alone, and I was.

He and his two friends walked toward the bar, and I turned back to Tommy, not wanting to make eye contact with Corey. I took two large gulps of the new seven and seven Tommy had made for me and willed it to work faster. Just as I was about to take another sip—a sip that would get me closer to finishing my drink so I could leave—I heard his voice. The voice that traumatized me as a kid.

"Well, shit. As I live and breathe, boys, it's Rhys Cole!"

I closed my eyes, not turning toward him. Instead, I reached for my glass again.

Someone—probably Corey—slapped me on the back. "I haven't seen you in …"

"Not long enough," I spat, still not looking at him.

"What, you're too famous for your old high school pal?"

I drank the rest of my drink and called to Tommy, "I'll take my bill now."

Corey laughed. "You're running like you did in high school?"

I stood and once again got within inches of a person, my blood racing. I was now two inches taller than him, and after the day I'd had, I would love to smash his face in. "Like in high school?" I mocked. "You were a fucking prick in high school, and just like then, I want nothing to do with you."

"Here you go, Rhys," Tommy said. I looked over to see he was trying to hand me my credit card, the bill, and a pen.

"Aw, you running home to Mommy?"

I took the stuff from Tommy and scribbled my name. Then I turned back to Corey. "You're pushing forty now. Grow the fuck up."

"You ain't shit, Cole. You may have taken my position on the ice in high school, but neither one of us made it to the pros."

I didn't stop as I kept walking toward the door. Apparently, he was still bitter that I'd taken his starting position in high school. I had no idea what he did after high school, but if he were good enough, he would have been drafted. It wasn't my fault.

I assumed Corey would follow me and we'd fight. I was ready. My fists were clenched as I walked in the direction of my place, but when I turned around a few feet down the street, there was no one behind me. Snow started to cool my anger, and when I made it to my building, I took the elevator up to my floor wanting to crawl into bed and wake up in the morning to start a new day. A day that would hopefully be better. But as I made my way down the hall toward my door, I noticed someone sitting on the floor.

"Cupcake." I knelt down in front of her and saw tears streaming down her face. "What's wrong?"

Her teary eyes looked up at me. "I'm so stupid."

"Did that guy hurt you?" I brushed a tear away with my thumb as my heart clenched in my chest waiting for the answer. After today, I'd kill this guy especially for hurting the person I cared so much about.

She shook her head. "No, but he was going to."

My blood that had thawed during my walk home in the snow started to boil again. "What do you mean?"

"Everything was off about the date, and when I was going to the restroom to call Jaime so she could call me back and get me out of the date, I saw him slip something in my wine."

My heart stopped and my muscles tensed. "Did you drink it?"

She balked. "Of course not! I left."

My body instantly relaxed and I moved to sit beside her. "Good."

"He knew about you and my ex."

"What?"

Ashtyn shrugged. "He said he Facebook stalked me, but my profile has always been private. Plus, I deleted every picture of me and my ex."

"Maybe he did this before the day you met him?"

"Oh, and he's the guy from Judy's who tried to pick me up when you pretended to be my boyfriend."

"Hmmm …" I rubbed my chin as I tried to process everything she was saying. She rested her head on my shoulder, and I brought her closer to me. "So let me get this straight. The guy that came up to you at Judy's the night we met is the same guy who you ran into getting coffee?" She nodded. "And he knows about your ex and obviously me?"

"Well, I think he knows about you since he knew who you were that night too."

"But you deleted all old pictures of your ex on Facebook?" I never checked because I didn't want to see if she had. We were only using each other for sex, and even though I wanted more with her, I couldn't bring myself to look because I knew it would hurt since she obviously still had feelings for him.

"Yes, and I've never posted anything personal on my business page."

"I never want you seeing that guy again," I stated. I didn't care that we were only friends. This guy seemed crazy, and I didn't want anything to happen to her.

"I won't. I'm freaked out." She looked up at me, her eyes red from crying. "Can I stay here tonight?"

"Of course, Cupcake." I stood and reached my hand down to help her up. "You can stay as long as you want."

We went inside my place and straight to bed. There was no stripping each other of clothes or touching of feverous hands. I loaned Ashtyn a T-shirt, and after I changed into pajama pants, we both crawled into the bed, and I held her spoon style. I was almost asleep when she spoke.

"What if I wouldn't have seen him put the shit in my wine, or what if he'd acted normal?"

"I don't think you should worry about that. You did see, and your instincts were on point."

"Almost a little too late."

"But you're here now."

She sighed. "And I never want to leave."

I raised up and peered down at her. Ashtyn rolled to her back, and in the darkness I could faintly make out her face with the light coming from the clock on my nightstand. It was just enough for me to find her lips. I kissed her lightly. "Then don't."

"I can't just move in with you."

"I'm not asking you to move in with me. I'm asking you to be my girl."

"Your girl?"

"Yeah, Cupcake. There's not a chance I'll ever let you go out with another man again, so you might as well be mine."

"Be yours? You're ready to start dating again? Bridgette's—"

"Bridgette and I are over, and I want to be with you."

A slow smile curved her lips. "I want to be with you too."

"Good, and I promise to never drug you."

"Little too soon, babe."

"Sorry." I rolled over onto my back.

"Since we're dating now, want to tell me about your night?"

I sighed. *Not really.* "It actually kinda sucked."

"Really?" I felt her turn over to face me.

"Well, for starters, the Blackhawks lost."

"Aw man."

"I know. And I went to Judy's for a drink, and fucking Bridgette showed up."

"She did?"

I nodded in the dark. "Told her that if I see her another time, I'll get a restraining order."

"Good."

"Yeah," I sighed. "Then my night got worse."

"How so?" She started making circles on my bare chest, and I never wanted her to stop.

"Ran into my high school bully."

Her finger stopped. "You were bullied as a kid?"

"I was bullied as a freshman," I corrected. "The asshole liked to roam the halls and pick on those smaller than him. Got worse when coach made me starting center and not him."

"What happened tonight when you saw him?"

I chuckled. "I called him old."

"You didn't!" Ashtyn snorted and rolled to her back.

"I did. I hadn't seen him since I was a freshman and he was a senior, and tonight he was trying to act as though we're best buds. He made some comment about me being on TV, and I was two seconds away from punching him in the face."

"But you didn't?"

I shook my head. "No. I told him to grow up, and I left."

Ashtyn moved again, but this time she placed her head on my bare chest. My arm went around her back, and I started to run my fingers along her arm. "I'm proud of you."

My heart swelled. "That means a lot, Cupcake."

She snuggled in closer to me. "Tonight was crazy for both of us."

"Yeah, it was." I sighed, though falling asleep with Ashtyn in my arms was the best way to end a shitty day.

A few days later, Ashtyn went to her parents' for Thanksgiving, and I went to mine. Our parents only lived about twelve miles from each other. It was weird to think that the girl of my dreams lived so close to me growing up and I'd never met her.

"Hello," I called out, walking in through the front door. Instantly, the smell of turkey hit my nose and my stomach growled. Everyone knew you didn't eat breakfast or lunch on Thanksgiving. It was all about the dinner, and this morning I worked up a sweat with Ashtyn before we'd parted ways, so I was extra hungry.

"We're in the kitchen," Mom called back.

My parents still lived in the two-story house I grew up in, and sometimes I missed living in a quiet neighborhood, but now I wouldn't change it for the world. How many people could say they lived across the street from their girlfriend? This guy. And it was fucking awesome because I didn't have to get in the car and drive thirty minutes or whatever to her place.

I shut the door and made my way to the updated kitchen that looked out onto a giant backyard. My sister and her husband were already there, and when I rounded the corner, Romi rushed to me.

"Is it true?" she asked, engulfing me in her arms.

"Is what true?"

"Are you dating Ashtyn Valor?"

I broke free from her grasp and looked from her to my mom and back. "What the hell is the big deal about Ashtyn?"

"Because she's not that skank Bridgette." She rolled her blue eyes that were just like mine.

"Romi!" Mother scolded.

"What? It's true!"

I nodded and agreed with my twenty-nine-year-old sister that still liked to gossip. "It is true."

"So are you and Ashtyn …?" She proceeded to prod me for the answer she was dying to hear.

I chuckled. "Well, now we are."

"You are?" Mother stopped stirring something on the stove and looked at me with a huge smile spread across her face.

"Yes," I confirmed again as I reached for a carrot on the tray on the kitchen island.

"That's the best news I've heard all day," my mother gushed.

"We can top it," Romi stated looking back at her husband with a huge smile on her face. "We're pregnant!"

Aw fuck. No doubt my mother was going to start hounding me more.

CHAPTER THIRTEEN

Ashtyn

Breaking News: Ashtyn Valor has moved on from Corey Pritchett and is now dating Rhys Cole—officially.

The Monday after my horrible date with Philip, I arrived at work to hear twenty voicemails from him. I kid you not. Twenty!

"Ashtyn, it's Philip. Where'd you go?"

"Ashtyn, it's Philip again. I'm worried."

"It's Philip again. Please let me know if you're okay."

They kept going and going ...

"The coat girl told me you left. You could have at least told me."

"You know what? Fuck you, bitch!"

And finally …

"I only wanted to fuck you anyway. You're probably a lousy lay."

I saved every single one just in case something were to ever happen to me, but didn't tell anyone. What was there to tell? I didn't know his last name or anything about him, and he technically never did anything to me. It was too late for them to test if there was anything in the wine. He also stopped calling after that day.

Thank God.

Like clockwork, Abby walked up to my desk with a flower delivery. "They're black," I stated, looking at the bouquet in her hands.

"I know! Crazy huh?"

I'd never seen a black rose in person before now. I pulled the card from the middle of the flowers after Abby set them on my desk.

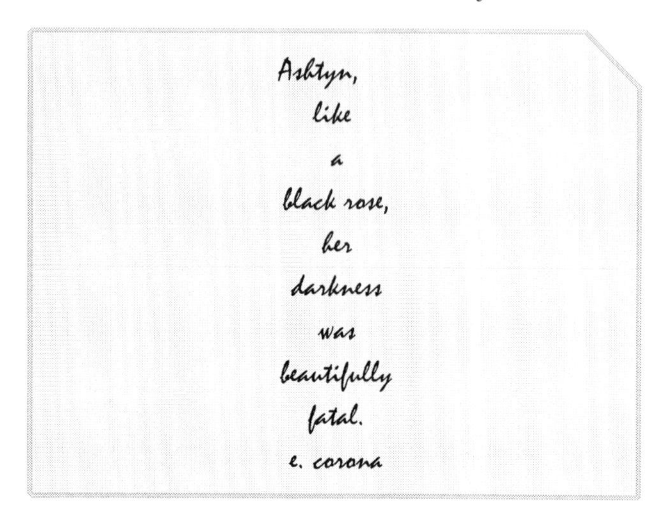
Ashtyn,
like
a
black rose,
her
darkness
was
beautifully
fatal.
e. corona

I had no idea what the note actually meant, but the black roses were beautiful, and even though they didn't say they were from SA, I knew they were.

Once again, I showed up alone to Thanksgiving at my parents. This year I had planned to bring Corey with me. Obviously, that was no longer the case, and since Rhys and I had just officially started dating, we decided to stick with our original plans and do our own Thanksgivings. It was a little too soon to meet the family even though for the past three nights I'd stayed over at his place because I was scared to be alone. Tonight would be no different because we had plans to meet up after dinner.

"Are you doing okay?" my mom asked, giving me a one-armed hug as I peeled potatoes.

"I'm fine." I smiled.

"Are you doing okay after everything with Corey?" Her hazel eyes squinted a little as she frowned, sad for me.

"Now I am."

She perked up at my omission. “Good. And what about that young man who does the shows before the Blackhawks games?”

“Rhys Cole.” My grin grew wider just thinking about him.

“Yes, him. I saw your picture on Facebook.”

“Everyone saw that picture.” I laughed. *Probably even Philip … somehow.*

“He’s very handsome.”

“Then if I tell you that we’re dating, you’ll be happy?”

Her eyes widened, and she smiled. “Yes.”

“Then we’re dating.”

“Who are you dating?” my sister-in-law Jessica asked. She was married to my older brother Ethan.

I turned to her, a potato in my hand, and proceeded to tell them that Rhys and I had just started to date after weeks of *talking*. That conversation led to my dad and brothers begging me to get them free tickets to a Blackhawks game until it was time to eat. Now that I was dating someone in the industry they assumed I had perks. I wasn’t even sure if Rhys could get free tickets, so I just told them I’d see what I could do.

“Hey, Daddy,” I greeted, coming into the living room where he and my brothers were watching football. Their wives and my mother were in the kitchen getting the pies ready, and my three nephews were doing something somewhere else in the house.

I’d snuck away from the kitchen because I wanted to talk to my dad for a few minutes. He used to be a police officer and then a detective for Chicago PD for most of my life. He’d retired almost seven years ago, but he’d know what to do. Ethan was currently a detective, but I didn’t think I needed to involve him yet. I just needed advice from my father.

“Kiddo,” Dad greeted back and draped his arm around my shoulders.

"Can I ask you a question?"

"Of course."

I raised up and turned slightly to face him. "When you were on the force, did you have any stalker cases?"

His steel-blue eyes widened. "Why? Do you have a stalker?"

I swallowed. "I'm not sure."

"What did you just ask Dad?" Ethan asked. I'd assumed he was too engrossed in the game to hear me talking to our father.

"Its fine." I waved him off.

"It's not fine," my other brother Carter snapped, joining the conversation.

I sighed. Sometimes I hated having older brothers. Ethan was six years older than me, and Carter was three. It was great in school until all my friends wanted to date my older brothers, especially when they went off to college. My high school friends loved the fact that they knew college guys. Little did they know that my brothers were assholes. At least to me. Now that we're all in our thirties, we loved each other, but they could still be jerks. They never missed an opportunity to tease me about something.

"Who's stalking you?" Dad asked.

"I'm not sure if he's stalking me, but I went on a date with this guy, and the whole thing was creepy."

"I thought you were dating Rhys Cole?" Ethan asked.

"I am. This was a few days ago before Rhys and I made it official."

Ethan leaned toward me from where he sat on a loveseat. He'd apparently forgotten about the football game and was now in detective mood. "How was this other guy creepy?"

I shrugged. "Don't worry about it. It's fine."

"Ashtyn, you better tell us," Dad threatened.

"I'm a big girl."

"And there's a lot of sick fucks out there," Ethan stated.

"Do we need to pay this guy a visit?" Carter asked.

I rolled my eyes. "No. I don't know anything about him or where he lives. I don't even know his last name or phone number." I'd thought I'd at least get his phone number on our date, but since that was cut short, I literally knew nothing about him except his first name and that he worked as a nuclear engineer. I didn't know where either.

"Just tell us why you asked me about stalkers," Dad pressed.

I sighed and told them how Philip was the guy at the bar when I met Rhys, how I ran into him at Starbucks, how I went on a date with him, how he knew about Corey even though I thought I'd deleted all traces of him, and how I saw him slip something in my wine.

"He tried to date rape you?" Ethan stood, anger lacing his face.

"I got out of there, so he didn't."

"I wish you knew more about this guy so we could handle it," Dad stated.

"I just want to know if he sounds like a stalker."

"He sounds like something," Carter mumbled.

"If you see him again, you call me." Ethan crossed his arms. "Even if you run into him at Starbucks again."

I nodded. "There's something else too. I get flowers once a week at work from a secret admirer."

"Flowers? What kind of flowers?" Dad asked.

"Roses."

"Are there cards?" Carter asked.

I nodded. "Yeah. They usually say stuff about how pretty I look."

"And you don't find them weird?"

I balked at Ethan's question. "No, I thought they were sweet. It's nice getting flowers from a fan."

"Do you think it's the same guy?" Ethan kept questioning.

I shook my head. "No, I've been getting them for about a year now, and I just met Philip a little over a month ago at Judy's."

"I suggest not going back to Judy's," Dad suggested.

"Okay. It's probably for the best." I could do that.

"Pies ready," Mom said, peeking her blonde head around the corner.

We started to walk toward the kitchen to grab a slice. "Just call me if something else happens." Ethan squeezed my shoulder.

I nodded.

"Yeah, then we'll go beat this guy up like we used to do to those kids in high school." Carter smirked.

I rolled my eyes.

"Now, it's a felony." Dad shook his head.

"If we get caught." Carter laughed.

Me: Are you home?

Rhys: Almost. Are you?

Me: I'm sitting in my car.

Rhys: Are you coming over?

Me: I need clean clothes. How about we stay at my place tonight?

Rhys: I'm on my way.

Ten minutes later, Rhys walked into my building. I was waiting in the lobby talking to Jose, one of the doormen. We had a few doormen who opened the door for us when we arrived or left, delivered packages if they arrived when we weren't home, and screened visitors who they'd never seen before. It made me feel a little safer knowing we had someone watching the front doors of the building.

"Hey, Cupcake." Rhys kissed my lips lightly. "You waited for me?"

"Just catching up with my good friend Jose." I winked at Jose and waved goodbye.

Rhys swung his arm around my shoulders as we walked to the elevator. "How was Thanksgiving?"

"I can't wait to get out of these jeans. I ate too much," I groaned.

"I did too, but I still need dessert."

It was on the tip of my tongue to ask why he didn't have pie. Dessert was always a part of my Thanksgiving, but then I looked up to see him smirking, and I knew exactly what he meant.

Most women love to shop. Especially when it's with their friends and they mix in cocktails—at noon. That was on my agenda while Rhys had a game. I needed to buy a dress for the Emmys, and I didn't want to go shopping alone in fear I might run into someone I didn't want to see.

The girls and I decided to shop for my dress first before grabbing lunch. I didn't trust us to pick a dress for me if we were tipsy. The Emmys were like—well, the Emmys. Each year we walked the red carpet, and then when we got inside, there was an open bar followed by the awards ceremony.

"I like that one," Kylie stated as I came out of the dressing room.

I looked in the mirror and twirled, looking at myself in the knee length, black, halter neckline cocktail dress. It was perfect. Unlike the Prime Time Emmys for the actors of all of our favorite TV shows, I didn't need to spend thousands on my dress. Granted they were probably paid *to* wear those dresses.

I turned to face the other girls. "I think so too."

"I agree." Colleen nodded.

"You look hot," Jaime agreed.

I chuckled. "I'm not going for hot. It's a work function."

"Yes, but your boyfriend will be there." Jaime sang the word boyfriend, and I rolled my eyes.

"We're not going together," I corrected. "He's bringing his mom."

"So you get to meet the family already?" Kylie asked.

"Just his mom." I moved to go back to the dressing room.

The planners of the event made the seating arrangements, and usually they sat each network together unless there was a special request. We were less than a week away from the Emmys, so I figured Rhys and I wouldn't be sitting next to each other.

"If you get her approval, I'm sure you'll be invited for Christmas," Jaime called out.

I started to unzip the dress after closing myself into the fitting room. "You guys are stressing me out with all this family talk. Let's go get a drink."

After paying for my dress, we went to the Cheesecake Factory where, after a glass of wine, I told them what happened with Philip. Jaime already knew what happened on my date because I'd called her when I was in the taxi heading back to my condo. She had been seconds away from coming over, but I'd told her I was going to see Rhys instead of heading into my empty place. Colleen and Kylie were shell-shocked, but after I assured them that I was okay because I was sitting in front of them drinking a margarita, they breathed a sigh of relief.

Now that everyone knew, I never wanted to think of Philip again.

CHAPTER FOURTEEN

Rhys

The Emmys.

Honestly, I just went for the open bar.

Of course, over the past few years, it was nice to actually get a few awards. If I had a fireplace, I'd display those babies so everyone could see them. Instead, I kept them in my office. I wouldn't mind adding to my collection. I even wore the same black and white tux every year because I was hopeful that it was good luck.

Since my parents lived almost an hour from the city, my father drove into town with my mother, and they checked into a hotel—that I'd paid for—where the Emmys were being held. My dad was going to watch TV while we were downstairs. He'd probably order room service and something on Pay-Per-View, but I didn't mind.

Ashtyn and her co-worker, Abby, were going together, and we had plans to meet up inside the ballroom. Once everything started, we were probably going to be at different tables, unless my mother talked someone into switching. I wouldn't put it past her. Once they met, I was sure my mom was going to tell me to marry her tomorrow.

I rode the elevator up to the floor my parents were staying on, walked down the hall until I found their room number, and then knocked on the door. My dad opened it, dressed in his boxers and nothing else.

"So not painting the town red tonight?" I teased as I moved past him and into the room.

He closed the door and followed behind me. "Not a chance. I get to order whatever I want for dinner, watch whatever I want on the TV, and not have your mother nag me to death. I'm staying right here."

"I heard that!" Mother yelled from the bathroom.

Dad rolled his eyes as I asked, "Are you almost ready, Mom?"

The white bathroom door flew open, and my mom walked out in an emerald colored dress that had long sleeves and went to just past her knees. "Yes. I'm so excited!"

I chuckled as I kissed her on the cheek. "You look beautiful, Mom."

"Thank you. I wasn't sure what to wear to meet your girlfriend."

"You've met almost all my girlfriends. Why would this be any different?" I looked to Dad for confirmation, but he wasn't paying any attention to us. Instead, he was laying on the king-sized bed, his ankles crossed as he flipped through the stations on the TV.

"Yes, but this is a local celebrity." She moved to grab her purse.

"You don't need your purse," I reminded her. "We're going downstairs to the ballroom."

"I have my camera in here."

"You mean your phone?"

She pulled out a digital camera she'd had for at least ten years. "No, my camera."

I laughed. "No one takes pictures with cameras anymore."

"I want to get a picture with Ashtyn."

I smiled. "Trust me. We'll get pictures with her, but we'll do it with my phone." I patted the chest of my tux jacket, indicating I had my phone on me.

"And if you win another Emmy?"

"I'm sure Ashtyn will have it under control."

Mother sighed and put her camera back into her purse. "Okay, then I'm ready."

The traditional red carpet was in front of the ballroom with The National Academy of Television Arts & Sciences – Chicago/Midwest backdrop. We made our way down the carpet, stopped for a picture, and then I was stopped by a journalist who wanted to ask me about the Blackhawks' season. My answer was always the same. *"They have a good chance to go all the way."*

"Want a drink, Mom?"

"Sure."

We moved to the bar where I ordered a beer and my mother ordered a glass of Rosé. As we stood, sipping our drinks, I looked around for Ashtyn. I didn't see her anywhere. I pulled out my phone to text her.

Are you in the building?

The three dots automatically started to dance on the screen.

Ashtyn: We're walking in now.

"Ashtyn's here," I said out loud as I texted her back.

We're by the bar to the right.

"Where is she?"

"She'll be here in a few minutes. She's just walking in." I chuckled.

Mom turned her gaze toward the front doors, and my girl walked in wearing a black dress that showed her bare shoulders. Bare shoulders that I'd kissed the first night I met her.

"She's even more beautiful in person."

I nodded my agreement and watched as Ashtyn scanned the crowd in our direction. When her gaze met mine, we both smiled. She said something to her friend and then started toward us. My smile hadn't faltered one bit in the time it took her to walk across the room.

"Cupcake," I greeted, kissing her lips softly. "You know what your shoulders do to me."

She shoved me playfully and hissed, "Be good."

"I am being good or I could—"

"You must be Mrs. Cole." Ashtyn reached out her hand to my mother.

Mom waved off the handshake and moved to Ashtyn with opened arms. "It's so nice to finally meet you. And please, call me Claire."

"Right. So, Mom, this is Ashtyn. Ashtyn, this is my mother, Claire," I introduced them sarcastically. I meant to do the introductions before they hugged but seeing Ashtyn in a tight dress that showed a lot of skin was killing me. It was causing me to have thoughts of dragging her in the restroom and having my way with her.

"It's nice to meet you too." Ashtyn smiled.

"You want something to drink, Cupcake?"

"Cupcake? That's a cute term of endearment," Mother cooed.

Ashtyn's gaze flicked to mine, and I smirked at my mother's words. *Yeah, I wanted to lick Ashtyn's cupcake right about now.*

"I'll have what your mom's having."

I turned to the bar and ordered a Rosé for Ashtyn while she and my mother chatted about God knew what. Mother was probably asking her how she felt about a spring wedding. They were both laughing, and it struck me that it was the first time my mother had laughed with one of my girlfriends.

The bartender placed the pink wine in front of me, and after tipping him, I turned and moved back to the ladies. "Where did your co-worker go?" I asked, handing Ashtyn her drink.

"To mingle with some people."

"You know who I'd also like to meet?" Mother asked.

"Who?" I questioned.

"Barbara from the evening news. She's been on for years, and I'd like to just meet her once."

"I can introduce you," Ashtyn offered.

"Really? I'd love that."

Ashtyn scanned the room. "She's over there. Want me to do it now?"

Mom looked at me, and I shrugged. "I don't mind. In fact, I need to visit the little boy's room." The women started to move away, but I grabbed Ashtyn's wrist, halting her. "After you introduce them, meet me by the men's room."

"And leave your mother?" she asked in a whisper.

I nodded. "Trust me. She'll talk Barbara's ear off, and I want to show you something."

Ashtyn's eyes brightened. "I'm intrigued."

We parted ways, and I walked out the door in the direction where I assumed the restrooms were. I actually didn't care. I was going to find a quiet place where I could finally kiss her and not the sweet-hello-how-ya-doing one I gave her earlier.

I found the restroom, and instead of going inside, I waited against the wall for Ashtyn. I hadn't seen anyone go in or out, and when I saw her walking down the hall, I smiled.

"What do you want to show me?"

"Well, it's more I show you mine if you show me yours kinda thing," I teased, but actually the more I thought about it, and the more I figured no one was in the restroom, other thoughts entered my mind.

She groaned. "Rhys."

"Come on, Cupcake. I'll make it fast." She didn't move, so I walked the few feet back toward her. "It will be like when we were on the booze cruise."

"When we were on the booze cruise, people couldn't walk in on us at any moment. People we may work with."

"True." I ran my fingers along her cheek and brushed her long blonde curls off her shoulders. "But that makes it more exciting, right?"

"My boss is a guy. What if he walks in?"

"Then you better not be loud."

I took her hand, and she willingly walked behind me. I heard her mumble, "I can't believe we're doing this, especially with our co-workers right down the hall." She stopped. "And your mother!"

I pressed the door to the women's restroom open. "Fine. We'll do it in here."

She stared at me for a few seconds while I held the door. Finally, she stepped forward, peeked her head in and then tugged me inside. "Is this going to be a thing when we go out in public?"

I smirked. "Do you want it to be?"

Ashtyn bit her bottom lip. "It does turn me on."

"Of course it does, Cupcake. The thought of being caught excites everyone. They just don't admit it." I pulled her into the largest stall.

"What if someone who needs this stall comes in?"

"Then we better fucking hurry now shouldn't we?" I closed and locked the door behind us. "Take your panties off."

Ashtyn hesitated for a moment and then did as I asked. I took them from her, stuck the lace in my pocket and started to unzip my pants. She faced me, her back against the wall and after I slipped a condom on that I had in my wallet, I picked her up and teased her opening with my cock as she wrapped her legs around my hips.

"You ready, baby?"

She moaned her response as I used my cock to circle her clit.

I took that as my greenlight and guided myself into her. Ashtyn threw her head back, exposing her neck and while I thrust into her, I sucked and licked her skin. She moaned again, this time louder.

"Shh unless you want someone walking by to hear us."

"Feels. Good," she panted.

"Yeah, baby." While sex always felt good, especially with Ashtyn, there was something about thinking that at any moment someone could walk in and hear us. It only fueled my drive which caused me to thrust harder over and over, Ashtyn's back sliding up and down the wall.

Then it happened.

I didn't hear the door open, but I heard the females talking.

"I hope the food's good this year. Last year the chicken I got was dry."

Another woman replied, "I know. I hate that."

Ashtyn looked at me, her eyes wide. I smiled and placed my hand over her mouth. I didn't slow down as I pumped into her until she moaned deep in her throat. I followed behind her with a low groan of my own and then kissed her until I heard the door close and no more voices in the room.

After cleaning up, we walked back into the ballroom and found my mother. She was still talking to Barbara as if they'd been best friends since kindergarten. For all I knew, they were best friends now. My mother had a way of making everyone feel like friends or family. She could also sell ice to an Eskimo. I was certain I got my personality from her, and that was why I was comfortable in front of the camera.

"There you two are. I found our tables, and since we weren't all sitting together, I switched Ashtyn with someone. I hope that's okay?"

I chuckled. "Yeah, Mom, it is."

"I also heard dessert is cupcakes from that baking challenge show on TV: Cupcake Battle."

"I love that show!" Ashtyn exclaimed. "I bet the cupcakes are delicious."

I smirked. I'd never look at a real cupcake the same now.

Dinner was served during the awards ceremony. Ashtyn and I each won an Emmy, and pictures were captured on our phones and by the hired photographers. Now, every time I looked at my Emmy for this year, I'd think about the restroom and this night.

It was a fantastic night.

We walked my mother back to her room. My father was snoring logs, so we whispered and hugged our goodbyes. Then Ashtyn and I grabbed an Uber and headed home.

"Want to display our Emmys over your fireplace?" I asked in the backseat of some stranger's car.

"You want to keep it at my place?"

"I want to put it out in the open so we can brag to our friends how awesome we are."

"If I recall, this isn't your first one."

I shook my head. "Nope, but it's the first time my girlfriend won one in the same year. It can be like bookends or … mantel ends."

Whatever the hell mantel ends were. Hers could go on the right, and mine could go on the left.

"You're silly, but okay. Whatever. Does this mean we're staying at my place tonight?"

"Sure. Just let me run home and get my phone charger and change so I'm not doing the walk of shame in a tux tomorrow."

Ashtyn laughed. "Walk of shame, huh?"

"You know what I mean."

"Okay. I'll get the shower ready." She smirked.

I groaned. "I'll be quick."

A moment later, the car pulled up to Ashtyn's building. She took my Emmy from me, and we got out on opposite sides of the car. The car drove off, and as I started to walk across the street, I called out, "Leave the door open and wait in the shower for me."

"Just go!" Ashtyn shooed me away as she laughed and turned to walk into her building.

As I was rushing into my condo to change, a thought occurred to me. I called Ashtyn.

"Hello?"

"Hey! Want to go to Garfield Park tomorrow?"

"To the conservatory?"

"Yeah. We both have tomorrow off. It can be our first official date." I heard a faint knock in the background as I made my way to my bedroom to change.

"Sure. I haven't been in years."

"I'll just grab a change of clothes too, and we can do breakfast beforehand."

"Did you send me flowers?"

I stopped dead in my tracks and scrunched my eyebrows at her question. "No, why?"

"There's someone here holding up flowers."

A weird feeling went through my body. The only way to describe it was a sinking feeling in my stomach. "This late?"

"It's probably Jose. He sometimes brings up packages if he's on break and misses me when I walk through the door. Hold on."

"Why—" I started to say but stopped when I heard Ashtyn speak again.

"Philip, what are you doing here?"

"Who's Philip?" I asked, but she didn't respond.

"Ashtyn, Ashtyn, Ashtyn, did you think you'd get away from me that easily?"

"Ashtyn!" I yelled.

She didn't respond again. All I could hear was the wrestling of what I assumed was the phone.

My feet started to move on their own as I listened. I was running down my hall toward the elevator as fast as my feet could go. I wasn't sure if I'd even closed my door. I pressed the damn button over and over, but it wasn't coming fast enough. My heart was beating to the point I thought it would jump out of my chest, wanting to run across the street and beat me to Ashtyn's. I took the stairs, needing to hurry—needing to save my girl.

With every step I took, I could hear Ashtyn screaming for the person to let her go.

CHAPTER FIFTEEN

Ashtyn

I opened the door like an idiot.

Before he'd knocked, I only had enough time to take my coat off and put the Emmys on my mantle. It was as though he was waiting down the hall to make his move—make sure I was alone.

The moment the flowers were pulled away, and I saw that it was Philip, my nerves were on high alert. How did he know where I lived? And how did he get past Jose? But when I arrived home Jose wasn't at his desk. Was he on break? Went to the restroom?

"Philip, what are you doing here?"

"Ashtyn, Ashtyn, Ashtyn, did you think you'd get away from me that easily?"

Before I could close the door or run, Philip threw the bouquet of red roses and stepped inside. The phone slipped from my hand, and I felt as though my lifeline had fallen with it. I had no idea if Rhys was still on the other end, or if he even knew Philip was here and moving toward me. I'd never told Rhys Philip's name, and even if he did hear me ask Philip why he was here, it didn't mean that Rhys was on his way to help me.

Everything was happening in slow motion.

I took a step back. Philip took a step forward. I took another step back. Philip took another step forward. His steps were slow, calculated, as though he didn't want to scare me. I was starting to panic deep inside, praying Rhys would barge through the door and save the day.

"What do you want?" I whispered, looking into his brown eyes. My pulse was beating so hard that it was echoing in my ears. My body started to shake as I kept taking slow steps backward. I didn't want to turn and run because I knew he'd catch me. Plus, there was nowhere to go.

"Isn't it obvious?" He licked his lips. "I want you."

"So you thought drugging me was the way?"

"Is that why you left dinner? You saw me put the Rohypnol in your wine?"

I nodded.

Philip huffed as though he'd just realized his mistake. "I should have waited longer. Then you'd be at my place right now."

"I would?" I kept retreating backward in the direction of my kitchen hoping I could make it and I could grab a knife. I wasn't sure what I would do when I had it in my hand, but I'd at least feel as though I had the upper hand and not the other way around.

"Yeah, but instead, you're still fucking Rhys Cole, and we can't have that." He pulled at his hair as though he was frustrated.

"Wha—what?" Had he been watching me? Was he sick enough that he'd somehow had a bird's eye view of what Rhys and I did in the bedroom? Or was he only speculating because he'd seen me with Rhys before he came up to my door?

He grinned. "I know more than you think. You ran from me and straight into his bed. How do you think that makes me feel, Ashtyn?"

"Why do you think that?" I asked, even though it was true.

"You didn't go home."

"That doesn't mean I went to Rhys's."

He snorted. "You think I'm that stupid?"

"I—I don't know. We don't know each other."

"I know you. I also know your dad used to be a cop and your brother is currently a detective. You have another brother who became a doctor. Oh, and let's not forget your mother—"

"Stop!" I took another step back. "Why are you doing this? If you wouldn't have tried to drug me then I would have stayed, and who knows what would have happened."

"I know what would have happened, Ashtyn. I've seen you with him."

"You've … seen me with him?"

"Judy's, walking to your place, walking to his. In your place. Even out on Navy Pier."

"You're following me?" I could feel my palms starting to sweat. Hearing that Philip was stalking me confirmed my suspicions. Then a part of what he said struck me deeper: *in* your place.

"Of course. I had to wait for the perfect time to make you mine."

"I'll never be yours!"

"You are!" he roared.

I was a few feet away from the kitchen, ready to make my move, when Philip grabbed me by the arm, spun me around and placed something over my nose and mouth. Just as everything was going dark, I heard Rhys call out for me from the doorway.

But it was too late.

CHAPTER SIXTEEN

Rhys

By the time I made it across the street, I'd already dialed 911 and told them what I'd heard. I wanted to stay on the phone with Ashtyn, to listen as I ran, but calling for help was more important. The operator wanted me to stay on the line with them too, but I knew I'd need my hands free.

Jose was nowhere in sight as I waited for the elevator, thinking to myself that I was buying a fucking house because the wait for the damn thing to descend was taking *years*. There was no way I'd make it up fifteen flights of stairs running in less time either. It didn't matter that there were two elevators because each one was taking forever to come down—or at least that was what it felt like as I pictured Ashtyn fighting for her life.

"Fuck!" I groaned, stabbing the fucking button as though the more I pushed it, the faster one of the cars would come down.

"Is something wrong Mr. Cole?"

I looked over to see Jose standing beside me. "Did you let a man walk in here with flowers for Ashtyn?"

Jose scrunched his dark eyebrows. "No, but I just got back from my dinner break. Why, is there a problem? Flowers usually don't—"

"Yes, there's a fucking problem!" I hissed, cutting his rambling off. "Ashtyn is getting attacked right now, and I'm down here talking to you about fucking flowers while I wait for the *fucking* elevator to hurry the *fuck* up!"

His black eyes became huge. "She's getting attacked?"

"Yes!" I roared just as the elevator dinged. "Call the fucking police!"

I didn't care that I'd already done it. Maybe they'd hurry if more than one person called. I didn't know. What I did know was I was going to beat the ever-loving shit out of this guy. It wasn't only because he could be hurting Ashtyn—or worse. It was because when I was a kid and Corey pushed me around, I'd go home and lift weights. I never wanted to be in the position where I couldn't defend myself again. And now, I had my woman to protect.

Just as the doors started to close, I saw another man walk up. Usually, I'd do the polite thing and hold the door. *Not tonight, man.*

The elevator felt as though it was crawling toward the sky. The seconds felt like hours before the car finally stopped on her floor. When it did, I exited the doors before they opened fully and ran down the hall, praying to myself that I'd made it in time.

"Ashtyn!" I yelled, crossing over the threshold. I ran past the roses on the ground and toward the man in front of me. "Let her fucking go!"

He turned, Ashtyn's limp body pressed against his front as he held her up with a cloth pressed against her nose and mouth. Was she dead? Did he fucking kill her? Was I not fast enough to save her?

I couldn't believe that this was happening.

"I knew you'd show up." He reached behind his back with his free arm and pulled a black Glock.

I stopped in my tracks and held up my hands as he pointed the handgun at me. I had every intention of being the hero. I wanted to run in and save the day, be Ashtyn's savior. That was until I was standing with the barrel of a gun pointed at me. "What the fuck are you doing? Let her go!" I yelled though I knew he wouldn't because no bad guy did that.

"I can't do that," he growled. "You have what I want."

I realized then that Ashtyn wasn't dead. It was clear he wanted to be with Ashtyn, and if he killed her, then neither one of us could be with her. What I needed him to do was drop Ashtyn. Sure she'd have some bruises, but then I could charge at him and hopefully grab the gun.

"Fine. Just let her go. She's a forgiving person. I'm sure you two will be happy together."

"Then leave."

"I can't do that. At least let me know she's okay."

"She's fine," he hissed. "Ten or so minutes after I remove this cloth from her face, she'll wake. It's only a little ether to knock her out so I could get her home."

"Just take the cloth off. Let me stay with her until she wakes up so I can say my goodbyes." I thought I faintly heard sirens. I never understood why police did that. That was how they got in foot chases with criminals. It was like they needed to announce their presence when, in reality, they should make a stealth attack.

"She left me without saying goodbye the other night. You don't get the pleasure either."

"How are you going to get past me?" The way he was holding her, there was no way he could move forward. He'd need to drag her behind him or carry her, and that would give me the chance to make my move.

"Well, I'm going to shoot you then leave like I'd planned."

"Then do it!" The moment those three words left my mouth, I realized I was standing in front of a man who was pointing a gun at me, and I wasn't scared. All I cared about was Ashtyn because I loved her. I didn't know when it happened, but I knew I'd do anything for her and that included taking a bullet.

Philip started to smirk as though he would gladly shoot me, but then his head twitched to the side slightly. "You called the police?"

"Of course I called the cops."

He brought his arm up higher, and I knew deep in my gut that he was seconds away from pulling the trigger. They say that when you're about to die, your life flashes before your eyes, but what flashed before mine was the night I met Ashtyn. Meeting her had turned my shitty night into the best night of my life. I'd met the person I wanted to bring coffee to in bed.

There was a flash of our silly date on the booze cruise in the middle of the day, and then a flash of us going down to have hot bathroom sex. And then there was one of me telling my mother that I was going to propose to Ashtyn. It didn't matter that it had never happened. It still flashed because that was what I wanted for my life. I didn't care that we'd just met two months ago, or that we'd just started dating. She was the one who made my world complete. Being with her made everything in my life whole. She made me happy.

"Drop your weapon!"

I turned to see the guy I hadn't held the elevator for move into Ashtyn's condo, a gun raised at Philip.

"Well, this is turning into quite the family affair." Philip chuckled.

I stared at the man dressed in jeans and a black coat, my arms still raised in defense. *Family affair?*

"I said, drop your fucking weapon!"

"Not gonna happen," Philip replied. "If I do, then you'll definitely have the upper hand because I know you won't shoot your sister."

Sister? Well, this was an awkward first meeting.

"Get behind me, Rhys."

I moved behind Ashtyn's brother. I'd never met her brother, but given what Ashtyn had told me, he'd watched my broadcasts before. I had no idea why he had a gun though, but using him as a shield was in my best interest. The sirens were getting closer now, and I just wanted the cops here already. The longer this was taking, the more I feared it wouldn't end the way we wanted.

"All you need to do is drop the gun, and no one gets hurt."

"No—"

I jumped at a loud pop. Philip stared at us, a hole now in the center of his forehead. Slowly, crimson blood started to trickle out of his head. Ashtyn's brother had shot him. He fucking shot him in the head!

Philip fell back with Ashtyn in his arms, and then she rolled as his arms loosened around her, the cloth falling away from her face. I stood in shock, still wondering how her brother had the guts to shoot Philip. Ashtyn's brother moved, kicked the gun away from Philip's lifeless body, and then picked Ashtyn up and placed her on the couch.

"Are you okay?"

I blinked.

"Rhys."

I blinked again, this time realizing I was staring at Philip with my mouth hanging open. "You—you shot him."

"Of course. He had a gun pointed at us, and my fucking sister's unconscious."

I snapped out of it and rushed to Ashtyn. Her brother was checking what I assumed was her pulse on her neck. "But you killed him." I didn't know why it shocked me because I'm pretty certain I would have killed the bastard too. Maybe it was seeing a man lose his life in front of my eyes that stunned me.

"I have to say that was a first for me, but I wasn't going to let him hurt any of us. Ashtyn's breathing, and the paramedics should be here any second." He took his cell phone out of his pocket, pressed a few buttons and then held it to his ear. "Yeah, dispatch. This is Detective Valor, badge number 57689. I responded to the call at," he rattled off Ashtyn's address while I brushed her hair away from her face. "Please be advised that I'm in plain clothes, shots were fired, and suspect's deceased."

"You're a cop?" I asked, looking up at him as he slid his phone back into his pocket.

"Yeah."

"Not that I'm not grateful, but how did you get here before the other cops?"

"Ashtyn told me about this guy when I saw her on Thanksgiving."

"She did?" I looked back at her, and if I didn't know any better, I'd think she was only sleeping on the couch, not unconscious from ether.

"Yeah, and I just got off duty and wanted to check on her to see if she had any more info on this guy. The doorman almost didn't let me in, but I showed him my badge, and he told me you said Ash was getting attacked."

I stood and took a deep breath, trying to calm the adrenaline that was still coursing through my veins. "If you would have been a second later, he would have shot me, so thank you."

He turned to me and stuck out his hand. “You’re welcome. Next time hold the fucking elevator for me. I’m Ethan, by the way.”

I took his hand. “I will, and damn, I wish we could have met under different circumstances.”

CHAPTER SEVENTEEN

Ashtyn

I woke to a room full of people.

Right away, I realized that I was lying on my couch, and a blanket was over me. From the quick look at my chest, I was still in my dress and shoes from the Emmys. I didn't know what had happened, but I wasn't chained somewhere with Philip looming over me.

When I turned toward the voices, the first person I saw in my haze was my brother. "Ethan?"

He looked over at me when I called his name, and as he moved, there was movement from my right side. I turned my head to see Rhys was moving toward me as well. Something tugged my arm, and I noticed a female paramedic was by my side with a blood pressure cuff around my upper arm.

"How are you feeling?" the paramedic asked.

"Foggy. What happened?"

"Your head should clear soon. Ether only stays in your system while it's being administered. And you'll need to ask a detective about what happened. I don't know."

"How long was I out?" I felt as though it had been hours, maybe even days.

"Maybe twenty minutes," Rhys answered.

"What happened?" I asked Rhys this time. I noticed he was still in his tux.

"I'll fill you in once you've had time to get all the ether out of your system."

I turned my gaze and looked at my brother. "What are you doing here?"

"It's a long story."

Rhys handed me a bottle of water that he was already holding. "Drink some water."

"Yes," the paramedic agreed. "You need to rest, and we need to get you to the hospital, but let's bring you closer to the window so you can get some fresh air first. That will help clear your head faster."

"Do I need to go the hospital?"

"I would advise you do go."

Rhys and Ethan helped me off the couch and then brought me to a window where the paramedic placed a chair. Rhys opened the window, and a rush of winter air blew in, sending a chill over my body. I took a few sips of the water.

"But I don't *have* to go to the hospital, right?"

"Well, given it was only ether and all your vitals are stable, you don't have to, but—"

"I don't want to." I took in another deep breath of the fresh air. I was already starting to feel a little better, and given what I knew about ether, doctors once used it like they used Propofol as a general anesthesia. "My other brother's a doctor and if I don't feel better, I'll have him check me out."

"Okay," the paramedic said. "Just promise me you'll get a lot of fresh air and drink plenty of water."

I nodded. The paramedic took my blood pressure one more time. "What happened to Philip?" I asked both Rhys and Ethan, not caring who answered.

Rhys and Ethan looked at each other, but my brother was the one to answer first. "He's—"

Rhys knelt beside me and brushed a strand of my blonde hair behind my ear and spoke before Ethan could finish, "He can't hurt you anymore, Cupcake."

"He's in jail?" I looked up at my brother for confirmation.

Ethan took a deep breath. "No. I shot him."

I gasped, and my eyes widened in shock. I hadn't realized Ethan arrived while everything was happening. I assumed that he was called in afterward. "You did?"

"Shit went down, Ash."

"Apparently," I replied dryly. My stomach started to feel a little queasy, so I turned back toward the window and took a deep breath of the chilly, fresh air.

A detective came over and pulled Ethan away. Rhys started to rub circles on my back. "You want to walk over to my place?"

"Yes." I definitely didn't want to stay at my place.

Rhys looked toward the paramedic, and she nodded. "If you can walk, that should be okay. Just go slow."

"Let me see if we're allowed to leave." Rhys stood and spoke to my brother for a few seconds. After it looked like they exchanged numbers, he came back. "We can go. Ethan pulled some strings or something, so the detectives will come over to get your statement tomorrow morning."

I nodded and started to stand. Rhys reached out and guided me as though I was a ninety-year-old woman. I actually felt as though I was. It didn't dawn on me until I noticed the lump on the floor that Rhys was taking me the long way around toward my front door. My breath caught as I realized who was under the white sheet.

"Is that …"

"Yeah." Rhys moved to block my view.

"He's dead?" Ethan had said he'd shot him. I didn't realize that he meant he'd killed him.

"Yeah." Rhys laced our hands together, and we walked past investigators and out my front door. When we got downstairs, Rhys muttered, "Crap. I didn't grab you a coat."

"It's okay. We're only walking across the street. I think I'll survive."

Rhys took off his tux jacket and wrapped it around my shoulders. It was warm and smelled like him. As we walked out of the elevator, Rhys pulled me to him, draping his arm across my shoulders.

"Ms. Valor!" I looked over to see Jose rushing to us. "Are you okay?"

I nodded. "Yes, I'm fine."

He breathed a sigh of relief. "I can't believe this happened while I was on my dinner break."

I stopped walking. "Honestly, Jose, I think he was waiting for that moment."

I didn't know if that was true or not, but it seemed it was the only way it could have happened. Plus, my stupidity thought I'd had flowers delivered while I was at the Emmys, and that it was Jose who was bringing them up to me. But, of course, it was late at night, and deliveries usually don't happen after five. Foolishness had clouded my judgment.

"I know, but if—"

"You're a doorman, not a security guard."

"I know, but I know who comes in and out of this building at all times."

"Except when you're off duty or on break," Rhys reminded him.

He gave a slow nod with a tight smile. "Right."

I grabbed his elbow and gave a slight squeeze. "It's not your fault."

Rhys and I stepped toward the door, and Jose opened it for us. "Have a good night."

We hurried across the street and then up to Rhys's condo. Once we were inside, Rhys led me to his shower and then told me he'd be back with a drink. I expected him to bring me more water, but instead, after I'd showered and dressed in one of his T-shirts, he handed me a tumbler with an inch or so of an amber colored liquid.

"Whiskey?" I asked as I sniffed it.

He nodded. "It will help you sleep."

"What about you? You had to have been there when Ethan shot Philip."

"I was." Rhys sighed and looked away from me. I got the impression he didn't want me to see how scared he really was.

"And you're okay?" In my foggy state, I hadn't even thought to ask earlier, but now my head was clearing, and I was feeling better, and more of what had happened was dawning on me.

"Well … I saw a guy die with you in his arms. That's not something I'm okay with."

"Ethan shot him while I was …" I whispered, but couldn't finish the thought.

He nodded. "Yeah. Drink up, and I'll tell you what you want to know."

Rhys undressed and moved into the shower as I went to the bedroom and took sips of the whiskey in bed. When he exited the bathroom with only a towel around his waist, he moved to his nightstand and gulped down his whiskey. I watched, still sipping the smooth liquor as Rhys stepped into pajama bottoms and then crawled onto the plush mattress and leaned against the headboard just like I was.

"Where do you want me to start?"

I felt my heart start to beat a little faster. I wanted to know what had happened, but it still made me nervous, as if I was standing on the edge of a cliff and just the thought of jumping made me anxious and uneasy.

"I guess start right after I was knocked out."

I was silent while I processed the entire story he told me, and then I sighed. "I think we need another drink."

CHAPTER EIGHTEEN

Rhys

"Hey, faggot!" I hurried and stuffed my books into my backpack, wanting to get to practice and out of the line of fire of Corey Pritchett. "I'm talking to you!" He grabbed the back of my backpack and slammed me into the set of lockers across from mine.

"I'm not a faggot!" I hissed.

"No? That's why you play hockey, right? You get to see all the boys naked in the locker room, and that turns you on."

"Fuck you!" I spat on him, not caring if he was going to pummel me.

"You want to fuck me, faggot?"

"Stop saying that!" I pushed him back, and before I knew it, he drew a handgun from behind his back. "What are you doing?"

"You think you can talk to me that way?"

"What are you going to do with that gun?" I continued to ask.

"What do you think? I'm going to shoot you then leave like I'd planned."

"Then do it!"

I heard a loud pop, and then a bullet appeared in the center of his forehead. It wasn't Corey, but Ashtyn's attacker, Philip.

I woke with a start, my pulse racing. When I realized that I was home and in my bed with Ashtyn, I laid back down and stared up at the dark ceiling. I expected Ashtyn to be the one who wasn't able to sleep through the night, but as it was right now, I was the one dreaming of crazy shit. My past and present had collided in a weird dream that never happened, and I didn't like dreaming about either one of them.

I'm not sure how long I laid there, staring up into nothing, but when Ashtyn stirred next to me, the sun was starting to come up.

"Morning, Cupcake." I rolled over and tucked a piece of her hair behind her ear.

"Is it?"

I smiled. "Yeah, but it hasn't been for long. Want some coffee?" She nodded, and I got out of bed, the cold wood floor sending a chill through my body that started at my bare feet. "I need a place with a fireplace."

"Turn the heater on."

"Oh, I am," I called out as I walked down the hall and stopped at the thermostat. After I turned the heat up, I continued to the kitchen and made two cups of coffee, then returned to the bedroom. "You still want to go to Garfield Park today?"

"No. Not really." Ashtyn sat up and took a mug from me. "I just want to lay here all day and do nothing."

I sat next to her. "Can't. Detectives will probably be here soon." She groaned. "And I think you should get some fresh air today."

"It's probably snowing."

"Yes, but I'm sure the conservatory has heat." I took a sip of the coffee.

"I really don't want to go anywhere. I don't even want to go back to my place if that's okay?"

"I don't want you to go back to your place either, but we should at least walk somewhere for lunch. I want to make sure you get fresh air like the paramedic advised." I knew she needed fresh air, but I wanted her to get out of the apartment to clear her head a little. I needed to clear my head as well.

She was silent for a few moments. "Okay, but only because we need to eat."

Ashtyn's phone started to blow up right at eight o'clock.

Word had gotten back to her parents, and also to her friends. While she reassured everyone that we were okay, I focused on getting caught up on the hockey world. It felt good to get my mind off of the previous night, though what I wanted to remember was the Emmys and not the horrific after party. Maybe my tux wasn't good luck after all? My friends had no idea what had happened, and all their messages on Facebook were about the Emmy I was holding in the picture I'd posted while we were still at the hotel.

After two hours of non-stop calls, two detectives showed up. Ashtyn and I each gave our statements separately. After, we sat on my couch, and the detectives sat in chairs at the two ends of my coffee table, they informed us of what they knew so far about Philip and his motive.

"Your father spoke to Captain Gordon. He wants us to put an undercover outside your place for a few weeks."

"Is that necessary? Philip's dead, right?" Ashtyn asked.

"Yes, he's dead, but your father is worried about you."

Ashtyn nodded.

"If I have to, I'll take her to work every day and pick her up," I offered. "Plus, I'll be with her at night. She won't be alone."

"While that probably won't be plausible given your work schedule, Mr. Cole, I also don't think it's necessary," Detective Cooper said.

"Okay, but I'd make it happen." I rubbed Ashtyn's knee. "I don't want you to be scared."

"I might have another stalker," she confessed.

"What?" I asked, raising my voice a little in surprise.

Ashtyn sighed. "Someone sends me roses at work every Monday."

"You don't know who they're from?" I asked.

She shrugged. "They sign it SA or secret admirer."

"They were from Philip," Detective Van Drake stated. "He was watching you for almost a year."

A chill ran through my body. How could someone have been watching her all that time and she didn't know? Was the meeting at Starbucks on purpose? I couldn't even imagine what was going through Ashtyn's head right now. I pulled her to me. "It's over now."

The room was quiet for a few seconds until Ashtyn asked, "How do you know it was Philip?"

Van Drake continued to take the lead. "We went over to his house this morning and found numerous pictures of you, of you and Rhys, you and other men you've been with, including live footage of your apartment."

"What?" Ashtyn shrieked.

"He had video cameras in the smoke detectors."

"He what?" I stood, ready to kill him even though he was already dead.

"It appears that he got into your condo somehow. Plus, credit card statements with charges to The Flower Pot every week indicates he was sending you flowers."

"How do you know that he bought flowers for me, though?"

"Why do you think it wasn't him?" I asked.

"It's not that I think it wasn't him. I just want to make sure I don't have another stalker out there."

"Before coming here, we talked to the owner of The Flower Pot. All orders they delivered to your work were linked to his credit card they had on file."

"So it's over?" Ashtyn asked.

"Yeah, we think so." Cooper nodded.

"I can't believe it was all him. I just met him two weeks ago, and now he's dead."

"You told me that you first ran into him at Judy's almost two months ago?" Van Drake asked flipping through his notebook.

"Yeah, but that was for a split second. I brushed him off."

Van Drake nodded. "Given what you've told me and what was seen at his house, we think he was watching you and waiting. When you went to Judy's, you were alone at first, right?"

"Yes."

"We think that was when he decided to make his move, but it backfired."

Ashtyn looked up at me. "Thank you again."

"Best decision I made was to go to that bar that night," I stated, and I meant it more than just because I'd saved her from some wacko. I'd probably be swiping left on some app right now if I hadn't met her that night.

"You're lucky the events played out as they did," Cooper chimed in. "If you hadn't seen him slip something in your drink the night you went on a date with him, then there's no telling what would have happened to you."

I didn't want to think about that scenario, and I was sure Ashtyn didn't either. Life has a strange way of working itself out the way it was meant to. I heard once that you never know how important something or someone is until you almost lose it. That was true with the way I felt about Ashtyn, and I wasn't ready to let her go.

After the detectives left, Ashtyn and I walked to a café down the street and grabbed lunch as planned. Her parents wanted to come over to make sure Ashtyn was okay. But Ashtyn wanted to be left alone. I understood that, but given that she needed fresh air, I all but forced her to walk to lunch with me.

The snow was falling, and with each word spoken, you could see the breath coming from our mouths. I was enjoying the fresh air, and Ashtyn seemed as though a weight had been lifted off her shoulders. She went from wanting to stay in bed all day to asking me if I wanted to catch a movie before we headed home.

Home.

The word struck me, but I didn't mind. When I was with Bridgette, it was as though she was invading my space. Now, with Ashtyn, I didn't want her to leave even if it was right across the street.

After we caught a movie, we grabbed a cup of coffee and then took an Uber *home*. Once the car dropped us off outside of my building, I asked, "Want me to go up to your place and get you some clothes?"

She thought about my question for a moment. "Yeah, I'll stay down here and talk to Jose if that's okay. I'm not ready to see what my place looks like."

"You know I love being of service to you." I winked and kissed her lips before we walked into the building.

"Ms. Valor!" Jose beamed. "How are you doing?"

After Ashtyn handed me her keys, I continued to the elevators while she stayed to talk to Jose. Once I was on the fifteenth floor, I stepped off and walked slowly down the hall. I wasn't sure what I was going to see because Ethan had been the one to lock up the night before. When I finally got to the closed door, I expected there to be yellow caution tape on the doorframe like I'd seen so many times on TV and in movies. But there wasn't anything. The door was closed as though a man hadn't died inside less than twenty-four hours prior.

I slipped the key into the lock, and just after turning it, I thought better of it. Instead, I pulled my phone out of my pocket and dialed Ethan's number.

"Hello?" he answered.

"Hey, Ethan. It's Rhys."

"Everything okay?"

I nodded. "Yeah. I was calling to see if it's okay to go into Ashtyn's condo and grab her some clothes."

"Is there yellow tape on the door?"

"No, there isn't."

"Then yeah. That part of the investigation is over."

"Okay cool." I reached for the door handle but stopped when he spoke again.

"Is Ash with you?"

"No." I shook my head. "I came up alone to grab her some clothes."

"Good. I've put in a call to a crime scene cleanup company, but they can't come until tomorrow."

"I'm not sure if she'll want to come back tomorrow after work anyway."

"Take care of her, yeah?"

"Of course." I fucking ran into a room with a crazy man who was trying to kidnap her. I didn't do much except distract him long enough for a cop to arrive, but I'd been ready to fight for her, and I'd take care of her until the day I died.

We hung up, and then I slowly opened the door. There was no chalk outline of Philip's body, and no brains splattered over the entire room. Instead, the only thing that looked as though there had been a person shot was a small pool of blood where I assumed his head rested until he was taken away by the coroner.

I knew the longer I stared at the dark crimson pool, the more I would relive what I'd seen. So, I hurried to Ashtyn's room and grabbed some dresses. I had no idea if they were anything she wanted to wear, but I didn't want to take too long. I rummaged through some drawers, grabbing underwear, and then went to the bathroom to grab some toiletries. Whatever I didn't grab, I'd buy for her until she was ready to come get the stuff herself. I also grabbed the two Emmys we'd won because I still wanted to display them, but this time it would be so we could remember the good part of the night.

"Ready?" I asked walking out of the elevator once I made it downstairs.

"Yep. Did you get everything I'll need for a few days?"

I waved goodbye to Jose as we exited the building. "Yeah, Cupcake, but I left the vibrator I found in your nightstand because that's my job now."

CHAPTER NINETEEN

Ashtyn

B*reaking News: …*

The thought of my own breaking news was too surreal to finish the sentence. It seemed that I reported breaking news almost every night, but when it involved me, I didn't want it to be true.

I knew there was a silver lining to what had happened. Even though I was attacked and almost kidnapped, Philip was dead. My big brother had come in and once again protected me like always. When I was younger, I thought my brothers were too overprotective, but now, I was grateful.

Tonight, though, would be the first evening I'd come home to an empty place.

Home …

I wasn't going to go back to mine. Rhys had given me a key to his place, but he wouldn't be there by the time I would arrive home. Most nights after there was a game, he wouldn't come through the door until after one in the morning. Tonight would be no different.

In the last week I'd been off work—boss's orders—I hadn't been alone. When Rhys worked, either Jaime, Kylie, or Colleen would come over and keep me company. I knew Rhys was the one coordinating everything with them, and that made me like him even more. In fact, I was certain I was falling in love with him. Rhys was the most caring, thoughtful, fun-loving man I'd ever met let alone dated, and it wasn't because he brought me coffee first thing in the morning. Whenever I was with him, he made me laugh, and when he was at work, I missed him.

"You want me to drive you to work?" Rhys asked coming into the bathroom where I was doing my makeup.

"You'd do that for me?" The entire time I was doing my makeup, I was trying to psych myself up about having to walk into parking garages alone. When I got off work, the garage would more than likely be empty because it was after the normal hustle and bustle of working hours.

"Of course. You know my studio is only a few blocks away, but do you think Abby can bring you home?"

"If not, I'll find a ride."

"If you can't, text me. I'll figure something out."

I turned to him and wrapped my arms around his neck. "Thank you, but I think I can manage."

"I'm sure you can, but that doesn't stop me from worrying about you."

I kissed his lips softly and stepped back to finish my makeup. "I'll text you as soon as I'm home." There was that word again. I liked the way it made me feel to think that Rhys's condo was my home too.

"Good." He kissed the side of my head and then started to walk back into the bedroom. "Let me know when you're ready to roll, Cupcake."

Rhys pulled his black Mazda SUV into the loading zone in front of my work building. It was snowing lightly, and people were walking the streets, but in just a few hours, the city streets would be bare.

I hesitated before getting out of the car. Maybe I wasn't ready to go back to work. What if I had another stalker and they were waiting to make their move? After the nightmare with Philip, it was breaking news that I was attacked in my home. Mine and Philip's names were reported as well as my brother's since he was the cop involved in the shooting. It felt weird to be the name in the news, but now a week later, the dust has seemed to settle.

Rhys grabbed my hand. "Try not to think about it too much. It's over. He can't hurt you."

I nodded and looked into his electric blue eyes. "I know. It's just a weird feeling."

"For me too. We're getting through this. Together."

I leaned across the center console and kissed him. "I know."

"I'll try to catch your broadcast tonight."

I smiled and opened the door. "Ditto."

Everything seemed like any other day. As I made my way toward my desk, people were on the phones or typing away on their computers as though I hadn't been away for a week.

"Hey, Ashtyn. How are you doing?" Mitch asked as he came out of the break room.

I turned to address him. "Hanging in there."

"I'm happy you're back, and I'm glad everything turned out all right for you."

"Thanks. I'm happy to be back."

"You got a delivery," Abby stated, walking up behind me.

My heart stopped, and thoughts of my Monday deliveries from Philip came to mind. "Flowers?"

"Yeah, but they don't look like your usual ones."

"What? How's that?"

She smiled. "Go look."

Everything the police had told me about the flower deliveries must have been wrong. They'd said they were linked back to Philip, but if I were to get more flowers after his death, then how could that be? Did he have it set up to deliver every week automatically? Were they delivered last week and no one had told me? If that was the case, why would the flower shop still deliver them after the cops looked into the charges from their store? Maybe they didn't care because money was money and everyone was always trying to make a buck.

When I finally made it to my desk, I realized that Abby was right. The flowers looked different. They were in a clear vase, and there were only a few stems, not the usual twelve. I stepped a bit closer. The flowers were made out of icing. I furrowed my eyebrows and pulled the card out.

Ashtyn,
For every way I want to lick you.
-Rhys

I clutched the card to my chest as though someone was reading the note over my shoulder. All worries about the mysterious flowers disappeared, and an instant smile spread across my face. Rhys had sent me a bouquet of cupcake flowers that looked like purple petunias, and that was one more reason why I loved him.

I thought about the revolution and realized I did, in fact, love Rhys Cole. I wasn't only falling. I'd fallen, and I was completely in love. That was better breaking news.

Breaking News: Ashtyn Valor is in love with Rhys Cole!

"Are those cupcakes?"

I looked over to see Abby walking up behind me again. "Are you a ninja today or what?"

She chuckled. "What are you talking about?"

"Always coming up behind me."

"You've never hidden the notes before. Rhys write you a dirty note or something?"

"Nooo!" I lied. "You just keep popping up out of nowhere."

"I just want a cupcake."

"Later." I laughed. "It's time for our meeting."

"You're killing me. I've been smelling these for an hour."

"They were here when you got here?" I asked as I grabbed my notepad and pen.

We started to walk to the conference room. "Okay, fine. I know all about them. Rhys asked me to pick them up for you."

"So you know what the card says," I stated.

"No, I swear I didn't look."

We walked into the conference room. "I'm not sure I believe you."

"I promise."

"All right. Does that also mean that you know I need a ride home since you've been talking to my boyfriend?"

"Yeah, and I've got you covered."

"Thank you." We took our seats, and the daily meeting commenced.

After we went over everything for our broadcast and leads for stories we wanted to break, everyone started to gather their belongings until Leonard spoke again.

"Before everyone goes I have an announcement. Barbara came to me this afternoon and gave her notice."

Everyone gasped and looked over at the greying woman. She smiled tightly.

"What station are you moving to?" Mitch asked.

Barbara shook her head. "I'm not. It's time to retire."

"Wow!" I breathed. I knew the time would come, I just didn't expect it to be so soon. Barbara had been doing the evening news for as long as I could remember. Even before I'd graduated from college.

"So we all know what that means, right?" Leonard asked.

My eyes widened with hope. Did it mean what I thought it did?

"Ashtyn …" I smiled at Leonard, waiting for him to continue. "Do *you* know what that means?"

I nodded. Since I'd been hired, Leonard knew I'd always wanted to broadcast the evening news and not the ten o'clock nightly news. It had the best hours for what I wanted in life—or what I wanted in life before Corey broke up with me—and had the best ratings.

"Will you be ready once the new year hits?"

That was in two weeks, but I nodded my head again. "Yes!"

"Then let's go talk in my office."

There were congratulations sputtered to Barbara and me as we all exited the room. I followed Leonard to his office, and he closed the door as I sat in a chair in front of his desk.

"So, your yes is a yes to move to the evening news?"

"Of course. That's where I want to be."

"Perfect, and just so you're aware, there will be a raise involved."

"Thank you so much!" I beamed.

"Tomorrow you can work on promos for the switch with the marketing team."

"Great. I'm excited."

"Good. And just for the record, I'm glad to have you back."

I smiled. "Thank you."

"Have a good show tonight."

"Thank you," I said again and stood to leave.

People say that when you hit rock bottom, the only way is up. I thought breaking up with Corey was my rock bottom when, in reality, it was the change I'd needed in my life for all the pieces to fall into place.

A few hours later, I was heating up a Cup Noodles—or what I called a cup of noodles because Cup Noodles sounded funny on my tongue—in the microwave for dinner. I'd already eaten a cupcake and was going to have another after I ate my soup.

My phone dinged with a text.

Rhys: You doing okay, Cupcake?

Me: Yes, thank you for my cupcake bouquet. I'm looking forward to all the ways you promised in your note ;)

Rhys: It's my favorite dessert.

CHAPTER TWENTY

Rhys

I wasn't sure what I was going to walk into when I arrived home, but two girls singing *Baby Got Back* with our new Emmys as the microphones wasn't it.

At first, they didn't hear me come in, so I stood just inside the door, leaning against the doorjamb with my arms crossed over my chest and a huge fucking smile on my face.

"Ooh, Rumpelstiltskin, *you* say you want to roll in my Benz? Well, use me, use me. 'Cause my booty says I'm juicy." Ashtyn turned around and shook her ass, the words Juicy spread across her backside.

I chuckled silently as Abby laughed. "That's not the words!" They moved their hips to the beat, and Abby turned, her mouth opened as though she was about to start to sing, but then stopped as her gaze met mine. She nudged Ashtyn, but Ashtyn continued to dance. I still had a huge smirk on my face because watching her finally laugh again was the best fucking feeling in the world. I knew without a doubt that I loved her. I just didn't want to tell her and scare her off because we'd just started dating. I would, though, once the time was right.

Ashtyn finally looked over at me and stopped dancing. When it registered that it was me standing with the door still opened behind me, she rushed over and threw her arms around my neck. "Tiger!"

"Tiger?" I grinned.

Ashtyn pulled her head back, her arms still around my neck. "Yeah. Rawrrrrr." She nipped at my ear as though she was the tiger and not me.

I chuckled. "All right, Cupcake. I take it you had a good night?"

Ashtyn broke free and started to sway her hips to the rest of the song. I closed the door as she motioned to Abby the best she could. "Abs and I played a game."

"What kind of game?" I started to unbutton my coat as I looked over to see Abby walking toward my stereo to turn off the music.

"When we got home, it was in the second period. We turned on the TV and watched your show like I told you I would," she slurred every word.

"Yeah?"

I hung up my coat and then watched Ashtyn's ass as she continued to shake it to no music. "We decided to play a drinking game where every time you or Jett said shot, we had to take a shot of Fireball."

"How many times was that?" I assumed a lot since I broadcasted hockey and that was what players did to try and make goals.

Ashtyn shrugged. "We lost track, but it was a *lot*."

"I can tell." I grinned.

"I better get going." Abby grabbed her purse.

"You can't drive home," I protested.

"I only had a couple of shots during the intermission a few hours ago. I faked the rest and let Ash have a good time." She opened the door.

"Thank you."

"Don't go, Abs!" Ashtyn reached out as if to grab Abby, but she had already walked through the threshold.

"I'll see you tomorrow, Ash. Eat some dinner, okay?" She closed the door and was gone.

"You didn't eat dinner?" I asked. It was a little after one in the morning.

"I ate a cup of raw men."

I laughed, doubling over. "A cup of raw men?"

"Yee-P. Chicken flavored."

"Well, I'm hungry." I really wasn't, but I needed her to eat and soak up the booze. I'd never seen her as drunk as she was. "How does breakfast sound?"

"What time is it?"

"Don't you know it's exciting to have breakfast for dinner, Cupcake?" I started to make my way to the kitchen.

"Will you make pancakes?" she slurred behind me.

"And bacon."

"You're the best boyfriend ever. You even send me cupcakes that look like flowers."

I smiled as I opened the fridge to pull out the raw bacon. "I'm glad you liked them."

I wanted to be the one to send her flowers now. I wanted to be her everything. I remembered the time Romi had made Mom a cupcake bouquet for her fiftieth birthday, so I'd called a local place and texted Abby to ask if she could get them on her way to work. Obviously, she had, and then she'd taken care of my girl all night. I needed to pay her back. Was she single? I could set her up with Kenny or Clark. I'd think about it.

Ashtyn slid onto the barstool at the breakfast bar. "I loved them. They were red velvet."

I took the bacon out and turned to the oven. "You going to show me how you licked the icing?"

She giggled. "Yes, I practiced on two of them."

As the bacon cooked in the oven, I took a quick shower hoping Ashtyn wouldn't join me—for once. Even though I wanted her to suck and lick my dick as though I was icing on a cupcake, I also feared she'd somehow mistake it for a real one and bite into me in her drunken state.

"Whatcha doin' down there?" I asked, a towel wrapped around my waist as I walked into the bedroom. Ashtyn was sitting on the floor, her T-shirt, bra, and one pant leg removed.

"I was coming to join you."

"It's almost time for breakfast."

"What time is it?"

I chuckled. "It's time for breakfast, and then we're going to bed. When we wake up, you're going to show me how you lick icing."

"Are you making pancakes?"

"Yep." I reached out with my hand for her to stand. I helped her out of her sweatpants and put her T-shirt back on. If she were topless as I cooked, I'd definitely burn the bacon. "Come on. The bacon should almost be ready."

We walked hand in hand down the hall, and when we got to the kitchen, I directed her to sit on a stool. I kissed the side of her head then moved to the oven to check the bacon.

"Do you always cook naked?"

I looked down at my bare chest and the towel wrapped around my hips. "I'm not much of a chef actually."

"But you're cooking now."

"It's not hard to screw up bacon in the oven as long as you set a timer. And pancakes are easy when the batter is already made and you just need to add water."

"You're the best," she gushed again. This time she rested her head on the cool granite.

"No sleeping, baby. You need to soak up some of that whiskey."

"But I'm tired."

"Tell me about your day."

She rested her head in her hand while I hurried and made the pancake batter. "So, I got promoted today."

I stopped shaking the bottle of the pre-made batter. "You did?"

Ashtyn smiled. "I'm gonna be on the five o'clock news starting next year."

"Holy shit, Cupcake." I pulled her up to hug me, and then I kissed her hard with a smack of my lips. She tasted faintly of whiskey. "I'm so proud of you."

"It's always been my hope to be in that time slot."

"Why didn't you tell me sooner?"

She shrugged. "I forgot. Fireball helps you forget."

I chuckled. "Yeah, it does."

The timer on the oven went off, and I checked the bacon. It needed a few more minutes, so I turned my attention back to the pancakes.

"You think I'll get a new stalker once I'm on that broadcast?"

I stopped pouring the batter onto the buttered griddle. "I hope not. You better tell me if you start getting flowers from a secret admirer again or some guy hits on you. The position is filled."

"You're my boss now?"

I smiled as I looked over my shoulder at her. "Yeah, baby, I am." I wasn't going to be controlling and shit, but she needed to know I wasn't going anywhere. If I had to make her bacon and pancakes every night at one in the morning, I would. I like what we had going now. Sure it started with sex and using each other to forget our exes, but now I couldn't imagine a night without falling asleep with her in my arms.

Things seemed to return back to normal. Or what Ashtyn and I thought normal was. She still didn't want to stay at her place, but I didn't mind. We'd gone to her condo and gotten more of her things.

When I was with Bridgette, I'd given her a key, but then instantly regretted it because her shit was all over my place. But having Ashtyn's stuff around felt completely different. I didn't mind seeing her toothbrush next to mine or seeing her bra lying on the empty chair in the corner of my room. In fact, I was giving it a month before I propositioned that we find a new place together. A home far away from the one Ashtyn hated to step foot in.

Ashtyn was at work, and I was setting up the poker table waiting for the guys to arrive when there was a knock at the door. I opened it to see Kenny holding up a six pack of Blue Moon.

"I'm early."

I nodded and chuckled. "Yeah, man. Help me set this shit up."

Kenny closed the door and followed me into my place. "So Ashtyn moved in officially yet?"

"Since you asked me yesterday at work?"

He laughed and gave a slight shrug after setting the beer on the kitchen island. "Yeah."

I opened the poker chip case and started to sort stacks. "Not gonna lie. I don't mind at all how things have turned out."

"She's not crazy like Bridgette, right?" Kenny popped the cap on a bottle of beer and handed it to me.

"I don't think anyone is as crazy as she is. Fuck, dude …" I trailed off not believing what was about to come from my mouth. "I think I love her."

"Ashtyn?"

"Yes, Ashtyn."

"Well, shit, man." Kenny clapped me on the shoulder with his free hand. "When are you going to tell her?"

I took a pull of the beer as I thought about his question. I wasn't sure. I didn't know how she felt, and I'd never truly been in love before. Sure, I'd told Bridgette, but that was in my lust-haze when I knew she wasn't wearing any panties under her dress, and I'd never uttered it again. When Bridgette would tell me that she loved me, I'd just nod and change the subject. She didn't seem to mind since she was living off my dime. But if Ashtyn were to tell me goodbye, I'd want to jump in front of the Blue Line as the train pulled into the station.

"When I know for sure she won't crush my heart."

"Well, I can't wait to go to Vegas for your bachelor party."

"Whoa!" I laughed. "Who the hell said anything about marriage?"

"I don't know, but you're all pussy whipped now."

"Don't be jealous I'm getting laid on a regular basis."

A knock sounded on my door, and Kenny turned to answer it. "I'm happy with the variety of pussy I'm getting thank you very much."

"Whatever. Just get the door."

I wasn't going to continue to argue with Kenny. He could have a different woman every night if he wanted. I wanted to crawl into my bed every night with Ashtyn and only Ashtyn.

The weekend after Ashtyn returned to work, we bought a Christmas tree. Since we spent all of our time at my place, we'd brought the tree there and decorated it. I had no fireplace for Santa to slide down, so I bought an electric one, and we hung our stockings on it. Plus, it was nice to curl up together and watch a movie with the illusion of flames dancing from a 3D effect. So many times it was on the tip of my tongue to tell Ashtyn how I felt about her. I wanted *many* more Christmas together. But if she didn't feel the same way, I feared she'd find someone better, so I needed to come up with a plan.

CHAPTER TWENTY-ONE

Ashtyn

As I walked down the darkened street toward Judy's, I continually looked over my shoulder to see if anyone was following me. I wasn't sure if that feeling would ever go away, but I wasn't going to live in fear anymore. Chicago was a walking city of sorts. I wanted to be able to go on a coffee run before my broadcast. I wanted to be able to walk down to Judy's if my friends wanted to grab a drink.

I wanted to be me again.

The last week or so had gotten me back to feeling a little normal. I was driving myself to and from work and going home to Rhys's by myself if he were at work. I still wasn't sleeping at my place, but it wasn't because I was scared anymore. It was because a guy had died in my living room. I was lucky Rhys wasn't sick of me yet.

Ethan had hired someone to clean up the place, but every time I walked through the threshold, my eyes went to the spot where I'd seen Philip under a white sheet. If the day came, I would move furniture around so it covered the spot where Philip died, and I'd sleep with every light on just in case he wanted to haunt me. Or I'd move. I wouldn't want to live across the street from Rhys if he were to break my heart.

I walked into Judy's and spotted Jaime sitting at a high top in the middle of the bar. "Hey, lady," I greeted her as I shrugged off my coat.

"I love Christmas shopping," Jaime joked as her hello and took a sip of her red wine. I noticed she'd ordered me one too.

"Yeah. Look at all the people fighting for the last Nerf Nitro Longshot Smash," I bantered back, remembering the hot toy for the year that we'd reported on.

"Please. I had my shopping done before Thanksgiving. I'm a pro."

I took a sip of the fruity wine. "When I finally have kids, I'll come to you for all your secrets."

"You and Rhys gonna pop out some babies?"

I snorted. "We've only been dating a few months. I have no plans to get knocked up."

"Fine, but I need a baby to snuggle with."

"You're capable of making some more."

Jaime shook her head. "Nope. I'm not doing any more shitty diapers. Thomas is almost potty trained."

"Then you should convince Kylie or Colleen."

"I see you more often," she stated.

"Fine. How about you ask me after a year of marriage?"

"Are you and Rhys getting married?" She folded her arms on the table and leaned slightly forward as though I had some huge secret to tell her.

"Not that I know of. Again, we've only been dating a few months." I rolled my eyes.

Jaime tsked. "Semantics. You two are perfect for each other, and I've never seen you this happy before."

"Well, thank you. I'm glad you finally approve of my boyfriend."

"You're welcome. So tell me about this plan."

"Don't forget to dress warm tonight." I kissed Rhys goodbye before leaving for work. It was Christmas Eve, and tomorrow we had plans to go to both of our parents' houses for lunch and dinner, so we decided to exchange gifts in the morning. The problem was, my gift needed to be done at night because that was when I was able to do it.

"Are you going to tell me what we're doing?"

I shook my head and grabbed my coat. "It will ruin the surprise."

"All right. Text me when you're downstairs, and I'll be ready."

This was going to be amazing!

CHAPTER TWENTY-TWO

Rhys

When I was dating Bridgette, I'd felt as though my life was in some sort of rut. I never wanted to break up with her because I thought my work schedule was too crazy and I wouldn't be able to date anyone else. What I didn't realize was finding the right person to date was effortless. It also helped that Ashtyn and I unofficially lived together. Bridgette had always wanted to go out and spend my money. Though looking back, I think she did it because she was hoping we'd run into hockey players that I knew. The problem with that was most of them were married. At least the ones with established careers who were making the big bucks. Also, did she realize that most of them had missing teeth? I mean, fighting was almost encouraged in hockey, and therefore, a lot of them practically had dentures.

My point in all of this is that when I thought about a Christmas present for Ashtyn, I contemplated getting her jewelry. I assumed I'd need to spend at least one of my paychecks on something that was gold for her, but the more I pondered about the perfect gift, the more I realized that wasn't Ashtyn. She didn't wear flashy things or expect expensive dinners every Saturday night. She wanted to curl up on the couch and watch a movie instead of getting dressed up for a night on the town. It was fucking perfect. She was fucking extraordinary.

So one morning, while Ashtyn sang in the shower, I thought of the most amazing gift. I just hoped she didn't laugh …

Too much.

Ashtyn: Be there in five.

I grabbed my coat, shrugged it on and then being the smart ass that I was, I grabbed winter gloves and a beanie. I'd also dressed in long underwear under all of my clothes. Ashtyn said to dress warm, and that was what I was doing. I just hoped I didn't sweat my balls off.

When I got downstairs, I waited inside the building until I saw Ashtyn pull up. Her blue Volvo was actually pretty sweet with a heated steering wheel, a heated windshield, heated wipers, and heated front and rear seats. And it also had some horsepower.

I opened the passenger door and stuck my head in. "Should I sit in the back so you can chauffeur me around?"

"No!" She laughed. "Get your ass in here and close the door. It's freezing out there."

I did just that. "It is snowing, Cupcake. Ice is literally falling from the sky."

"Yeah, so did you dress warmly?"

"Even put my thermal underwear on." I winked.

Ashtyn pulled away from the curb. "Me too."

I looked down to see she was wearing jeans and not the dress she'd reported the news in. "Are you going to tell me now where we're going?"

"Nope."

"Will there be booze?"

"Nope."

"Music?"

"Nope."

"Food?"

"Nope."

"Sex?"

She looked away from the road and over at me as we waited at a light. "If you're good."

I grinned. "Pretty sure I'm on the nice list."

"Yeah, you are. Just don't screw it up in the next hour and you'll get sex when we get home."

I bobbed my head in approval. I could totally be good. Especially if sex was on the table. Or on the couch. Or on the kitchen counter. Or in the shower. I wasn't picky.

Ashtyn drove us toward Grant Park. "Cupcake, I hate to burst your bubble, but the park is closed."

"I know," she replied and drove right down to the parking garage.

There was an attendant at the gate, and I expected him to tell us they were closed, but instead he nodded to Ashtyn and opened the gate. I turned to look at her, confused. She shrugged. "Perks of the job."

"Okay …" I hesitated as she drove and parked the car. "So, what are we going to do here?"

"Still a surprise."

Seeing as we were about to go frolic in the fucking park, my long johns were definitely the right decision.

After we parked and got out of the car, we grabbed our gloves, and Ashtyn took my hand and led me toward the section of Grant Park that was by the mini-golf course. "We're going to play mini-golf?"

"Nope." She shook her head and kept walking.

As we walked, I spotted the ice skating rink in the distance. It wasn't your typical ice skating rink. In fact, it was called a skating ribbon because the rink was interwoven into the terrain of the ground it sat on. You didn't just skate around and around in a circle. It had slight inclines and declines and followed a shape like a ribbon around the two rock climbing walls.

"We're going ice skating?"

"Kinda," she replied and tugged me until we were standing in front of the ice skate rental building. Another man opened the door, and as we passed, Ashtyn greeted him by name and thanked him.

"So, you just slip these guys some money, and they let you in?" I teased.

"I told you that I get perks."

"Do I want to know how?"

Ashtyn laughed. "Not like that. Jeez!"

I smiled and followed as she walked up to the skate rental booth. Two sets of skates were waiting for us. We slipped them on, and after lacing them up, Ashtyn asked, "You ready to race?"

"Race?" I laughed.

"Yeah. Loser has to do all the pleasuring tonight."

I snickered. "Is that so?"

"Yep."

"You do remember me telling you that I've played ice hockey since I was five?"

She shrugged slightly. "How do you know I haven't been practicing?"

"Have you?" I asked and stood. I stood easily on the blades as if they were normal boots I was wearing. Ashtyn, on the other hand, had to grab onto the side of the counter for support.

"You'll just have to wait and see."

"All right, Apolo Ohno. Let's see what you're made of."

I helped Ashtyn out of the building and across to the outdoor rink. After we slipped off the blade covers, I thought I'd need to help her not fall on the ice. However, she skated effortlessly.

"First one back here is the winner."

"Got it," I replied and stood next to her in a race-stance position. Should I let her win? I didn't mind doing all the pleasuring. She knew I loved to lick her cupcake. But then when a woman beats you at anything, especially sports, you never live it down. Romi beat me one-time at Horse when we were playing hoops, and to this day my sister thinks she's better at basketball than me.

"Ready?" Ashtyn asked, and before I could reply she bolted.

"Hey!" I shouted and took off after her.

I was right on her heels almost the entire way, but she gave me a run for my money. The fucking long johns under my jeans and coat were riding up in places I didn't want them to be. We laughed and groaned and laughed some more as we sped around the ribbon. I pulled ahead, and just as I was rounding the final turn, I saw people standing on the ice with a finish line ribbon across it. Ashtyn had gone all out on this night, but as I skated closer, I recognized one of the men. It wasn't the garage attendant or the guy who had let us into the skate rental building.

It was my idol, Jeremy Roenick.

Still skating, I turned my head to look over my shoulder at Ashtyn. She was smiling as she skated leisurely up behind me. She clearly wanted me to win, and now I knew why.

My gaze met Jeremy's, and he was smiling as I skated through the tape. I'd always known him to have a good rapport with his fans. Back in the day, I'd hear about how he would smile and stop what he was doing to sign autographs. I'd never gotten to meet him, but I knew if I were ever given the chance, he'd be a standup guy. And I was right because what retired hockey player would come stand out in the snow at midnight to meet a fan?

Apparently, Jeremy Roenick would.

CHAPTER TWENTY-THREE

Ashtyn

I couldn't believe that I was able to pull off such an amazing opportunity for Rhys. I knew a guy who knew a guy who knew a guy. And that guy knew Jeremey was in town, and because he caught the game the other night, Jeremy knew who Rhys was and was willing to make my Christmas wish come true.

Seeing Rhys's face the second after he saw Jeremy Roenick at the finish line was awesome. Seeing him talk to Jeremy and tell him how he had been his idol since he was ten was heart-warming. And seeing Rhys's face when I took off my coat, stripped off the Roenick Blackhawks jersey I was wearing, and handed it to Jeremy to sign was incredible.

When we got home, Rhys had forgotten that he was the one who won the race, so he did *all* the pleasuring.

I didn't wake to the smell of coffee. Instead, I woke to a hand caressing my parted thighs. A hand that slowly traveled up and then slipped into the waistband of my panties before I even opened my eyes.

I moaned.

"You should have slept naked, Cupcake."

"Cold," I panted.

"Are you cold now?"

"No." I wasn't.

Rhys tore the covers off of me and then did the same to my panties. His mouth was between my parted legs, and he ran his tongue from the bottom of my pussy to my clit in one fluid motion as though to drink every ounce of my arousal. I was his morning coffee or his breakfast, giving him the energy to go on for the day. They say breakfast is the most important meal of the day and I knew of one source of protein that I was looking forward to in just a few minutes.

Rhys slipped a finger inside of me and then two, fucking me with them while his tongue flicked my clit. My hands gripped the sheets as I moaned, bowing my back as the orgasm was building quickly. My bent knees started to wobble and shake as he worked me like I was a bass guitar for a rock band. Each strum was the right cord. My hands gripped the sheets tightly, and then as I came, my grasp tightened, and I heard a rip.

We were silent for a few moments as my breathing returned close to normal.

"You ripped the sheets, baby."

"I did what?"

Rhys nudged his head toward my hand. I followed his gaze, and sure enough, there was a tear in the cotton.

"I'll buy new ones."

He smirked as he pressed his lips to mine. "I'll buy three hundred and sixty-five sets if that's what it takes to make you come like that every day."

"Well, it is Christmas."

"That wasn't your present."

I chuckled. "Then what is?"

"Santa left you something under the tree."

"How did he get in? We don't have a real fireplace."

Rhys grinned. "He knows a guy who knows a guy."

I shook my head and laughed.

Stepping into his PJ bottoms, he said, "Let's open your present and then since we both need to shower before we head out, we can save water and shower together." He winked. I wasn't going to argue. Shower sex was hot. I was extremely curious what he'd gotten me for our first Christmas.

After I threw on my T-shirt and PJ bottoms, I walked down the hall and found him in the kitchen. "First, I need coffee," he said.

"Why do you need coffee for me to open my gift?"

"You'll see. I'll bring you a cup."

I turned and walked to the couch and sat down. A minute later he handed me a big steaming mug. "Thank you." I took the cup from him.

He took a few sips of his coffee and then set it on the coffee table before grabbing a medium sized wrapped box that had recently appeared under the tree. I was in charge of wrapping the presents for our family, and when I'd put them under the tree a few days ago, that box wasn't there. "Did you buy this yesterday?" I teased.

He grinned. "No. But I wrapped it yesterday."

I reached out my hands and took the box from him. It was heavier than I thought it was going to be. "Jesus. Are there bricks in here?"

Rhys laughed and reached for his coffee again. "Just open it while I finish my coffee."

I tore through the paper, and once enough was torn away, I balked, surprised at what it was. "You got me a karaoke machine?"

"I thought you liked to sing. The other night with the Emmys…" He trailed off, smirking at me.

I rolled my eyes. "I was drunk."

"Clearly, but you sing in the shower."

"I can't use this in the shower." I laughed.

"True, but this isn't all of your present either."

"Oh?"

He took a deep breath as though he was nervous. "Yeah, the machine is just the vessel."

"The vessel?" I furrowed my eyebrows in confusion.

He downed the rest of his coffee and reached for his iPad that was sitting on the table. "I'm actually going to put on a concert for you."

I snorted. "You're what?"

He exchanged the karaoke machine with his iPad. "I'm gonna sing to you."

"You're kidding!"

"I'm not." He opened the box, and I realized it wasn't taped completely. He'd already opened it.

"Why are you going to sing to me? And why now?"

"You'll see." He did some things on the machine and then said, "Open the karaoke app and follow along."

I looked down at the iPad and noticed it was the only app on the screen. I touched the icon, and it opened to a list of songs. I looked back up at Rhys, not paying any mind to the titles.

"Are you ready?" Rhys asked.

I chuckled. "Are you?"

He grinned. "Well, I'm no Ed Sheeran, so you can't make fun of my voice."

I smirked. "I won't."

"Now, for the next twenty-three minutes or so, you can't stop me."

"You're going to sing for twenty-three minutes?"

"Yep. I have six songs to sing to you."

"Okay." I smiled and sat back on the couch. I threw a blanket over me and sipped my coffee as I waited for the show.

Rhys took a deep breath, cleared his throat, and then pressed something on the machine. "I'm also going to record this so you can listen anytime you want."

I laughed, but it died off when I heard the strum of a guitar of a country song.

Rhys started to sing, a smile on each of our faces. He nudged his head toward the iPad, and I looked down to see the words scrolling across the screen. He sang about meeting a girl who makes him smile. One that crosses the street and when she moves, it changes the whole world. Though he changed the lyrics to sing about my green eyes and not the baby blues in the song. I realized as he sang that he was talking about meeting me and my smile didn't falter. It actually grew bigger, and I had to resist the urge to sing along with him.

After the song ended, another one started right away. As soon as he started to sing about being a call away, I realized that the songs that were on the list on the main screen of the app were specifically put there by Rhys. It was like his own concert set list.

Rhys continued to sing about being a call away if I needed a friend, that Superman had nothing on him and no matter where I went, I wasn't alone. His voice was beautiful. I hadn't realized in the months that we were dating that he had a good singing voice.

I swayed my upper body as I listened to the words, wishing I had a lighter to hold up. Rhys started to move a little as though he was finally getting comfortable singing in front of me, and I caught myself as I quietly started to sing the words along with him.

The piano faded out, and the strum of a guitar started to play as the next song queued. My eyes widened when I realized what song he was singing. "JT?" I whispered-hissed.

Rhys nodded his head, not missing any words. My ears perked up at the mention of falling in love. I knew it was just a song, but it was clear that he'd chosen it and now he was singing that it was okay to fall in love with him. He was telling me that not only was it okay to fall in love with him, but that he'd be the guy to heal my heart. He was the guy who had healed my heart. The previous two songs were a timeline of our relationship, but now he was singing that I should fall in love with him. Did he actually mean it? Or was I reading far too much into these songs?

He sang the lyrics about being the last voice I'd hear at night and that he wanted me to be the one staring back at him when we woke each morning. I continued to sway in my seat as he did the same singing next to the Christmas tree. Listening to the words, I realized that it wasn't bad to fall in love with him. I needed to tell him that I did love him, but before I could get a word out, the next song started, and Rhys quickly took a sip of my cooling coffee.

"Throat's dry," he whispered.

I nodded, not able to say anything. Then the song picked up, and realization once again dawned on me. "Savage Garden?" I whispered.

He nodded and started to sing. I definitely knew the song. It was one that was popular when I was in high school. All the girls wanted their boyfriends to fall truly, madly and deeply in love with them, and I was one of those girls. Now here I was with the perfect man, and he was singing how he'd be my dream, my wish, my fantasy, my hope, my love and everything I'd need. He was all of those things, and as he sang the slow song, a lump started to form in my throat.

Rhys was telling me through all of these songs that he wanted to be with me forever. I wanted to be with him forever too. I wanted to sing along with him, but there was no way for me to even whisper the lyrics or I would cry. I felt my heart expanding in my chest, and I was paralyzed, not wanting to ruin this moment because he was finally telling me that he loved me.

When reality was, I loved him too.

The guitar faded away, and before I could stand to rush into his arms, another one started. I had no idea what number we were on. He'd said that there were six songs he wanted to sing to me. Six songs of him expressing how he was in love with me—or so I now assumed.

The song that started next was another country song like the one he had started with. This one was about me finding my Prince Charming and how I liked romantic movies. Then he sang about how he could love me like Romeo loved Juliet. He sang that I just needed to give him a chance, but that was exactly what I was doing. Even though I was brokenhearted when we'd met, I'd opened my heart again, and it was all because of him.

Rhys sang about moving Heaven and Earth and making me his world if I'd be his girl. I was his girl, and as I listened to him finish the song, I realized that he must have fallen in love with me before he asked me to be his girl. Or so I assumed given the timeline of these love songs.

So where did that mean we were on the timeline? He met me, he was one call away when I needed him to forget my past—but he sang that it was okay for me to fall in love with him before he sang about loving me deeply and being my Prince Charming. Then I grasped that it wasn't just him singing to me that it was okay for me to fall in love with him.

He was giving himself permission to fall in love with me.

Tears pricked my eyes. Even though we'd met when we were both broken and scared, we'd fallen in love with each other. I didn't know how or when it had happened, but the game of love always goes on. It had for us, and here we were on Christmas morning having our own Christmas miracle.

"This one's important," Rhys stated, holding the mic away.

I hadn't noticed that the song had ended, so I nodded, still paralyzed and unable to move. I didn't care what number song we were on. Rhys was telling me he loved me and I wanted this moment to last forever.

More guitars strummed as the next song started to play. I furrowed my brow when it dawned on me what song it was. Or better yet, who sang the original. "One Direction, really?" I laughed.

Rhys cracked a smile, but all laughter stopped when he moved, sat next to me and started to touch each part of my body when the lyrics matched them. And then the moment he sang that he loved me, the tears I was trying to keep at bay spilled over my lids. I wasn't even sure what most of the lyrics were because each time that he sang he was in love with me, everything seemed to fade away except those words.

"You're in love with me?" I whispered as the song ended.

Rhys was still sitting beside me, and he slowly smiled. "Yeah, Cupcake. I love you so fucking much."

A tear slid down my cheek and onto the blanket. "I love you too."

He brushed the tears away with his thumb. "Don't cry."

"I'm crying because I'm happy."

He chuckled slightly. "So that means you loved my show?"

I rolled my eyes at his ridiculous question and tackled him. We fell back onto the couch and eating breakfast was replaced with something else entirely for the second time that morning.

And then again in the shower.

Rhys's Love Concert

I Met a Girl – William Michael Morgan – 3:22

One Call Away – Charlie Puth – 3:14

Not a Bad Thing – Justin Timberlake – 4:26

Truly Madly Deeply – Savage Garden – 4:37

I Can Love You Like That – John Michael Montgomery – 3:55

Little Things – One Direction – 3:40

We arrived at Rhys's parents' house around noon. I was starving since breakfast was forgotten, and by the time we finished what replaced breakfast, it was time to get ready to leave. But I'd skip breakfast every day if all mornings were like the one I'd just had.

When we walked in through the front door, Rhys's mother was standing in the entry as though she'd been looking out the window all morning for our arrival.

"Ashtyn!" She beamed and wrapped me in her arms.

"Merry Christmas, Claire."

"I'm so happy you could come." She pulled back.

"Thank you for having me."

"Hand me your coat," Rhys said.

I shrugged out of my wool coat and handed it to him. Claire gestured for me to walk into her home, and as we headed toward the kitchen, we passed a lit fire in the fireplace and little bit of pain scorched my heart. I had a fireplace in my condo, and I knew Rhys wanted one. If only I could stand to be in there for more than ten minutes while I grabbed clothes …

I turned my head to look at Rhys as he followed behind us and nudged my head toward the flames. "We should find a place with one."

Rhys's mom stopped walking. "You two are going to find a place together?"

My gaze darted to Rhys, realizing I had just said we should move in together. We practically were living together, but it wasn't official yet. There were things that needed to be done before we had the same address. Like selling my condo. And if we decided to find a bigger location with a fireplace, then we'd need to sell his home too.

"It's a possibility." Rhys winked at me as he answered his mother.

"Did you hear that, Romi? Your brother and Ashtyn might move in together!"

We finally rounded the corner, and I saw a few more people standing at the kitchen island and eating what looked to be cheese dip.

"Don't embarrass the girl, Mom." A woman who looked a lot like a younger version of Rhys walked over to me and stuck her hand out. "I'm Romi, Rhys's sister."

I smiled. "It's nice to meet you."

"This is my husband, Shane." She gestured to a man behind her. We shook hands as well.

"And this big guy is my dad," Rhys stated.

"It's nice to meet you, Mr. Cole."

"Please call me Andy." We shook hands as well.

"I'm not trying to embarrass Ashtyn, Romi. I'm just saying that your little bun in the oven might not be my only grandchild."

"Whoa!" Rhys held up his hands in mock surrender. "We haven't even had sex yet." My eyes widened as Rhys threw his arm around my shoulder and whispered, "Don't be embarrassed, Cupcake. They know I'm joking."

I wasn't sure if that was worse.

One down. One to go.

Being with Rhys's family was amazing. I felt comfortable, and I think I fit in well with everyone. His mom continued to be wonderful, and so was his father. His sister couldn't stop glowing, and I was jealous that she was finally starting a family. It wasn't that I was thinking Rhys and I should start right away just because we were in love. It was because I was going to be thirty-four and time was ticking.

Rhys drove us about twenty minutes to my parents' house for Christmas dinner. I was already stuffed, but this was how I assumed all Christmases would be in the future. At least that was what I'd always wanted, or maybe next year we could do Thanksgiving at his parents and Christmas at mine then switch the next year.

"I know you've met Ethan, but I have another brother. Plus, my dad," I reminded him.

Rhys looked over at me as he put the car in park. "I'm not scared. Ethan loves me."

"Right." I snorted. I wasn't sure if either one of my brothers would ever approve of a boyfriend of mine. They were too protective and acted as though I was still in high school and some guy only wanted in my pants.

"Well, he knows I'm taking care of you, and that's all fathers and big brothers want."

"I hope so," I sighed. What if they didn't like Rhys? What if Ethan was only being nice because Rhys had tried to save me? It's not every day you're almost kidnapped and your boyfriend is almost shot. But they loved hockey and hockey was Rhys's life. Plus, every game they watched Rhys on TV just like his family caught my broadcasts.

We got out of the car and walked up to the front door. It was unlocked, so we entered. Dad, Ethan, and Carter were sitting on the couch ready for the rare Christmas day football game. It didn't happen often, but it was happening this year, and they were excited. It wasn't even two teams they liked. It was just sports, and they were men.

Dad stood as we entered the room. "Dad, this is Rhys. Rhys, this is my father, Glen."

Rhys stuck out his hand. "It's nice to meet you, sir."

"Likewise."

Carter stood and stuck out his hand. "I'm Ashtyn's brother, Carter."

"Nice to meet you, too."

Ethan came up with his hand out as well. "Rhys."

"Ethan." They shook too.

"Mom and the girls are in the kitchen?"

Dad nodded. "Dinner should be ready soon. I hope you're hungry."

I groaned inwardly thinking I was going to gain ten pounds in one day and I'd eat so much that they'd need to wheel me out because it would be too uncomfortable to move a muscle. "Let's have you meet the women, and then you can come back here and do man stuff."

"Man stuff?" Rhys laughed.

I waved my hand at the TV. "Watch men hit each other as they try to get a ball."

"Football," Rhys stated as though I had no clue.

"Don't let this one fool you, Rhys. She knows about every sport," Dad chimed in.

I knew the basics because of my job. I had no idea of stats and stuff like a lot of guys knew when they talked sports over beers. Now, ask me anything about Scandal or How to Get Away with Murder and I'd be all over it.

"I know she knows more than she lets on. She got Jeremy Roenick to meet me last night and sign a jersey for me."

All the men looked at me, and I shrugged. "I know a guy who knows a guy."

"I can't wait to see what you got us for Christmas," Carter beamed hopefully.

I frowned. "Nothing." Then I looked at the door where we'd set a few bags down that had wrapped presents in it.

"Don't be like that, Ash. I saved your life," Ethan stated.

He had, and even though I got them signed jerseys too, it would never be enough.

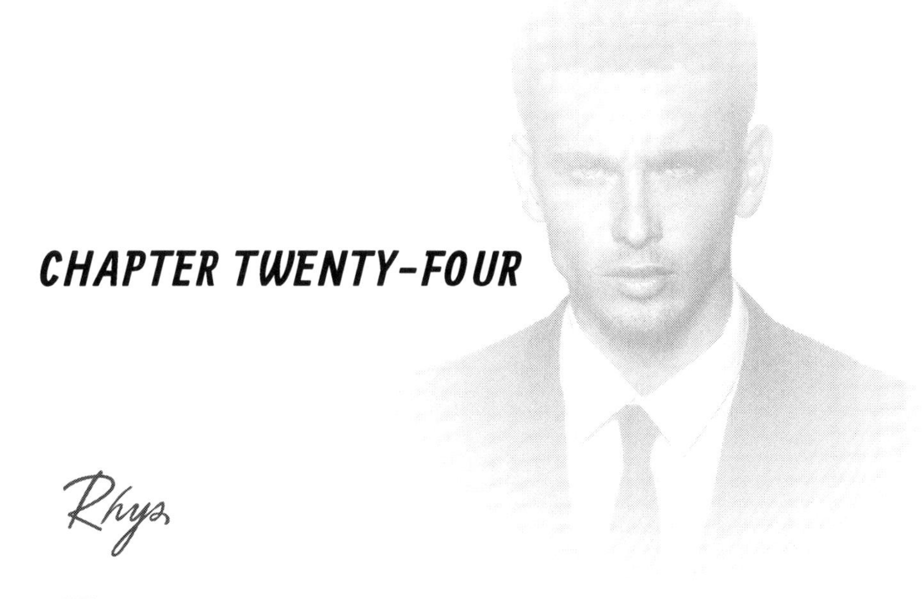

CHAPTER TWENTY-FOUR

Rhys

It's crazy to think that one night and a decision to walk to the closest bar instead of going nuclear on a bitch was the best decision I'd ever made.

Ever. Made.

I can't even think what my life would be like without Ashtyn in it. Sure, I might be dating—might even have another girlfriend—but I knew that she was the best thing to ever happen to me. I knew it in my soul. I knew it in my bones. I knew it in the core of my being.

I just hoped she felt the same way too.

While Ashtyn was at work and I was watching her broadcast, I grabbed my laptop and started to search for homes for sale. She'd mentioned finding a place with a fireplace, and I wanted that too. I didn't want to remind her that she had one in her condo because it was clear that she never wanted to sleep there again. I would be more than happy for her to permanently move in with me and why not buy something to share? However, in a few months, we wouldn't even need a fireplace because the weather would start warming up. Maybe we needed a place with a pool and a fireplace. The best of both worlds.

But would I be willing to sell my condo and buy something together? Would she? What if we broke up? Of course, I never wanted to break up, but sometimes fate has other plans.

I had to be smart about this.

A few hours later, a key in the lock turned, and Ashtyn walked in.

"Hey, Cupcake."

"Hey."

"How was work?"

"Counting the days down until I get home at a decent hour." She shrugged out of her coat and hung it on the hook by the door.

"Speaking of, you still want to go to a game?"

Ashtyn smiled. "Yes."

"Okay. I'll get you and the girls some tickets."

The Blackhawk games usually started about seven-thirty at night. When Ashtyn moved to the evening news, she'd be able to make it to the game on time if she went straight from work. I, of course, had to do my shows and wouldn't be able to join her but she could have a girl's night.

"I'm so excited!" she exclaimed and sat next to me on the couch.

I kissed the side of her head, my laptop still on my lap from doing shit the last few hours. She was finally starting to be her old self again. I could tell by the way she was no longer scared to be alone. And she hadn't mentioned any more flowers being delivered or people stalking her. Hopefully, all the crazy people were in our past.

"You going to shower and get ready for bed?"

"In a few minutes. I just want to cuddle with you."

"We can cuddle in bed." I smirked.

Ashtyn grinned. "I know, but give me a few minutes to unwind."

"Okay. While you're resting, I have a question."

"What's that?"

I rubbed the back of my neck nervously. "Were you serious the other day when you said we should get a place with a fireplace?"

Ashtyn tilted her head slightly and bit her lip. "Well …"

I set the laptop on the coffee table and turned to face her. "If I tell you that I want to, would you agree?"

She nodded and didn't speak.

"Good because I think we should."

"Yeah?" She grinned.

"But I'm not saying we should get rid of our condos."

"I don't understand." She furrowed her brows.

I grabbed her hand and brushed my thumb across the back. "We practically live together now, and while I want us to keep coming home to each other every night, I'm not sure selling our places would be the right decision."

"Oh." Ashtyn frowned.

I smiled, trying to put her at ease. "I'm not saying I don't want to. I think that if we can afford it, we should find a place that's ours and rent out our condos. I think we can rent them out for more than our mortgages, and if two of us are paying a mortgage on a house—"

"A house?"

I nodded. "I don't know about you, but I don't need this scene anymore," I stated, meaning living in the city and having everything within walking distance.

"So, you want to move to the suburbs?"

I chuckled. "Yeah, but only if we find a house with a pool and a fireplace."

She thought for a moment. "You know what I was thinking?"

"What's that?"

Ashtyn grinned. "The same thing. Well, I wasn't thinking of renting out my condo, but I think you're right."

"Yeah?"

"Yeah."

I stood, pulling Ashtyn with me. "Good. Now let's make sure we fuck in every inch of this place before we move."

The snow was falling—again. It was cold as fuck, and yet my dumb ass had agreed with my friends that going on a fucking yacht for New Year's Eve would be fun. But Kenny had come across an ad for a Speakeasy cruise and wanted us to go. Besides ringing in the new year with my girl, I was looking forward to the poker tournament that was being held on the boat. The guys and I had practiced for years, though we didn't know that we had been practicing. I wasn't sure how the boat was going to be set up for the tournament, but I hoped that at the final table my friends and I would be playing each other. At least then I could read their tells and have more of a chance of walking away with some money.

I was dressed in a black pinstriped suit, a black button-down shirt, a red tie, black and white Oxfords and a black and white fedora. I legit felt like I was a gangster. Maybe dressing up in a getup from the twenties wasn't all that bad. Plus, the way Ashtyn looked …

She was dressed in a gold, satin evening gown that clasped around her neck. The material hugged every inch of her curves, but what I couldn't stop staring at was her bare shoulders. There was something about the way the curve of her neck sloped to her slender shoulders that made my mouth water and call my name. All I wanted to do was run my tongue along every inch of her skin and not stop until we were both naked and sated.

But there was no time for that.

"Ready, Cupcake?"

She grabbed her clutch. "Yep."

We took an Uber down to Navy Pier and met up with Kenny, Jett, Clark, and Abby. Everyone was dressed as though the year had changed back to a time where alcohol was illegal, and there were a lot of underground clubs where you could drink and play cards. Most of the women were dressed in flapper dresses, but I preferred the way Ashtyn's gown hugged her curves, though I wouldn't mind a knee-high flapper dress I could slip my hand under.

"Isn't this the same boat we took for the booze cruise?" Ashtyn asked as we all walked aboard.

"Sure is."

"Maybe they'll have Jenga set up so Abs and I can play something."

"You don't want to watch me win?" I smirked.

"I'm winning tonight," Kenny stated.

"Please. You lose every week," Jett put in.

"There can only be three winners, and tonight one of them is me," Clark stated. He was right. There would only be a first, second and third place. Third place would walk away with five hundred bucks, second would take a grand and first place was getting five thousand.

I rolled my eyes. "You fools know I'm the better player."

"While I would love to see you four have a catfight, I would love a drink more," Ashtyn indicated.

"Right," I agreed. "Let's get a drink then figure out the dinner situation."

Dinner was in our bellies, and a few drinks had been consumed by the time the tournament started. There were ninety-nine of us playing for first place.

There were eleven tables, each with nine players. There were six tables on the bottom level, five on the middle level and the final table on the upper level. The winner from each table would move to the main event, so the final table would consist of eleven people. The seats were chosen randomly, and I was at a table with Clark. I won.

"You're going to the final table?" Ashtyn asked, a huge smile on her face.

"Of course I am."

She shoved my shoulder. "Don't be so cocky."

"I play every week, Cupcake. It's like second nature to me."

"Isn't it the luck of the cards?" Abby asked. She and Ashtyn had watched our game for the past hour or so until I'd won.

"There's more than just luck. You need to know when to hold 'em and when to fold 'em." And now that song is stuck in my head. "Plus," I leaned closer and whispered, "I'm a good bluffer."

"A good bullshitter he means," Clark chimed in.

"Don't be mad 'cause you lost."

He snorted. "I'll get you back next week."

"Right." I grinned.

"Do you ladies want to grab another drink while we wait?" I asked.

"You guys don't want to see how Kenny and Jett are doing?" Ashtyn asked.

I shook my head. "Nah, I don't want to distract them. Let them do their thing."

We made it to a bar on the top deck, and each ordered a drink. A couple of minutes later, Jett walked up.

"Well?" I asked.

"Beat 'em."

I nodded my approval. "I won too."

He looked at Clark, and Clark shrugged. "Asshole cheats."

I laughed. "I don't fucking cheat. You suck."

"Let's go tour the boat," Ashtyn said to Abby. "Let the boys compare—"

"Watch it, Cupcake. You know what happened last time we were on this boat."

She slowly turned her head toward me and narrowed her eyes, but before she could respond, Kenny walked up.

"Who do I get to beat at the final table?"

"Me," Jett answered.

"And me," I affirmed.

Kenny looked at Clark, and Clark shook his head. "Rhys cheats."

"Dude, I don't cheat."

My gaze turned to watch Ashtyn walk away. When I said that her dress hugged every curve, I meant it. Watching her ass sway in the satin was causing my dick to strain in my pants. It didn't help that this was a boat where we'd once fucked in the bathroom. I still craved her like warm soup on a cold night.

Kenny moved next to me and leaned in as he whispered, "You gonna hook me up with Abby?"

"I'll talk to my girl."

"You're a true best friend."

"Yep," I agreed.

"You gonna let me win later too?"

"Nope."

"I need to look good for Abby."

I laughed. "You're gonna need more help than winning at cards."

The key to having better odds of winning was to not be drunk when it was time for the final table. The problem was, the moment he walked into the room, I wished I was wasted off my ass.

My body went rigid, and anger laced through my veins.

Corey Fucking Pritchett walked into the room and moved toward the final table. I didn't know where Ashtyn was and that was probably for the best because I didn't want her to witness me losing my shit. The last time I saw Corey, I was alone and knew if he tried something, I would more than likely get my ass kicked. Now I had my boys with me, and there was nowhere to go. We had at least two more hours on the cruise, and now that I knew Corey was on the same boat, it was going to be the longest two hours of my life.

I narrowed my eyes in his direction, wishing looks could kill. He looked around the table after sitting, and when his gaze met mine, recognition registered on his face.

He smirked.

He fucking smirked at me, and I wanted to do nothing more than fly across the table and beat his ass.

"Cole," he said dryly.

"Pritchett," I clipped. I could feel my friends look at me, but I didn't take my death glare off of Corey.

"Didn't know you were here."

"Same."

I watched a woman move up behind him and place her hand on his shoulder. She leaned down and asked, "Can I get you anything to drink, sweetie?"

Sweetie? She has no clue.

Fuck! Where was Ashtyn?

I wanted Corey to see me with her. To know that I was winning because Ashtyn was mine. I was dating someone everyone knew and not this chick who looked like she stood on street corners. Okay, that might be a little harsh because I didn't know this woman, but she was dating my bully from high school, so all cruel names were a go.

I watched him look up at her and have no emotion whatsoever. He looked at her as though she was hired or that he knew nothing about her other than maybe her name. I'd bet it was Cinnamon or some shit. So I decided to do what my mother taught me. I was going to kill him with kindness.

"Yeah, bring me a Jack and Coke, will ya?"

"Anything for you." She kissed his cheek and then his attention moved back to me.

"You know this guy?" Kenny asked, hooking his thumb in Corey's direction.

I smiled. I fucking smiled as though Corey and I were fucking bros. "Yeah. Corey and I go back to high school."

"You going to introduce us?" Jett asked.

No. That thought had never crossed my mind. Fine. I sighed and did the introductions. Everyone else at the table took that to mean we were getting to know each other and the other six people shook hands. I didn't fucking touch the asshole sitting across from me.

The dealer shuffled the cards and dealt out two to each of us. Pocket kings. Fuck yeah. I slow played my starting hand, only calling one of the guy's bets. Kenny, Jett, and Corey all called as well. The others folded. The dealer turned over three cards: two of spades, ten of hearts and king of clubs.

I didn't show any emotion as I stared at the cards, knowing I had a three of a kind. It helped that I was pissed. Never in my life had I thought I'd run into this asshole, and now within a month or so, I'd run into him twice.

Twice.

The original better bet again and the rest of us called. The dealer turned over a two of hearts. I had a full house.

As I contemplated how much to bet, Ashtyn walked in through the door that led outside. It was as though everything was right in my world. We smiled at each other as our gazes met and then, just as I was grabbing chips to raise, Corey spoke and changed my entire world with one word.

"Ashtyn?"

I watched her turn at her name, and it felt as though a knife was being stabbed in my heart. "Corey?" she asked. Clearly, she knew who he was.

I went all in, not caring about slow playing anymore. As I watched the exchange, not reading my opponents, Corey smiled and spoke to Ashtyn as though he couldn't care less about the game. "I had no idea you were at this party."

The knife went an inch deeper.

"Now I wish I wasn't."

My gaze snapped to Ashtyn. She seemed to get along with everyone. Plus, being in the public eye, you had to put on a smile even when you wanted to stab someone in the eye, especially now that everything can be live streamed. How did she know this jackass?

"Aw, don't be like that." Corey folded his cards, throwing them in the center of the table.

Ashtyn's gaze turned to me, and I asked, "Are you okay?" I didn't know what was going on other than I was starting to think we both hated this guy. But why did she?

"Remember the last time we were on this boat?" she asked me.

I nodded. "Yeah …"

"Now it's my turn to run into my ex."

The knife in my heart twisted and caused the most tormenting pain I'd ever felt as I realized the one person I hated the most used to date the one person I love the most in the world.

I needed to get away from the table.

I actually wanted to jump off the boat and swim to shore so I could be alone, but that wasn't logical or plausible.

Corey Fucking Pritchett was her ex. He knew what it was like to hold her. Taste her. Hear her moans. He'd been inside of her, inside of what's mine. My heart that was sliced in two was trying to leave my chest. Pressure tightened around the area, and I felt as though I was going to keel over and die. I wanted to die knowing someone so evil could be loved by someone so sweet. What did that say about her loving me?

I looked at the table and noticed my friends were still in. "One of you call me."

"What?" Jett asked.

"I'm folding after the river."

"What are you doing? You're just going to tell us to bet it all and hope you fold?" Kenny asked.

"I'm trying to give you all my money."

"What?" Jett and Kenny said in unison. I saw Clark beside Ashtyn and Abby eyeing me as though I had two heads. Maybe I did, and that was why Ashtyn loved me because she had once loved the devil.

"I need to get out of here." My gaze moved to Ashtyn, and she furrowed her brow, probably wondering why I was having this sort of reaction toward her ex. Maybe she assumed I'd thrown the chance of winning five grand away so I could fuck her in the bathroom to make her forget Corey. That wasn't the case. I needed to get as far away as possible given we were on a fucking boat.

The guys stared at each other as my leg bobbed up and down, waiting impatiently for them to decide what to do. In the end, Kenny called me, and Jett folded.

The dealer turned over a four of spades, and without hesitation, I folded, throwing my cards in the center of the table. Then I stood, needing to get fresh air. Ashtyn moved to me, but Corey spoke and stopped me from walking out the door.

"You two dating?"

I jerked my head toward him. "That's none of your business."

Corey smirked. "Only fitting you get my leftovers."

"Shut the fuck up."

He grinned. "Aww, I'm ruffling your feathers. You going to run home to Mommy?"

"Leave him alone, Corey," Ashtyn hissed.

"Your girlfriend fighting your battles?"

"Is that what you think?" I laughed.

"Doesn't matter. She was only a hole to stick my dick in."

I snapped.

My hands grabbed fistfuls of his shirt, and I was in Corey's face. My hat fell off my head as I roared, "What the fuck did you just say?"

"Whoa!" I heard behind me, and arms started to try and pull me away from Corey. I didn't budge.

"Security's gonna throw you out, dude," Kenny stated.

I glared at Corey. "Not likely since we're in the middle of the fucking lake. How about I throw you overboard instead?"

"Sir," someone else said. I didn't know who. Didn't care who it was.

"You think you can talk about my woman like that?" I hissed.

"She was mine first."

"Sir," someone said again. I ignored them, still with Corey's shirt in my grip and hands trying to pull me back.

Realization dawned on me as I processed his words. It didn't matter that he was hers first because I was with her now and I fucking loved the shit out of her. "And I'm the one who's going to be with her the rest of her life." I pushed him back as I released his shirt. When I turned around, Ashtyn's gaze met mine, and I honestly didn't know what to do at that moment. I was angry, and it wasn't toward her, but I wanted to be alone.

"Sir." I heard again and turned to see a woman dressed in a pantsuit with a radio in her hand. "We're going to need you to leave this room."

"Already planning on it," I clipped as I picked up my hat and walked out the door. The cold air hit my face, but it wasn't enough to cool me off. I needed another drink. I heard heels behind me.

"Rhys."

I turned and looked over my shoulder, seeing Ashtyn. "Not now."

"Are you mad at me?"

I stopped walking and turned to face her. "No, but I want to be alone right now."

"I'm not going back to him," she stated.

"I know," I sighed. At least I'd hoped that was the case.

"I don't understand why you're so angry. He was only running his mouth because he's an asshole who thinks he's God's gift."

I sighed again, trying to calm down. "Can we talk about this later? I really need a fucking drink."

"Yeah. Sure. Whatever."

Ashtyn started to walk away, but I grabbed her wrist, halting her. I stepped closer to her and cupped her face tenderly. "I'm not mad at you, but he's a part of my past too."

Her eyes widened. "How?"

"I don't want to talk about it right now. I need a drink, and then I need to be alone for a few minutes while I process everything."

"Why are you pushing me away?"

"I'm not trying to push you away. I just need to gather my thoughts."

Her emerald eyes stared into my blue ones, and it was her turn to sigh. "Okay, but we're good?"

I smiled. "Of course. Just give me some time."

"Okay. I'll go back to Abby and then come find you when it's almost midnight."

I leaned forward and pressed my lips to hers. "Thank you. And don't worry about me. It's nothing whiskey can't fix."

Ashtyn smirked. "I think we're supposed to have sex right now."

I nodded my understanding. "While I would love to bring you down to the bathroom where we fucked before, I think we've passed that stage. Don't you?"

"You're right. My future is you."

"And my future is you. I love you."

"I love you too."

"I'll see you in a few." She went to turn, but I stopped her again by grabbing ahold of her wrist.

"Talk to Abby about Kenny."

"What about him?"

I grinned. "He wants us to hook them up."

Ashtyn's eyes widened. "He likes her?"

"I think he thinks she's cute. Not sure they've even spoken more than a few words to each other."

"This makes me excited. I've wanted to hook her up with someone."

"Good. Go talk to her, and I'm going to get a drink."

I kissed her again and then she left while I turned back in the direction of the bar. By the time I got there, I was already relaxed, but I still needed to process that the love of my life used to date the guy who beat me up in high school.

CHAPTER TWENTY-FIVE

Ashtyn

I had no idea why Rhys was acting as though he wanted to kill Corey. Sure I wasn't all that happy the few times we'd run into his ex, but I never wanted to harm her. Well, okay, maybe I wanted to slap her, but I would never act on it. But Rhys had been in Corey's face, and I knew in my gut that if they were the only ones in the room, fists would have been thrown. Rhys told me that Corey was a part of his past too. How? What could Corey have done that would cause this sort of reaction from Rhys? From what I knew about Rhys since we'd been dating, he was sweet, kind, and didn't have a mean bone in his body.

I walked back into the room where the poker game had resumed. The table was full except Rhys's seat, and Kenny looked at me as I made my way to where Abby and Clark were.

"What the hell was that?" Kenny asked me.

I shrugged. "He won't tell me."

The hands of cards kept being dealt as we all spoke.

"I'll tell you," Corey stated, stopping me in my tracks. "Bitch always runs because he's scared of me."

My gaze cut to Corey. "Scared of you? How do you even know him?"

"Yeah, man. Enlighten us," Jett chimed in, acid lacing his words. "Tell us how you get one of the nicest guys I know all riled up."

Corey threw some chips into the center of the table. "Your boy's a pussy. Has been since high school."

High school? They've known each other since high school?

Kenny stood, causing the chair to scoot back against the wood floor and tip over. "Fuck you, man!" He pointed at Corey. "Who the fuck do you think you are?"

"Oooo, Kenny getting all feisty is kinda hot," Abby whisper-hissed next to me.

With each word that Corey was saying, the more I wanted to be the one to get in his face. But, I was in the public eye, and I didn't want to get fired if something were to end up on the internet, so I had to keep my cool even though I wasn't.

"Gentlemen," the dealer warned, "if this continues, I'm going to have to ask you all to leave the table."

"He should be the one to leave," Kenny spat, throwing his arm in Corey's direction.

"Let's just all calm down," Clark stated to them. "Get the game over with, and when we dock, we can all leave."

The players I didn't know all nodded their heads and muttered agreement. Kenny sat back down, and my gaze moved back to Corey. He was smirking. What did I ever see in him? How did I ever think that we could get married? I didn't need to know the full story about Rhys and Corey to know Corey and me breaking up was the best thing that had ever happened. It caused all the dots to connect, all the stars and all the moons to line up. I'd dodged a bullet, that was for sure.

I wanted to run to Rhys and comfort him, tell him that I didn't care about Corey and, in fact, I never wanted to speak of him again. It was killing me to be patient and give Rhys time, but clearly, something had happened to cause Rhys to act like this after all these years.

I shot daggers in Corey's direction the entire time the poker game was going on until he was out. The only people left at the time Corey was eliminated were Kenny and Jett. Kenny and Jett were good, and it became clear that Rhys was right. It wasn't only about having luck, it took skill. I wished that he was still playing because I wanted to see him smile and play with his friends like he does at home.

"I'm going to go find Rhys. Come find us when this is over, or in thirty minutes before the clock strikes midnight," I said to Abby.

"Okay. I'll just watch—"

"Kenny." I winked at her.

Abby smirked. "You know me too well."

I chuckled and moved toward the door. Rhys wanted me to talk to Abby about them two getting together, but there was no reason to. They'd eventually figure it out.

I made my way toward the bar where Rhys had said he was going to be. It had been thirty minutes or so and if he needed more time, then … Well, I didn't know what I'd do because we were on a boat for Christ's sakes.

The snow had stopped falling, and when I got to the outdoor bar, I saw Rhys standing under a heat lamp talking to an older man. Rhys turned and smiled when he saw me. Apparently giving him some time had paid off. Everyone processes anger differently and learning that Rhys needed time to cool off was good to know.

Rhys reached out his hand, and I took it when I got close. "Otis, this is my girlfriend, Ashtyn."

Otis stuck out his hand, and I shook it with my free hand. "Of course. You do the nightly news on—"

"Actually she's moving to the evening news," Rhys stated.

I smiled. "Tomorrow's the first day."

"Congratulations," Otis beamed.

"Thank you."

"Otis owns a karaoke bar."

My eyes widened, and I look to Otis. "Really?"

"I do, and I heard you love to sing."

My face heated. "I wouldn't say that. This one," I hooked my thumb in Rhys's direction, "is actually the karaoke singer."

We all laughed. "Well, if you two ever want to come and sing your hearts out, give me a call." Otis handed Rhys his card.

"Thanks, man. I'm sure we can do that one night," Rhys replied.

"I better go find my wife. Get ready for midnight and all that. It was nice meeting you two." We shook hands again.

"Want a drink?" Rhys asked after Otis left.

"Sure."

He turned toward the bar and released my hand, raising his finger to indicate another drink. I had no idea what he'd ordered until the bartender set a glass of Rosé on the bar top. "Who's left at the table?" Rhys asked as he handed me the flute.

"Kenny and Jett."

"Not Corey?"

I shook my head. "Nope."

"So he's lurking around?"

I took a sip of my wine and placed the glass on the high-top table next to us. "I guess he is."

Rhys took a deep breath. "I can't believe your ex is Corey Pritchett."

I sighed. "I can't believe you went to high school together."

"He told you?"

I nodded. "Yeah, but that's all he said."

"We only went to high school together my freshmen year."

"Really? And you still remember him after all this time?"

He looked off into the distance, and took a few minutes before responding. "Kinda hard to forget the guy who used to beat me up for no reason."

My eyes widened as my stomach dropped. "He was the one who bullied you?"

"Almost every day." He took a sip of his drink.

My throat started to close as I remembered what Rhys told me before about his bully and how he ran into him a few weeks back. The same night Philip tried to date rape me. "Now I know why you hate him so much."

Rhys sighed. "It was a long time ago, but fuck if it doesn't make my blood boil to know he's your ex."

We were silent for a few moments. I didn't know what to say because I couldn't change my past just like he couldn't change his. I also didn't know what I would do in his position. I wasn't bullied as a kid. In fact, I was one of the popular girls. What I did know was that I loved Rhys. He had come into my life and was like the sunshine after a rainstorm. The thought of him leaving me would end my world. I wouldn't be able to move on with my life if he wasn't in it. It was Rhys I needed to make me happy.

I stepped closer, and Rhys wrapped his arms around me. Before I could come up with what to say, the devil himself walked up.

"Are your panties still in a bunch, Cole?"

I felt Rhys's body go taut against me. "Fuck you," he hissed.

Corey chuckled again. "Just remember that paybacks are a bitch and I've waited many years to get you back."

And all the anger that I was keeping at bay came barreling out. I spun around and shoved Corey. "Just shut the fuck up, Corey!" Corey stumbled back, and Rhys grabbed my waist, trying to pull me back, but I kept pushing as I yelled, "We want nothing to do with you. Leave us alone!" At that moment, I didn't care who was around, and I didn't care if my outburst was all over the internet. I was so over Corey's bullshit.

A girl appeared at Corey's side. She was pretty, blonde, big boobs, and a fake tan. A tan in fucking winter. "Don't touch my man!" she hissed.

I balked, and it wasn't because she thought we were going to fight over her man, but I'd realized Rhys and I were better than this. Better than the trash these two people were. "Fine." I threw up my hands then grabbed Rhys's hand. "Corey, take a flying leap off the front of the boat."

I towed Rhys behind me. I had no idea where we were going, but I didn't want to stand there with them. We went to the back of the boat where people were standing around. The places we could go were becoming less and less, and I couldn't wait to get on land. God, I wish we weren't on a boat.

"Take a flying leap off the front of the boat?" Rhys chuckled.

I groaned and looked up at the dark sky. "I'm so pissed right now. I don't know what I'm saying."

Rhys wrapped his arm around my shoulders and pulled me to him. "If you hadn't stepped in, I would have decked him, and the cops would probably be waiting for me when we got back to the pier."

I rolled my eyes out of frustration. "What are the fucking odds?" I could still feel the heat coursing through my veins. I hated Corey. Hated. What if he'd never broken up with me? What if he'd asked me to marry him like I thought he'd do one day? Would I have seen his true colors?

"How about we never come on this boat again?"

I nodded against his shoulder, staring out at the twinkling skyline. "I was thinking the same thing."

We stayed like that for a few minutes until our friends came up behind us.

"There you guys are," Kenny said.

We turned, and Rhys spoke. "Who won?"

Jett smiled. "Yours truly."

A waiter came over with a tray of champagne. "It's almost midnight."

We all grabbed flutes, and I'd realized I'd left my Rosé on the table at the other end of the boat. Oh well. We were minutes away from returning to the pier and for us to go home.

While we waited for the clock to strike midnight, I stole glances in Abby's direction. Her and Kenny were laughing and chatting. I knew they'd figure it out. It probably also helped that we were on a fucking boat.

Yeah, I never wanted to do this again.

No more boats.

Not long after, people started to count down from ten. When it got to one, we all toasted to the new year and Rhys and I kissed. Fireworks started to go off in the distance, and when you kiss the right person, you can't tell who is kissing whom.

And it was clear to me that this person was Rhys.

Switching to the evening news wasn't much different from the nightly news except I got off earlier. The daily meeting was still at the same time as it was before, but now when I arrived at work, I did the promo videos first thing instead of doing the meeting and then doing promo.

Freshening up my makeup in the one dressing room we had in the studio, I sent Abby a text. Rhys was working tonight, and I wanted to find out about Kenny and Abby. I know they'd hung out together after we left on New Years a few days ago, but I wanted to know if they really had figured it out.

Me: What are you doing on your dinner break?

Abby: I brought a boring salad to eat in the break room. Why?

Me: Take your lunch early and come to dinner with me.

Abby: Okay. What's up?

Me: Nothing. I just miss my friend.

Abby: Okay. See you after your show.

I was waiting for Abby at my desk after my broadcast when I got a text. I balked when I read who it was from.

Corey: Congrats on moving to the evening news.

I stared at the words on the screen, and my fingers hovered over the letters wanting to text back. But I didn't. What was there to say? Thank you?

Fuck. That.

"Ready?" Abby asked, stopping at my desk.

I stood. "Yeah. Guess who just texted me?"

"Who?"

"Corey!" We started to walk toward the elevators.

"What did he want?"

"To congratulate me on moving to the evening news."

"Did you text him back?" Abby asked as she pressed the down button.

"Hell no." We walked into the car, and Abby pressed the button for the lobby.

"He probably broke up with that hooker."

"Oh my god!" I laughed, grabbing my stomach as the laughter coursed through me. "She was a hooker, huh?"

"She was something. Kenny kept—"

"Speaking of Kenny." I wiggled my eyebrows. "You two…?"

"I don't kiss and tell."

I squealed as the elevator stopped and the doors opened on the ground floor. I didn't think a thirty-three-year-old could be this excited when her co-worker told her that she was dating her boyfriend's friend.

But I was.

"Can I wear your Roenick jersey to the game?" I asked Rhys. It had been a few weeks since I'd moved to the evening news and Rhys had gotten me four tickets. I'd invited Jaime, Kylie, and Colleen. My brothers were, of course, jealous. I even think Ethan called Rhys and told him that Rhys owed him and needed to hook him up.

"No," he said flatly.

I frowned. "Really?"

"It's not that I don't want you to wear my jersey. It's because it's signed and I don't want to get it messed up."

I nodded my head in understanding. "Right. I didn't think of that."

"I do have Toews, Kane, Crawford and Tootoo jerseys. Pick one."

"Why do you have so many?"

"They were given to me. Not going to turn jerseys down."

"Which one is the best player?"

"You know I can't answer that. I have to be unbiased for a living."

I groaned. "Then which one should I wear?"

"Well, Toews is the Captain—"

"I'll wear that one."

Rhys smiled. "And Crawford is the goalie."

"Oh …" I realized he was going to tell me who was who.

"Tootoo—"

I giggled at the name. How could you not? Rhys stopped and glared at me. "What?" I asked.

He rolled his eyes. "Never mind. Just pick a jersey. You can't go wrong."

I thought for a moment. "I'll go with Crawford. He plays the entire game, right?"

"Usually."

"Good. Can the girls wear the others?"

Rhys nodded and turned to the closet. "Of course."

The girls and I walked down the stairs, closer to the glass. Rhys had gotten us rink side seats against the glass, so I had to make sure I thanked Rhys properly. Once we were seated, we took a selfie of the four of us, and I sent it to my brothers with the ice in the background. I also posted the picture on Facebook and sent Rhys a thank you text.

During the first intermission, the girls and I went to grab a beer and nachos. My phone buzzed in the back pocket of my jeans.

Corey: Saw you on TV. Your boyfriend get you those seats?

I rolled my eyes as I shoved the phone back into my jeans. I focused on the conversation the girls were having about how funny it was we were having a girl's night at a hockey game, and their husbands were at home with the kids. My heart ached at the thought. Deep down inside, I wanted to be included in the conversation. I wanted to know what it felt like to love someone before you'd ever met them. To know what it was like to feel them move around inside your tummy. And what it felt like to look at someone and know you created them.

Was I serious? Did I want a baby—now?

CHAPTER TWENTY-SIX

Rhys

Two nights ago, I had another nightmare. Running into Corey apparently did that to me. Though this dream was different. Instead of Bridgette cheating on me with a no-named guy in my bed, it was Ashtyn and Corey together. The only thing that made me get past that nightmare was waking up next to Ashtyn and knowing that she was with me.

Just like this morning.

She stirred next to me, and I took that to mean that she was waking. Taking my finger, I connected all the freckles on her arm lazily, feeling her soft skin.

"What are you doing?" she asked sleepily.

I smirked and looked up to meet her gaze. "You know."

Reaching over, I grazed my finger against her hard nipple that was poking through her sleep shirt and twirled it around the peak before moving on to do the same to the other. She shivered next to me, and I took that as my cue to cover her with my body, using her stomach to get me harder. Harder to the point that I could slip in and fuck her a proper good morning.

I pressed my lips to hers. Ashtyn opened and sought my tongue. My tongue worked in her mouth and then I pulled my head back slightly and bit her bottom lip lightly. Every inch of her was sugar to me, and once I had my first taste, I knew I couldn't stop. Her shirt came off, my boxers next, and then I pulled her panties down and off her body.

We were now both naked, and I ran my tongue down her throat and to the side of her neck until she moaned and tilted her head back. I latched on to her throat with my mouth, feeling her pulse beat against my lips. If I wasn't careful, she'd need to cover up my mark before going on the air. Or she could let the entire town of Chicago know that she was fucked good morning.

Either way, I was going to do my job.

And well.

Moving slightly to the side, I ran my hand down her chest and didn't stop until I found the heat I was seeking. Christ. Always fucking ready. She was so ready that I felt her pushing on my chest, and before I knew it, we'd switched places. Ashtyn grinned down at me as she straddled my hips and then took my lips.

I could feel her warmth as she slid against my dick. "Condom," I croaked. That was the best I could do because if I wasn't inside of her soon, I would come like a boy the first time he fooled around with a girl.

Ashtyn reached over to my nightstand and pulled one out. I expected her to hand it to me, but instead, she opened it and then did the honors. Her mouth returned to mine, and I guided myself home.

She gasped for air, breaking our kiss as I filled her. "Oh shit. Yeah," she moaned and continued to do so as I rocked up into her. We were like a well-oiled machine as I thrust into her over and over and over. She'd moan, I'd groan, and just as she was about to come, I latched onto her nipple and sucked hard.

"Fuck!" she hissed as she came.

I wasn't done.

I stayed inside of her as I rolled her to the side, me going behind her and lifting her leg to spread her open. Her hand reached around my neck as she held on.

"Christ, baby," I groaned. "Watching your tits bounce from this angle is going to make me come in two seconds."

"No," she protested as a moan.

I smiled, still pumping into her. I knew she wanted to come again, and I was going to make that happen. Quickening my pace, we rocked together, and then I sought her clit with my hand and started to create circles in rhythm with my thrusts.

"Rhys," Ashtyn moaned.

"That's it, Cupcake." Good God, hearing my name on her lips as a moan was almost enough to make me lose it.

"Faster," she panted. My fingers pressed down harder against her clit. "So close."

I sped up my thrusts, hitting the very end of her until I felt her start to spasm again. This time, instead of sucking her nipple, I bit on her earlobe, and a shiver raced down my spine as I spilled into the latex.

I was spent.

We were both a little sweaty, but I knew she was fucked good.

Ashtyn had started to officially move her stuff into my place. We'd decided to rent her condo first, then find a place to move to before we put mine up as a rental too. Once she found a tenant, we planned to put her stuff into storage. This was another reason why I knew that she was with me and only me.

In the middle of January, the cops told Ashtyn that the investigation with Philip was over. He had definitely stalked and obsessed over Ashtyn for at least a year. The police found hours and hours of footage of her at home, and what looked like a bedroom made for her in his basement. It was something you'd see on TV or some shit. Thankfully, it was over.

"What do you want to do today?" I asked as Ashtyn and I sipped our morning coffee and read the newspaper.

She looked over at me and shrugged. "I don't know. What do you want to do?"

I thought for a moment, looking out the window at the sun shining above. "How do you feel about heights?"

"Heights?" Ashtyn choked on a sip of her coffee. "Why?"

"I have an idea."

She folded the newspaper and propped her chin in her hand. "Enlighten me."

"Let me make a call." I set the paper down and grabbed my phone as I headed to my office.

"You have to make a call out of the room?" she called out.

"It's a surprise."

"Why?"

"You'll see." I made my call and headed back to the kitchen island. "It's a go."

"What's a go?"

"Still a surprise." Ashtyn groaned, and I laughed as I sat back in my chair next to her. "Payback for Christmas."

"Yeah, but that was meeting your idol. Am I meeting Channing Tatum?"

"What?" I exclaimed. "Channing Tatum is your idol?"

She laughed. "No, but I wouldn't mind meeting him."

"What does he have that I don't?" I crossed my arms over my chest.

She sat up and grinned. "Dance moves for one."

"I've got moves."

"Show me."

I grunted. "Okay, I don't have his moves. What else?"

She thought for a moment. "Nothing I care about."

"Good." I smiled.

"So, you going to tell me what you have planned for today?"

"Nope." I took a final sip of my coffee.

Ashtyn groaned. "Ahhh! I'm not sure I like surprises."

I stood. "Sure, you do, Cupcake. Everyone likes surprises."

I was excited to see her face when she figured out what we were doing today. I'd done it before, but not with a girlfriend. It was with Kenny, and I was certain this time would be much better.

"Do I get to know now?"

"Nope," I replied, popping the P.

"When will I know?"

"When we get there."

We slid into my car, and I pulled out, heading toward the Chicago Executive Airport. We weren't joining the mile-high club.

At least not today.

"We're flying somewhere?" Ashtyn asked as she looked at the control tower in the distance.

"Not exactly."

"What does that mean? You're pulling into an airport."

"Ever flown a plane?"

She snorted. "Can't say that I have."

"Well, you will today."

Her eyes widened as I glanced at her to see her response. "Are you serious?"

"As a heart attack."

"I'm about to have a heart attack."

"You better not. You have to fly a plane."

"How?"

I pulled up to the building they'd told me to go to over the phone. "I know a guy who knows a guy."

Ashtyn rolled her eyes. "Using my line?"

I laughed. "I do know a guy who knows a guy. Usually, you have to book this three weeks in advance."

"Really?"

"Yep," I confirmed, and we opened our doors to exit.

As she waited by the window, looking out at the tarmac, I checked her in. She had to sign some papers and then we met with an FAA certified flight instructor. He covered the ins and outs of the airplane's mechanics with Ashtyn as I watched. They went over the instruments panel and then did a pre-flight inspection of the small plane. Afterward, the three of us climbed inside the aircraft. Ashtyn and the pilot sat up front with me in the back. I had a smile the entire time as I watched her learn everything she needed to know about flying the plane. I could see the joy radiating from her body as she soaked in everything, and I knew my plan for this Saturday was the right decision. It was a crazy spur of the moment plan, but seeing Ashtyn beam was what I always wanted to see from her.

We buckled into the cockpit of the four passenger, single-engine airplane, and Ashtyn taxied us to the runway. Steering a plane was essentially the same as driving a car, but of course, there were more controls once you actually had to get it to go in the air.

Once we got the all clear for take-off from the control tower, the pilot took over due to the FAA safety regulations. The pilot still had control of the aircraft as we rose to the cruising altitude, and Ashtyn turned her head to look at me.

"This is amazing!" She smiled.

I grinned back, both of us speaking in the headsets we had to wear. "I know."

"All right, Ashtyn. The controls are all yours," the pilot said.

Ashtyn turned back around and took over. She didn't hesitate as the pilot instructed her to do various things. We ascended, descended, did several turns, and once we were close to our destination, Ashtyn radioed to the control tower to see if it was clear for the pilot to land.

We landed at the Grand Geneva Airport where a black town car was waiting for us. "Where are we going?" Ashtyn asked, fluffing her hair.

"Lunch."

"Lunch?"

We slid into the car. "We're going to the Grand Geneva Spa and Resort here in Wisconsin for lunch before you fly us home."

"How is this real life right now?" Ashtyn laughed. "I feel like a celebrity or something."

"Well, you are a celebrity."

"Only in Chicago."

"True, but, technically anyone can book this experience."

"I had no idea it was possible. Thank you." She leaned over and pressed her soft lips to mine. "This beats sitting at home and catching up on shows on the DVR."

I grinned. "Sure does."

After the car dropped us off at the entrance, we made our way to the Grand Café for lunch.

"Thank you for doing this." Ashtyn smiled, looking out the window at the lake.

"You're welcome, but it's fun to take a little getaway, right?"

"It's amazing."

"Speaking of amazing, I found a few houses we should go look at."

"Yeah?" She smiled.

"Here, I'll show you a few." I took my phone out my pocket and pulled up the realtor's website where I found some houses. I went to the first one and handed Ashtyn my phone. "What do you think of this one?"

She scrolled through the pictures. "There's no fireplace."

"But there's a pool."

"But we want a fireplace and a pool, right?"

"Okay." I reached for my phone. "What about this one?"

Ashtyn took the phone back and looked at the pictures of the next one. "I think we should go look because if the closet's small, it's an automatic no."

I chuckled. "Okay. How about I call my realtor and have him set up a few places for us to go see next weekend?"

She leaned across the table and pressed her soft lips to mine. "I'd like that."

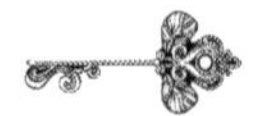

The next Friday, Ashtyn groaned and shut the door behind her after returning home from work.

"Bad day?" I asked, taking a pull of my beer.

"No, I had a great day." She hung up her coat.

I set my beer on the coffee table. "So, what's all the groaning about?" I was watching the San Jose Sharks and Minnesota Wild game that had just started. We were playing a doubleheader next against the Sharks to make up for the game that was canceled in October. Doubleheaders usually weren't a thing in hockey because of how strenuous and exhausting hockey is, but it needed to be done.

"Corey—"

"Corey? What the fuck?"

Ashtyn sighed and plopped down on the couch. "He keeps texting me."

I stilled, the game on the TV forgotten. "What do you mean he keeps texting you?"

"He keeps sending me texts about random shit."

"Like what?" I was trying to keep cool, but honestly, hearing that Corey was communicating with Ashtyn was testing my patience to the limit. Who fucking does that? A fucking asshole motherfucker who saw with his own eyes that Ashtyn had moved on, that's who. What could he possibly have to say or want?

Ashtyn unlocked her phone and began reading them. "Saw you on TV. Your boyfriend get you those seats? You're too good to text me back now? How was your day? Isn't today the day we met? I miss you—"

"He what?" I snatched the phone from her grasp and read the rest of the texts.

Corey: I miss you. Call me.

Corey: I love you. I know I said I was lying, but that was a lie.

Corey: Please at least text me back. I made a mistake.

Corey: I can't stop thinking about you.

Corey: Baby, break up with that loser and marry me. I love you.

"Marry him?" I hissed. "He asked you to marry him?"

"I can't say that a texted proposal is legit."

My body was tight as anger radiated through my veins. I was going to kill him. I was going to beat the shit out him like he had to me all those years ago, but I wouldn't stop until he wasn't breathing. "I don't give a shit. Who fucking does this?" I threw the phone on the couch.

"Does it matter? I've never texted or called him back."

"Why haven't you told me he's been texting you?"

"Because he just started after New Years."

"It's been almost a month," I hissed.

"I didn't want you to be mad like you are now."

I stared at her, processing what she'd said. "I'm mad because he's only doing this because you're dating me. Think about it." I started to pace back and forth in front of the TV.

"It doesn't matter. I'm with you."

"You think he'll stop?"

"I'll just block his number."

"Good." I paced a little more and then yelled slightly, "Wait!"

"Wait?"

I reached out my hand. "Give me your phone."

"Why?" Ashtyn held it to her chest away from me.

"Because I'm going to call that motherfucker."

"What? Why?"

I moved to her, my hand still outreached. "Because, Cupcake, he had his chance. He let you go, and I'm never letting you go. He needs to know that."

"I'll just block his number, and that will be that."

I stood in front of her. "Until he shows up at your work or some shit. We've already been down that road with a stalker. We don't need another."

"If he's going to stalk me—which he won't—then he'll do it even if you call him. Hell, it might make him do it more."

"I need to do this."

"Why?"

I ran my hands down my face and sighed. "Because he can't win."

"He's not winning. If anything, you are." Ashtyn waved her hand in my direction.

"Just let me do this. I need to do this," I pleaded.

She stared at me for a beat and then handed me the phone. "Okay."

"Really?"

"Yeah. After finding out that he was your bully, I did some research and read that confronting a bully is good for the bullied. Of course, I was never going to tell you that because of who he is. I thought it would be better to just let it be."

I didn't know about that. Having him once again try to ruin my life was the last straw. We weren't kids anymore.

Before I talked myself out of it, I took the phone from her hand, found his number in her contacts and hit the button to call him. It rang twice before he answered.

"Ashtyn! Thank you—"

"It's not Ashtyn."

"Cole."

"Yeah, it's me. Stop calling my girlfriend!" I started to pace again. This time around the entire living room because I couldn't stand still.

"I can call whoever the fuck I want."

"Dude, she ain't interested in you anymore."

"You're just her rebound."

"I'm glad you think so, but I know differently."

"I've known her longer, and she was mine first."

"Why do you even care? You moved on with that blonde."

He tsked. "I don't care about her."

"Okay, well leave Ashtyn alone or—"

"Are you threatening me?"

"Do I need to?"

He laughed. "I wouldn't or I'll—"

"Or you'll what? Beat me up like you did in high school? I'm much bigger now, asshole, and like it or not, Ashtyn and I are together."

"Not for long."

"Yes, for long. Forever." My gaze met Ashtyn's, and she smiled. I tried to smile back, but the laughter in my ear caused me to close my eyes in frustration.

"So she showed you her Pinterest board? You two getting married now?"

"I don't know about her damn Pinterest board." Ashtyn rolled her eyes and sighed, shaking her head. "But yes, to answer your other question, if she'll let me."

"Not if I stop you." He hung up, and I took the phone away from my ear. I had no idea what he meant, but it felt as though our little game wasn't over.

CHAPTER TWENTY-SEVEN

Ashtyn

A few weeks ago when I was at the game with my friends, I thought I wanted to have a baby. That was short lived because being able to jump in an airplane and fly to a spa on a whim was more my style. At least for now. My biological clock was ticking, but I loved what I had going with Rhys, and I didn't want to scare him away.

Also, how could I bring a baby into this world when there was so much drama? Fucking Corey. I just wanted him to leave me the hell alone. All of his texts were confusing, and after Rhys called him, I thought that maybe Corey was only doing it to break us up.

"If I'll let you do what?" I asked.

"Nothing. What is he talking about Pinterest?"

I took a deep breath. If he got scared away because I was a planner, then it was better to know now. "I have a wedding board on Pinterest."

He was silent for a few seconds. "That's it?"

I nodded. "Yeah. Corey—"

"Fuck, Corey. I don't want to talk about that asshole again."

"Okay. Hand me the phone back."

"What are you going to do?" Rhys asked.

"Block his number."

I did just that.

Over the next few weeks, Rhys and I went and viewed several houses. I didn't need the hustle or bustle of the city anymore. I wanted the fireplace and pool. Hell, I wanted a fireplace next to the pool. None of the places we looked at were the one, but I went ahead and found a renter for my condo. It was weird knowing some stranger was living in my place, but ever since Philip died in it, I didn't feel like it was my place at all. The new tenant didn't seem to mind that a man had been killed in my living room. In fact, she was a paranormal author and seemed to think that it would help her with her writing. To each their own I suppose.

Some might think that buying a house together after only four months of dating is too fast. Maybe it is for some, but when you know, you just know. It was different with Rhys than with any man I'd dated before. He made me smile, he made me laugh, and I felt safe when I was with him. And he almost took a bullet trying to protect me. If that's not true love, then I don't know what is.

"The girls are coming over tonight after work. We're going to watch the game."

Rhys stared at me for a beat as we lay in bed. Something we did a few times a week. It was as though we felt the longer we stayed in bed, the more time would slow so we could have more time together. "Are you trying to be late to work?"

"What?" I chuckled.

"You just made me hard again by saying that the girls are coming over to watch the game. I'm pretty sure with that sentence I fell more in love with you."

"Well …" I blushed.

"Next you're going to be telling me that they're coming over for poker night."

My eyes widened. "Yes! Let's do that. Let's have a poker tournament when we buy a house. Like a housewarming party, but with poker."

"Do you even know how to play?" He laughed.

"No, but you can teach me. We have time."

Rhys grinned and rolled on top of me. "You, Ashtyn Valor, are going to be the death of me."

"I'm going to be late," I reminded him.

"You won't be late. I'll be quick." He kissed me feverishly and true to his word, I wasn't late to work. I made it with a few seconds to spare.

After work, I was going to stop at the liquor store and grab a couple of bottles of vodka. Since it was a Friday night, the girls and I might drink all of it. I wasn't driving, and Rhys had the secret breakfast that cured hangovers. Plus, I could talk him into making it in only a towel again.

As I was brushing mascara on my lashes to freshen up for my broadcast, I saw Abby walk by. "Hey!" I called out.

She peeked around the corner. "What's up?"

"Anything you want to share?"

She smirked. "About what?"

I put the tube of mascara down and turned toward her. "You know how Rhys and the guys have poker every week?" I leaned a hip against the makeup vanity and crossed my arms.

She nodded.

"And you know how I live there now?"

She nodded again.

"Well," I chuckled and shook my head slightly in amusement, "to give the guys time alone to play, I go in the bedroom and read or do whatever, but I can still hear them."

"Okay …"

"And you know what I heard on Wednesday night?"

Abby started to smirk slowly as though she knew what I was going to say. "Do tell."

"Let's just say that I know Kenny's not sleeping at home."

She shrugged. "I don't kiss and tell."

I laughed. "Apparently Kenny does."

Abby started to walk away. "Men!"

I turned back to the mirror. After fluffing my hair, I made my way to get mic'd and then I took my seat next to Everett, the current lead anchor for the evening news. Once he retires, I'm in line to take his position just like I had when Barbara signed off.

"Have big plans this weekend?" Everett asked, smoothing down his suit jacket.

"Don't think so. Rhys and I will probably catch up on The Blacklist."

"Ah. Good show."

"Hey, Everett?" I heard our Producer, Chantel's voice in my ear.

"Yes?" Everett answered back.

"We have breaking news of a shooting that just happened thirty minutes ago. We're going to start with that."

"Sounds good," he responded and then looked at me. "Want to take it?"

"Really?" I grinned.

"Sure, why not?"

"Thanks."

"We're live in five," Chantel said again in my ear.

I cleared my throat and waited for the signal.

"Good evening, I'm Everett Johnson."

"And I'm Ashtyn Valor." I read the monitor not knowing what the story would be about, "We start tonight with breaking news out of the River North area. A man driving a red Ford Mustang opened fire on another vehicle before speeding away. Authorities are on the lookout and have asked for you to contact them if you have any details on his whereabouts. The victim driving the black Mazda ..." I trailed off as I caught a glimpse of the car with a Blackhawks sticker on the back that was being shown on live TV. My heart started to beat faster.

"Ashtyn," Everett whispered.

I couldn't speak as I stared at the monitor. The one that was showing footage of Rhys's car. The one with yellow police tape blocking off part of the street, and the one showing dozens of cops walking around doing their investigation.

This wasn't happening.

Everett took over. "The victim driving the black Mazda SUV was rushed to the hospital. There's no word on their condition at this time."

"Red Mustang. Rushed to the hospital," I said out loud. It was only a whisper, but again I felt Everett look over at me as I continued to stare at the monitor. "I have to go." I stood and started to take my mic off. Everyone was silent as they continued to air my departure. They stared at me, and I faintly heard Everett talking to the camera, but all I could think about was that Corey had shot Rhys. Or at least I'd assumed given he drove a red Mustang. How the fuck did that happen? I'd just seen Rhys this morning, and now I was reporting that Corey shot him when he was on his way to work. Shot him only a few blocks from my work.

"Hey, what's wrong?" Abby stopped me as I made my way out of the newsroom.

"Corey shot Rhys."

"What?"

I moved around her to rush to my desk to grab my purse and car keys. "I have to go Abs."

"I'll call Kenny."

I didn't wait for her even though I could sense she was following me. I briefly heard her talking on the phone, but I didn't pay any attention. My focus was getting to Rhys. I knew that Carter was a trauma surgeon and he'd once told me that all gun shots go to his trauma center. That was where I needed to go to look for Rhys, but how was I going to manage driving heavy machinery as my heart raced a million miles an hour and I couldn't get the crime scene out of my head?

"Kenny had no idea. He said they've been trying to call Rhys since he didn't make it to work."

"Because he was shot!" I yelled and snatch my purse out of the bottom drawer of my desk. I had to go.

"Let me drive you. I'll drop you off in front of the Emergency Room."

"Okay," I agreed. "Hurry."

Abby rushed to her desk while I went to the elevator and pressed the call button repeatedly. Just as it dinged and opened, Abby ran up to me. We got in, and once again I was pressing a button over and over. This one was for the parking garage, and if the car didn't hurry and descend, I was going to lose my mind.

"I'm sure he's okay."

My head snapped in her direction. "We don't know that."

"I know, but he has to be."

I sighed. "Yeah, he does."

We made it to Abby's car, and we slid inside. As she drove, I thought about what could have happened to make Corey shoot Rhys. Then images of Rhys dying entered my mind. Tears started to stream down my face.

"Everything will be fine." Abby patted my knee.

I didn't turn to her. Instead, I looked out at the darkening sky and prayed everything would be fine.

"How do you know it was your ex?"

I blinked at Abby's question. "Shit!" I hissed and started rummaging through my purse for my phone. "I need to call my brother."

"I'm sure it can wait."

"He's a cop. I need to tell him I think it's Corey."

"Oh. Yeah, call him. We're almost to the hospital."

I hit the button to call Ethan. He answered after a few rings. "Ash …"

"Are you working the shooting near my work?"

"No, why?"

"Rhys is the one shot."

"Are you serious?"

"Yes!" I screamed. "And the person driving the Mustang is Corey, my ex."

"Are you sure?"

I sighed heavily. "He drives a fucking Mustang, Ethan, and he and Rhys have a history."

"What's his last name?"

"Pritchett," I stated and remembered that Corey had never met my family. He never wanted to meet them.

"Do you know his address?" I gave him the location of the apartment I'd once been to. I didn't know the address, but I knew where it was. "How's Rhys?"

My throat started to close finally as the adrenaline was starting to diminish. "I don't know. I'm on my way to the hospital."

"Keep me updated, and I'll look into Corey."

"Thanks."

I hung up the phone and stared out the window at nothing as a tear slide down my cheek. "Is Kenny on his way?" I sniffled.

"Yes, of course."

I nodded, so many thoughts running through my head. "Good."

Abby pulled up to the Emergency Room. "I'll go park and meet you inside."

"Thank you." I reached for the handle and got out of the car, wiping my tears. I felt as though I was walking in quicksand as I rushed inside the hospital. My legs were trying to move, but my heart was telling them they weren't fast enough. When I finally made it inside, I went straight to the check-in desk. "I'm looking for my boyfriend. He should have been brought in with a gunshot wound," I said when the nurse looked up at me.

She blinked at me as she realized who I was. "Ms. Valor. Who's your boyfriend?"

"Rhys Cole." I started to look around nervously searching for any sign of Rhys. Maybe even Carter. I wasn't sure if he was working or not, but I knew he worked in the ER.

She started to type on her computer, and I heard my name being called from behind me. I turned around to see Kenny and Abby running in.

"Have you heard anything?" Kenny asked.

I shook my head.

The lady looked at me sympathetically then said, "Mr. Cole's in surgery." I knew that was all I was going to get as far as information. Hell, I was lucky she even told me that much since I was only his girlfriend.

"Surgery?" Kenny asked.

"I'm sorry, but that's all I can tell you unless you're family. You can go up to the surgical wing and wait if you'd like."

"Where's that?" I asked.

The nurse gave us directions, and we started to walk in that direction.

"Let me see if I can get ahold of my brother. He's a doctor here."

They nodded, and we kept walking as I dialed. The phone rang and rang, and he didn't answer. "He didn't answer."

"Do you think he's doing the surgery?" Abby asked.

I sighed. "I have no idea." I felt as though I knew nothing at that moment and I needed to know everything because I was so scared.

"Are Claire and Andy on their way?" Kenny asked as we walked into an elevator.

My eyes widened. "I didn't call them. Shit, I didn't call them."

"It's okay, Ash." Abby touched my arm. "Call them now."

"Right." I pulled my phone out of my purse. My hands were sweaty as I scrolled through my contacts, looking for Claire's number. As I pressed the button to call her, the three of us exited on the surgical floor.

"Ashtyn!" Claire exclaimed. "What happened? I was watching—"

"Did you recognize the car?"

She was silent for a moment. "What?"

"The car in the story I was broadcasting before I ran off." We made it to the surgical waiting room and took a seat near a wall.

Claire again took a few moments before she responded. "It looked like Rhys's car, but he's at work."

"No." I shook my head, tears forming again in my eyes. It was almost time for his pre-game live show, and no one would know he was missing until Jett went live. "He was the one shot."

"That can't be."

The tears dripped onto my blue dress. "It is." She gasped, and I told her what hospital we were at and that we were waiting in the surgical waiting room. "They won't tell us anything because we're not family."

"We're on our way."

"Want me—" Abby started to say just as Claire and Andy walked through the sliding doors.

The three of us stood, and I rushed to Rhys's parents, engulfing Claire in the biggest hug I could muster. "How did this happen?" she asked, sobbing into my arms.

It was on the tip of my tongue to tell her it was Corey, but I held off because even though I knew in my gut it was him, I wanted to wait until we knew for sure. Through my own tears, I simply said, "I don't know."

We broke apart, and I looked to see Andy talking to a nurse in the hall. I wasn't sure where she came from. Maybe he'd stopped her when she was walking by. Finally, he came back to us. "The nurse said Rhys went into surgery not too long ago and that once he's out a doctor will come give us an update."

I hugged Andy, and then Kenny stepped forward, giving them both a hug as I wiped my tears away.

After Kenny hugged them, he introduced them to Abby, "Andy, Claire, this is my girlfriend, Abby."

They shook her hand. "I'm sorry about Rhys," Abby stated with a tight smile.

"Boy's tough. He'll pull through," Andy replied a matter-of-factly.

He was tough. But it still worried me that something so tiny like a bullet could take the biggest thing in my life away from me.

"I'm going to go see if I can find us some coffee," Abby said, and I smiled tightly at her. I loved her and was happy she and Kenny had started something.

"I'll come with," Kenny offered, and the two of them left.

The surreal feeling returned as I sat down next to Andy and Claire. I couldn't imagine what they were going through. Kids are supposed to outlive their parents. What if that wasn't true in this case? I didn't know how long Rhys was in surgery for, but longer than a few minutes to remove a bullet was too long for my liking. I wanted to rush in and hug him, kiss him, run my hands over his entire body to make sure he was still alive.

But what if he wasn't?

What if he was shot in the head? What if he was shot in some artery and they couldn't stop the bleeding? So many scenarios rushed through my head again and again. The not knowing was killing me. Plus, what do you say to your boyfriend's parents in this situation? I wanted to tell them that everything would be okay, but I didn't know that, and I didn't want to give them false hope.

Abby and Kenny returned with five cups of coffee. I stared at Abby as she offered to make Andy and Claire's coffee the way they liked it and Kenny pulled cream and sugar from his coat pocket.

"Abby," I called, a thought hitting me.

She looked over at me. "Yeah?"

"Don't you need to get back to work?" I didn't want her to go, but we'd left in a hurry, and I didn't tell anyone.

"I called Leonard and told him what's going on. They told me to stay and take care of you."

I sighed, and my throat started to close again. "Thank you." We were all silent again, sipping our coffees when another thought occurred to me. "What about Rhys's work? Isn't the game on?"

"I took care of it," Kenny stated.

I nodded and took a sip of my coffee. It tasted like shit, but at least it gave me something to do while we waited.

Finally, a doctor came out. "Family members for O'Neill."

You could physically hear and feel the five of us sag in our seats.

"Why is it taking so long?" Claire asked.

Andy patted her knee. "Let's look at it as a good thing. They are still working on him, so he's not dead."

My heart clenched at his words.

"Don't say that, Andy!" Claire exclaimed.

"I'm just saying to think positive."

"I just want to know he's okay," she replied.

I looked at Abby and Kenny. He had his arm wrapped around her shoulder, and her head was resting on his. Why couldn't that be Rhys and me right now? I'd do anything to be in his arms and to know everything's okay. Instead, the love of my life might be fighting for his, and I might never get to hold him again.

As we continued waiting, two detectives arrived. "Mr. and Mrs. Cole?" the male cop greeted.

"Yes?" Andy spoke.

"We're Detectives Coulson and Bailey," Detective Coulson flashed his badge, and then Detective Bailey showed us hers. "We're investigating the shooting of your son," he said.

"Do you know what happened?" Andy asked.

"Witnesses say that he was shot by a white male driving a red Mustang. Do you know any men who fit that description?" They glanced over at me, and I stood.

"I don't think he knows anyone who drives that car, but we don't really know," Andy stated.

"I do."

Everyone turned to me. "Your brother, Detective Valor, mentioned that it may be your ex. Is that true?" Coulson asked.

"Yes, they have a history, and Corey does drive a Mustang."

"We've sent a team over to his apartment. We should know more in an hour or so."

"Do you really think that douche shot him?" Kenny asked.

"He's been texting me, and a few weeks ago Rhys told him to leave me alone. He mentioned something about stopping us from being together, but I didn't think he'd try to kill him."

"Is there anyone else you can think of?" Detective Bailey asked.

All of us shook our heads.

"Okay," Coulson noted. "We'll follow up on Mr. Pritchett, and if you think of anything else, call us." He handed us his business card.

"Thank you, detectives." Claire finally spoke up.

"We'll be back first thing in the morning to talk to Rhys and get his statement. We want to wait until the sedation wears off after surgery, but not too long."

Did that mean he was going to be okay? Did they know?

As we waited again for any update on Rhys, I knew deep in my gut that it was Corey who had shot him. I just didn't understand why. He broke up with me, but now that I was happily dating someone new, he wanted to screw it all up.

The minutes ticked by, and finally, another doctor came out. When he turned, I realized it was Carter. I stood and rushed to him. "Carter!"

"Hey, Ash." He smiled. He actually smiled even though I was in the fucking hospital wanting to know if my boyfriend was going to live. "Rhys is out of surgery."

I breathed a sigh of relief.

"Are you the surgeon?" Andy asked.

"I am."

"He's also my brother," I clarified.

"I am, and Rhys is going to be fine."

Claire gasped. "Oh thank God."

I bit my lip, fighting the tears back that decided to reappear. This time from relief.

"The bullet didn't hit a major artery, and we were able to remove it and repair the damage to his deltoid muscle, tendons, and the surrounding tissue. After some physical therapy, he should make a full recovery, but we're going to keep him here for a few days to monitor him."

"Can we see him?" Kenny asked.

"He's still sedated and hasn't been moved into a room yet. Visiting hours will probably be over by the time he wakes up, but once he does and we move him into a room, we'll let one of you go in."

"Thank you, Carter." I hugged him.

He shook Andy's hand and then left.

Rhys was going to be okay, but the thought that Corey was still out there running the streets, made me extremely nervous. I hoped that when the cops showed up at his apartment, he would be there and all of this would be behind us.

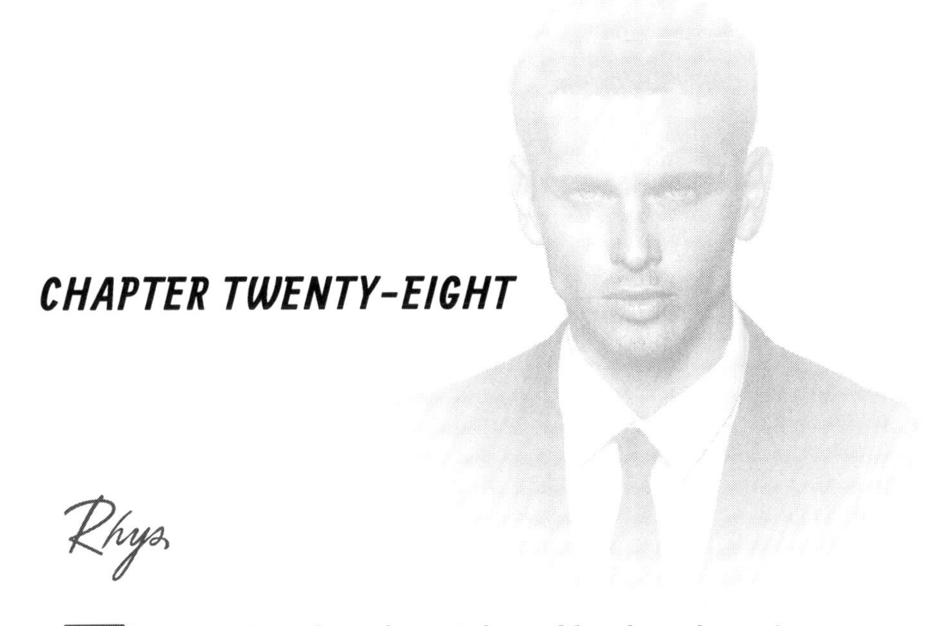

CHAPTER TWENTY-EIGHT

Rhys

This must have been how Ashtyn felt when she woke up after being knocked out by ether. Though, as I opened my eyes, I didn't see anyone I knew. The room was filled with people in scrubs, machines, and bright lights. Why were the lights so damn bright?

"How are you feeling, Rhys?" I looked to my right to see a nurse typing on a computer.

"Like I got shot," I deadpanned hoarsely. I could barely speak because my throat felt raw and dry.

She smiled tightly and nodded. "Because you were."

I actually didn't feel anything except extremely tired. Then it all came flooding back, and I remembered what had happened ...

I pulled out of the parking garage of my building and turned toward work. For once, it wasn't snowing, but it was cold as shit. Even though I'd lived in Chicago my entire life, the winters never got easier, but having Ashtyn warming my bed every night was an added bonus. Sure, for the past two years there had always been a woman in my bed—Bridgette—but Ashtyn was different. When I woke each morning, Ashtyn was touching me in some way. Even if it was her arm pressed against mine, I still woke up warm and had all those weird fuzzy feelings in my heart.

Love.

When the song switched on the radio, I smiled. One Call Away was streaming through my speakers and Christmas morning flooded my memory.

Yep, this was love.

Charlie was serenading me when I got the sense someone was staring at me. Turning my head to the left, my gaze fell on him. Corey Fucking Pritchett. He revved his Mustang, and I rolled my eyes. Fucking prick. What were the odds I'd run into him? Then I remembered that Ashtyn had seen him near her work, and that made me wonder if he was stalking us.

She was the most beautiful woman I'd ever laid eyes on, and any man would probably kill to be in my position. I knew that even though Philip was gone, there would probably be more, including Corey. Hopefully, any future stalkers wouldn't be so extreme. I was okay being the guy with the girl everyone wanted to know. The one who would hold her hand and wonder how I ever got so lucky. That would be me for as long as I was breathing and not Corey Fucking Pritchett or any other man because I was never going to let her go.

Corey rolled down his window and yelled, "Hey, faggot!"

I didn't respond.

Instead, I turned my head forward and waited for the light to turn green. When it did, I stepped on the gas. Corey did the same, but instead of slowly moving forward, he sped past me and then got in front of me in my lane. He slammed on his breaks, and I stopped hard, coming within inches of hitting him.

"What the fuck?" I shouted out of anger as we came to a dead stop.

Cars behind me started to honk, and cars in the left lane kept moving. I looked in the rearview mirror, looking for a break in the line of cars passing us so that I could go around Corey. Instead, out of the corner of my eye, I saw him get out of his car.

This was it.

This was the moment I'd waited my entire life for.

The moment I could finally stand up to the guy who thought I was a punching bag and not a human being.

Except as I stared at him as he walked toward my driver's side door, I saw him reach behind his back, and then, for the second time in my entire life, I was staring down the barrel of a gun.

"You've got to be fucking shitting me!"

"I told you I'd stop you," he spat.

My eyes stayed glued to the black hole. The one that at any moment could discharge the bullet that would end my life. How was this happening again? How the fuck was this my life? This time there would be no Ethan rushing in to save the day. I was alone and in my car.

"Put the gun down, Corey," I yelled, not rolling down my window as though that could stop a bullet. I held up my hands in surrender and faintly recalled the cars behind me had stopped honking, and no cars were driving past us anymore. Everyone was probably scared he'd turn the gun on them. I was the only lucky one though.

"Shut up!" he bellowed. "I'm tired of your fucking mouth."

"What are you talking about?"

"When you have Ashtyn next to you, you think you're some big badass. Well, who has the upper-hand now?"

"Okay, man." I was going to agree to anything while he was pointing a Glock at my face. "Just put the gun down, and we'll talk."

"You don't get it. You've taken everything from me."

"Ashtyn doesn't want you back."

"I don't want her back either. I want you to pay for ruining my life!"

It happened in a blink of an eye. I didn't see Corey fire the gun. What I did hear was my window breaking and then I felt a sharp, burning pain in my arm as I flinched. I grabbed my arm, trying to stop the sting, and the bleeding I assumed was coming from my shoulder and onto my shirt and coat. Then I watched, speechless as Corey ran back to his car and sped away.

I didn't know what to do. I was alive. I was conscious, and I was in so much pain when I moved my arm slightly that I wanted to pass out. Still clutching my arm, I startled when a man ran up to my door and flung it open.

"Are you hit?"

"Yeah," I breathed.

"Help is on the way."

"We're moving you to a private room in just a minute." I blinked and realized the nurse on the computer was still talking to me.

I nodded and fell back asleep, no longer able to keep my eyes open.

When I woke again, I heard more voices.

"He'll be in and out for a while until the anesthesia wears off."

"I won't be long."

I opened my eyes to see Ashtyn talking to a nurse. "Cupcake," I whispered gruffly.

Ashtyn turned her head toward me and then she rushed from the doorway and grabbed my hand on the uninjured side. "Hey, tiger. How are you feeling?"

"It was Corey," I responded even though that wasn't her question.

She nodded. "I know. I already talked to the cops."

"Did they catch him?"

"I'm not sure."

"Ashtyn." The nurse poked her head into the room. "I hate to do this, but visiting hours are over, and Rhys needs his rest."

"Yeah," Ashtyn replied. "I'll come back first thing in the morning."

"Not gonna lie, Cupcake. I'm gonna miss sleeping with you tonight."

She leaned down and brushed her lips against mine. "All the morphine in your system will help you forget."

"I want you to help me forget."

Ashtyn snorted. "I see having a life-threatening experience hasn't changed you."

"Not when you're involved."

She kissed me again. "Get some rest. I'll see you as soon as you can have visitors."

I held her wrist so she couldn't step away. "Are you going to be okay tonight?"

"I'm staying at Abby's."

"Good." I nodded.

She leaned down and kissed me again. "I love you."

"Love you too, Cupcake."

My pain meds were awesome. I didn't feel any pain, and I was sleeping like a baby. Nurses came in at different hours to check my vitals and shit. Each time they muttered how well I was doing and then they would leave and I would drift back to sleep.

True to Ashtyn's word, she came walking into my room before I was served breakfast. "Are you here to give me a sponge bath?" I grinned.

Ashtyn chuckled and shook her head slightly, a cup of coffee in her hand. "I see you're feeling well this morning." She leaned down and kissed my lips.

"Can't even tell I was shot."

"I think that's the morphine still pumping through your veins."

I shrugged my good shoulder. "At least I don't have the pain to remind me I was shot. I still can't believe it."

She sighed and sat in the chair next to my bed. "Me either."

"Any word on Corey?"

"I haven't heard anything, but the cops should be here soon."

My eyes widened as I realized I missed work the night before. "Does my work know?"

"Yeah, Kenny told them."

"Fuck ..." I breathed and looked up at the off-white ceiling, still not believing this was all happening.

"I was so scared," Ashtyn confessed.

I looked over to see tears in her eyes and grabbed her hand, lacing our fingers. "You can't get rid of me that quickly, Cupcake."

"I don't want to get rid of you." She rolled her eyes.

"I know. I was joking. You know that's what I do. Everything's okay."

At that moment a man and woman, both wearing suits, walked into my room. "Good morning, Mr. Cole. I'm Detective Coulson, and this is Detective Bailey. How are you feeling?"

Okay, that question was going to get old fast. "Drugs are working," I stated honestly.

Ashtyn slapped my arm—the one that wasn't stitched up. "Rhys!"

The detectives chuckled. "Ms. Valor," Coulson spoke, "It's good to see you again. And I have to say it's good to see you're in good spirits, Mr. Cole."

"Please, call me Rhys, and honestly, I'll be in better spirits if you tell me you've caught the fucker."

"I wish we could," Bailey stated, "but we're here to get your statement and to see if you know who shot you."

"Yes, I know. Corey Fucking Pritchett."

"That's what Ms. Valor told us. We're following up." Bailey looked over at Ashtyn.

"Saw him with my own eyes as I stared down the barrel of the gun."

"Do you know why he shot you?" Coulson asked.

"We've known each other since high school," I started and then proceeded to explain everything from how he used to beat me up, how he and Ashtyn dated, what happened New Year's Eve, and then my phone call with him. I also told them what he said before shooting me.

"Okay. Well, like I mentioned earlier, we wish we could tell you that he's in custody," Detective Bailey stated.

"How have you not caught him?" Ashtyn asked.

Bailey continued, "We haven't been able to locate him."

"He's on the lam?"

The detectives laughed at my use of the word. "We just haven't been able to locate him yet," Coulson replied. "He didn't come home."

"Did you go to his work?" Ashtyn asked.

"We're heading there next," Coulson stated.

"He used to work the late afternoon shift."

"We'll find him," Bailey stated.

They fucking better.

I was released from the hospital a day later. My parents and sister had come to visit me as well as Kenny, Jett, and Clark. No one could believe that this was my reality. I couldn't either, but what scared me the most was that Corey was still missing.

The cops came back the morning I was released from the hospital to give us an update and to see if we'd heard anything. We hadn't and explained that Ashtyn had blocked Corey's number. When they asked if she would be willing to unblock his number, I felt as though I might lose my shit. All we wanted was to be left alone, and it seemed that being together was a deadly combination.

Ashtyn unblocked his number in hopes he'd call, but to me, the only solution I could come up with was that we needed to buy a house stat and get far away from where Corey knew Ashtyn lived. Even though she wasn't living there, she was only across the street, and if we wanted to walk to Judy's or lunch or whatever, there was a chance Corey could come out of the shadows and strike again.

I couldn't let that happen.

I knew he could have access to get either one of us on the way to and from work, just like he'd tried with me, but we were going to do one thing at a time for now and get everything settled.

It had been a week since the shooting, and I was returning to work. The season would be over in a few months, and afterward, Ashtyn and I were going far, far away. I didn't care where as long as it was only she and I and all of our troubles were behind us.

"Are you sure you're ready to go back?" Ashtyn asked, zipping up her plum-colored dress.

I put my head in my hand and turned to her as I lie in bed. "I'm only a little sore. It's no big deal."

"Yes, but you're on Norco, and you fall asleep sitting up."

"That happened once."

"You were on the toilet."

"I was comfortable."

"You were high."

I shrugged. "Still am."

Ashtyn rolled her eyes and went into the bathroom still talking, "Exactly why you should stay home. You have to go on air and people will be watching you."

"It will be fine. Plus, I want to get out of this place." I waved my hand indicating the room even though she wasn't in it.

She walked back into the room. "Okay, but if you don't feel good, I'm sure Jett wouldn't mind handling everything again."

The day I got shot, there was no one to cover for me, and therefore, Jett had to do everything himself. I heard he handled it like a pro because he is one, and the last couple of games, we ended up getting Jeremy Roenick to fill in for me. Apparently, he'd heard what happened and offered his services. I have to say, watching him on TV again, talking about hockey, filled my heart. Or maybe that was the drugs talking. They made me feel good, and the pain was almost non-existent. Plus, the wound was getting better each day, and the stitches were almost dissolved.

Each night I'd go to bed and somehow wake up the next morning and not have a nightmare. I wasn't sure why, but I was glad because I didn't want to relive the shooting again. And each day I texted Ethan to see if they found Corey, but he'd always text back that they hadn't. They couldn't find him using the GPS off his cell phone, he wasn't using his credit cards, and he never went home. It was as though he'd vanished.

We could only hope.

"Everything will be fine. I'm already weaning myself off of them."

Ashtyn's phone chimed. "Abby's here." Abby was picking Ashtyn up each day for work, and we'd arranged for Kenny to swing by and get me on game days.

"Come give me some sugar, Cupcake."

CHAPTER TWENTY-NINE

Ashtyn

Corey had been missing for two months.

I was back to looking over my shoulder any time I stepped out of the house, but sometimes I'd forget that he could pop out at any moment. What made me a little more at ease was Rhys and I had bought a house.

Together.

Rhys had rented out his condo about a month ago, and things were moving along nicely. Our new home was a two-story, beige wood house with white trim and a red door. The front yard was luscious, and the backyard had a pool like we wanted. It also had four bedrooms, which meant we each got our own office, and a massive kitchen that Rhys made me breakfast in each Saturday morning.

It was perfect.

For our housewarming party, we ended up having the poker night like I'd suggested. And even though Rhys had taught me how to play, everyone, including Kenny, Jett, and Clark, ended up losing to him. They joked that we could take his winnings and buy something for the house. We were now looking into getting a hot tub for the back deck to add to our little paradise in the burbs.

Everything was perfect …

Except not knowing where Corey was.

We tried to not think about him, but it was always in the back of our minds. We'd stopped going anywhere except work and home, and I was okay with that because all I wanted was to have Rhys safe. If Rhys and I had never started dating, then none of this would have ever happened. I might be locked in Philip's basement or dead, but Rhys would have never been shot. It's crazy to think that one fluke meeting turned into a game Rhys and I were trying to win. The game of love. I just wished we didn't have to fight for our lives because this was not what love was supposed to be like. People shouldn't have to die for people to stay together.

Thankfully, both Rhys and I were still alive.

Over the last two months, I'd also decided I couldn't work in the field and do special reports or anything of that nature. I needed to stay in the studio where I was safe. I'd talked to Rhys and my boss, and made the decision to not do any field work until Corey was caught. That meant the story I wanted to do about the floating island would go to someone else. I was bummed, but Rhys told me he'd take me when they opened, and that was all I really wanted to do anyway.

Tonight, however, I was going to the last Blackhawks' home game of the season. Rhys got everyone tickets: Jaime, Kylie, Colleen, Abby, my brothers, their families, my parents, Rhys's parents, his sister, Romi, and her husband, Shane. He had set us up in a penthouse suite with food, drinks, TVs that broadcasted the game (and Rhys when he did his shows before and during the game) and a view of the entire ice.

It was going to be awesome.

He let me borrow his Crawford jersey again, and after I arrived at the stadium with Abby and Kenny, we met up with everyone else and waited to be escorted to the suite. A lady finally appeared, and after confirming our tickets were for the penthouse suite, she took us in groups up to the room. I was in the last group to go up.

"Sis," Carter said, slinging his arm across my shoulder as we walked into the room. We stopped in front of the muted TV where Rhys and Jett were broadcasting. "Rhys is the best guy you've ever dated."

I pushed him away playfully. "I know that, but you're only saying it because your dream of getting free Hawk tickets has come true."

"I saved his life," he countered.

"True, but he was only shot in the shoulder."

"Just be lucky we approve," Ethan chimed in.

"Leave your sister alone," my mother chastised, "and tend to your children."

They each had two kids, and said kids were leaning against the railing of the suite that overlooked the stadium. Tyson, the youngest of Ethan's, had his belly balancing on the black rail and looking straight down as though he were Superman. Cohen, Ethan's oldest son, and Jacob, Carter's youngest son, were all looking at Tyson as though they were two-seconds away from doing the exact same thing.

"Shit," Ethan muttered and went to save his son from falling. Carter followed.

I looked toward the bar to see both of their wives ordering a drink. I needed one too. "Thanks, Mom. Can I get you a drink?"

"Sure. A glass of wine. I'm going to go talk to Claire for a bit."

I smiled and turned toward the bar. My friends had already formed a line. "So, when are you two moving in together?" I asked Abby and Kenny.

Kenny's eyes widened.

"We don't move as fast as you and Rhys," Abby replied.

"Please," I snorted and hooked my thumb in Kenny's direction. "This one keeps gossiping with the guys weekly about how much he stays at your place and stuff. 'Abby has the best coffee.' 'Abby makes me an omelet every morning.' 'Tonight when I go over to Abby's—'"

"We get it." Kenny chuckled as though he were embarrassed.

I grinned. "So again, you two moving in together soon?"

They looked at each other and shrugged. I laughed slightly and moved up in the line after my sister-in-laws were done getting their drinks. "Ash, what are you having?" Jaime asked.

I stepped forward to stand next to her. "Two red wines, please."

The bartender started to pour a glass of the burgundy wine.

"How's the house?" Kylie asked.

"It's good. Big." I laughed.

"Have you christened the entire place?" Jaime asked.

My eyes widened, and I looked toward mine and Rhys's parents. Then I turned my head back to the girls and grinned. "Wouldn't you like to know?"

"That's a yes," Colleen stated.

I shrugged, not confirming that they were, in fact, correct. Even the pool once. It was still too cold to actually enjoy the pool, but I knew we'd spend a lot more time in there this summer.

Without further grilling and teasing, the lights over the ice dimmed, indicating the game was about to start. After sliding my mother her drink, I went to sit next to my dad and Andy in the front row seats of our suite.

"Hey, kiddo," Dad greeted me.

"Hey, Daddy."

"I was just talking to Andy about going to a Cubs game. Would you and Rhys want to come?"

I thought for a moment. In the past, I liked baseball more than hockey, but sports had never been my thing before Rhys. "I'll ask him."

My dad turned back to Rhys's father and they starting talking again. Watching them chat was warming my heart. This was what I'd always wanted. I had the guy, my family loved him, I loved him, and we lived together. Even my mother and Claire were having a conversation, both of them laughing. My heart swelled even more.

The Blackhawks each skated out of a darkened tunnel and onto the ice where they skated in front of the net and then to center ice where they stood in a line, facing the goal on the red line. After the national anthem was sung, the game finally started.

The puck was dropped, and the players started to skate, getting into whatever position they needed to get the puck in and try to make a goal. From where we were all the way up in the seats, we could still hear the skates cut across the ice as players stopped, when they checked other players against the boards causing them to rattle, and whenever someone shot the puck.

"Ms. Valor?" I looked up to see a lady in black pants and a Blackhawks polo shirt standing next to me.

"Yes?"

"Each intermission we have games for fans. We were wondering if you'd like to do the one during the second intermission?"

That meant I was going to miss Rhys's broadcast. I hesitated, but my family and friends all started to shout, "Do it! Do it! Do it!"

"You can win a couple of prizes. Maybe even a new jersey."

"Do it! Do it! Do it!"

I chuckled, figuring that I could maybe get my own Crawford or Kane or whoever else's jersey if I actually won. "Okay, sure."

"Great. I'll be back around the middle of the second period to get you and take you down to the ice."

I could see the headline now …

Breaking News: Ashtyn Valor sucks at ice games. She also fell on her ass on the ice.

The period ended, and everyone in our suite moved to the TVs. Andy turned up the volume, and Rhys's handsome face filled the screen. Watching Rhys do his thing was hot. Not gonna lie. Watching him in his element turned me on each night I caught his show. He owned the camera when he spoke. His intermission show only lasted about twelve minutes because intermission was only fifteen. On Tuesday, when it was the Hawks' final game, I vowed I wasn't going to miss a single second of Rhys's show.

After intermission was over and we returned to watching the game, I became even more nervous. Why couldn't I get some of the athletic genes that my brothers got? They played sports their entire childhood, but yet I was the one that was going to go down and play some sort of game. Maybe it would be Jenga. I could totally do Jenga. Of course, that wasn't likely because it needed to be something fast so the Zamboni could do it's thing before the fifteen minutes was up.

Lost in thought, I didn't realize it was time. "Ashtyn, are you ready?"

I looked up at her. "As ready as I'll ever be."

"Stop being a pansy ass and get out there," Ethan bellowed as he pointed toward the rink.

I rolled my eyes and stood.

"Good luck," everyone cooed as I followed the lady.

"I'm Brittany by the way."

"Nice to meet you." We made it to an elevator to head down. "What will I be doing exactly?"

"Shooting two pucks into the net."

"That's all?"

We stepped into the elevator and Brittany pressed the button. "You need to shoot from the blue line and then from the center red line. There's a prize for each line."

"Oh … What can I win?"

"You need to make the goals to find out."

I chuckled. "It's like that?"

"It's the rules." She shrugged.

"Can you give me a hint?"

She thought for a moment. "One of them may or may not be a jersey."

"And the other one?"

"Can't tell you that."

The elevator dinged and we walked out into the underground halls of the stadium. At least that was what I'd assumed. It was industrial with walls and walls of off-white concrete. We made our way down the hall and then we were in what vaguely looked like the walkway the players skated out to take the ice right before the game started.

Brittany and I stayed inside the tunnel, and she gave me a general idea of what to do. The buzzer sounded, and the players skated off toward their benches and into their locker rooms.

"Okay, here we go."

"Wait," I said, "don't I need skates?"

She smiled. "You can walk out onto the ice. Just go slow and you won't fall."

"I better not!" At least I was in my Chucks and not high heels.

"It will be fine. There are carpets where you'll take your shots."

I breathed a sigh of relief and then followed Brittany onto the ice as slowly as I could. It was slippery, but I made it to the first carpet at the blue line. I could hear my friends and family up in the suite to my left screaming and hollering their cheers for me.

"Ladies and gentleman, we have a special guest in the arena tonight."

Her words stilled me, but then I remembered that this part wasn't televised because people were watching Rhys do his thing and Corey wouldn't know where I was.

"You may recognize her as Ashtyn Valor from the evening news. She's going to try to make two shots. One is from the blue line and one if from the red line. Can we get loud for her?"

People cheered, and I moved to the center of the carpet at the blue line. As I tried to get a good grip on my stick, Tommy Hawk, the Blackhawks mascot that was a giant black hawk, skated out and stood in front of the goal as though he was the goalie.

I laughed and turned my head toward Brittany. "Not making this easy on me are you?"

She smiled and talked into the mic. "You can do it, Ashtyn!"

The crowd cheered again, including everyone in my suite. They were the loudest, which gave me the encouragement to do the best I could. I lined up the puck and slapped it with the stick. It was heavier than I thought it would be, but I watched it glide across the ice and through the legs of Tommy Hawk. He threw his hands over his eyes and faked being defeated. The crowd continued to cheer.

"One down and one to go!" Brittany announced into the mic.

I moved to the carpet that was farther away and did what I had the time before by adjusting my grip and the puck until I felt I was lined up with the center of the net. I swung and watched the puck once again slide across toward the net. I held my breath as it got closer and Tommy Hawk once again pretended to miss it as it went into the net. He threw his stick down and faked being upset. I laughed and turned to Brittany, ready for my prizes.

"I have one of them." She was holding a Blackhawks T-shirt in her hands. "And Tommy Hawk has the other."

I turned back to him, and he was standing in front of me holding what appeared to be a square jewelry box. Then Tommy

Hawk proceeded to take off his head. He was literally lifting the black bird's head off his body, and I blinked, realizing I was staring into the electric blue eyes I saw every day and night.

"Rhys?" I whispered.

He didn't say anything as he started to bend down on one knee. The crowd went crazy, just as wild as my heart beat in my chest. If I wasn't standing on carpet, I knew my feet would slip and I would fall on my ass. I didn't want that mishap to be in the story of how Rhys proposed, so I stayed absolutely still and covered my mouth with my hands.

"Cupcake—" he started, grinning up at me.

He was cut off when someone shouted, "We can't hear you, man!"

We both chuckled, and I thought that was the whole point. Neither one of us wanted to share this moment even though we were in front of nineteen thousand people or so.

Rhys continued, still holding up the box. Now I realized it was open and a big ass diamond was shining at me. I couldn't tell what it was or what it looked like because tears had started to form in my eyes, causing Rhys and the ring to become blurry.

"Like I was saying, Cupcake, from the moment we first met, I couldn't stop thinking about you. You were the light to my darkness, and I wanted to pretend that what we had going on was just you and me using each other to fill the sadness we were both feeling. But the more we spent time together, I realized you'd always held the key to my heart. You make me happy. You make me feel free. You make me feel alive. And while I don't mind being used, because let's face it, baby, you can use me anytime, I want to make you mine."

"I am yours," I whispered.

He smiled. "Then marry me and make it official."

I nodded and muttered a "yes" before I flung myself at Rhys. A diamond ring was much better than a jersey. Rhys caught me and stood and then we glided across the ice with my arms wrapped around his neck and my lips pressed to his.

The crowd cheered again, and Brittany spoke into the mic. "I think she said yes."

Breaking News: Ashtyn Valor said yes!

CHAPTER THIRTY

Rhys

Ashtyn was going to be my wife.

When I rushed to the arena after my first intermission broadcast, my heart was racing a million miles an hour. Kenny dropped me off at the back loading zone, and I rushed in. Being in the field has it's perks, especially when I got a discount on a suite for the night so I could have everyone that was important to us there to watch me propose. Everyone knew what was going to go down, and when I took off the mascot's head, and Ashtyn saw that it was me, I realized that no one had spilled the beans.

She was shocked.

Some might think that getting engaged six months after we met might be a little too soon. But when you know, you fucking know, and I didn't want another day to go by where she wasn't mine. Officially mine.

I was nervous because even though we'd bought a house together, I wasn't sure if Ashtyn wanted to be that committed in such a short amount of time. There was still a chance that in front of nineteen thousand people, she might crush my heart. Luckily for me, she said yes.

I skated off the ice with Ashtyn in my arms, and once we cleared the lip of the rink, I sat her down so I could walk in the skates.

"How did you do all of this?" Ashtyn asked, looking down at the round, pavé halo engagement ring that had a setting with small diamonds encrusted around the larger diamond and along the top of the white gold band. I wasn't sure if she'd like it, but the guy at the jewelry store said it was called the "Center of My Universe" engagement ring and Ashtyn was definitely the center of my entire galaxy.

"I know a guy who knows a guy."

Ashtyn laughed. "Pulling that line on me?"

"It's true." I smirked and took her hand in mine. "You know what this ring is called?"

She shook her head, still staring down at the sparkling diamond.

"The Center of My Universe."

She looked up at me. "It is?"

"True story. I had to get it because, Cupcake, you're the center of my universe."

Ashtyn smiled warmly. "I wouldn't want to be anywhere else."

I took her lips with mine and kissed her until I had to forcefully make myself stop because we had shit to do and I was in a fucking mascot costume. Taking her hand again, we walked to Tommy Hawk's dressing room and entered. He was sitting on a couch, watching the intermission show.

"Hey, man."

"Well?" he asked, standing. Ashtyn walked around me and flashed her hand. "Right on. Congrats!"

"Thanks," Ashtyn and I both replied.

I started to strip out of the costume and handed each piece to Tommy. That wasn't his real name, but I didn't need to know it. I only needed his getup to do my thing.

"Jett seems to be doing a good job without you," Ashtyn stated, watching the TV.

"He had practice when I got shot, remember?" Tommy's brows furrowed. "I'm kind of a badass."

"More like a lucky ass," Ashtyn corrected.

I chuckled. "I better be getting lucky tonight."

"Get it." Tommy laughed.

"We'll see. Do you have to go back to work?"

"Nope. Jett's handling everything."

"Okay. Then let's go to our people."

"Our people already know." I nodded goodbye at Tommy.

"True. Let's go show them my ring!"

For the past six months, Ashtyn, her mom, my mom, and Ashtyn's girlfriends have all been planning our wedding. Ashtyn mentioned she had some ideas on Pinterest and the girls went crazy. I stayed out of it. The only say I got in the matter was …

Who was I kidding? I didn't have a say in shit, and I was okay with that because all I cared about was marrying Ashtyn.

After the season ended, the Blackhawks were in the playoffs, but in the end, they didn't make it past round two and therefore, didn't go to the Stanley Cup. This year, the season was starting out strong and I was hopeful it would be their year. In my time off between seasons, I spent my days on the golf course with the guys followed by my nights with my fiancé.

Life was good.

I had my girl, my boys, and Romi had her baby. I was now the proud uncle of a little girl who I couldn't wait to spoil. Romi and Shane named her Margaret. I was going to call her Maggie or Mags. It was already a done deal.

Today though, I was making Ashtyn my wife. Our entire relationship has been on overdrive, but with all the action we'd faced, making her my wife on the anniversary of us meeting was the best fucking date ever.

Corey was still MIA, so to be safe, Ashtyn and I didn't have the traditional bachelor and bachelorette parties because we didn't know what Corey was capable of. I didn't feel like getting shot again, and with my luck, even with a large crowd somewhere, he'd open fire.

Being at home with Ashtyn was all worth it, though. While she addressed envelopes, we'd watch movies. When she'd look online for wedding dresses she liked, we'd catch up on our DVR. When she was making the seating chart, we'd cook dinner together. And when we were picking our first dance song, we danced on the back patio under the stars.

Life was definitely good.

Especially today.

"Here." I looked in the mirror of the bathroom I was standing in to see Kenny walk in. He was holding a drink. "Thought you could use a seven and seven."

"Thanks." I took the drink from him, took a sip, and then turned back to the mirror to straighten my black tie. I'd rented a suite at the Westin down the street from the venue, and Kenny, Jett, Clark, and I were using it to get ready before heading to the sports museum so I could get hitched. Ashtyn was in a suite of her own on a different floor getting ready, though my executive suite would be used to consummate our marriage—all fucking night.

"You getting nervous?"

"Should I be?"

Kenny shrugged. "I've heard some guys do."

"Not me, man. This is my girl."

"Well, drink up and let's seal your fate."

I rolled my eyes at his joke and chugged my drink, ready to start the next chapter of my life.

Not only had Ashtyn agreed to get married in a sports museum, but it was her idea. My love of sports was rubbing off on her.

The guys and I walked into the Chicago Sports Museum, and we were greeted by a guy in a black suit.

"Mr. Cole." He stuck out his hand. "Congratulations."

"Thank you," I said, shaking his hand. "Kenny, Jett, Clark, this is Matt. He'll be in charge of security tonight."

Two more guys dressed in black suits walked out from the museum. "Only people in there are workers setting up for the wedding, and the minister."

"Perfect," Matt replied. "This is Noah and Liam. They will help me be the eyes and ears tonight."

Ashtyn and I, including her father and brother Ethan, agreed that we should hire security for the night just in case since Corey was still in Chicago. It was better to be safe than sorry, and if that meant I had to hire security for the night, I would.

"Awesome."

"You're free to go in now," Matt gestured for us to enter the museum.

The night before for our rehearsal, Ashtyn and I had walked through the venue and was told where everything would be set up. But seeing it as I entered the venue felt surreal. There were interactive exhibits, we were going to have an open bar, and it overlooked the lake.

It was perfect.

As we made our way through the venue, we walked past tables that were set up alongside the memorabilia. Each table had white linens draped across them, and in the center were purple roses and what smelled like lavender. Votive candles were placed around the flowers, but not yet lit, and each place setting had a place card in gold stock paper with our guest's names written in purple. It was beautiful. The girls had outdone themselves.

I continued my way past the wood dance floor and to the back of the building where chairs were set up looking in the direction of Lake Michigan. A white cloth walkway separated two sides.

"Rhys," the minister greeted, extending his hand.

I took it. "Mason."

"Nice suits."

I looked down at myself, straightening the dark grey jacket of my suit. Under it was a dark grey vest, white dress shirt, and a black neck tie. The guys were dressed similarly, except instead of a black tie, theirs were purple to match Ashtyn's color scheme as well as purple vests. "Thank you."

"Guests should be arriving soon—"

"Shit," Kenny muttered, cutting off Mason. "I almost forgot." He ran back in the direction we came, and then a few seconds later he was running back with a small box in his hands. "Put this shit on your lapel."

I took a boutonniere he handed me. It had dried lavender and a purple rose arranged in a bundle. I pinned it to my jacket, and the boys followed suit.

"Like I was saying," Mason started again, "the guests should be arriving soon. Feel free to escort them all to their seats."

We nodded and went back to the entrance where we slowly took mine and Ashtyn's family and friends to their seats.

Then it was time.

The guys went back down the aisle, and then a slow melody started to play. They reentered with bridesmaids on their arms, two at a time. Each bridesmaid was wearing an eggplant-colored, haltered-style dress that matched the guy's ties and vests. We didn't have a flower girl or ring bearer, so I knew that the next person I would see would be Ashtyn. A different song started to play from speakers, and time stood still. I didn't know what song it was, but the woman was singing about how long she would love the person. The answer was as long as the stars are above them.

But all the other words faded away as soon as I saw Ashtyn.

I took in her white, strapless gown that had ruffles in the shape of giant roses on the skirt. Now I knew why men weren't allowed to see the dress before their fiancée walked down the aisle. They were trying to kill us. Ashtyn was fucking breathtaking, and I literally couldn't breathe as she took each step toward me with her father next to her.

Was this really happening?

I hope she doesn't trip.

I sucked in a deep breath, trying to fill my lungs with oxygen again, but it wasn't working. She was a vision. This was my best friend, and I wouldn't want to spend the rest of my life with anyone else. And I wasn't ever going to.

I was a real lucky sonofabitch to have walked into Judy's that night.

I took Ashtyn's hand from her father's and kissed her cheek. "You tryin' to kill me, Cupcake?" I whispered.

She furrowed her brow and whispered back, "What?"

"You took my breath away as you walked toward me." She probably thought it was a line, but I fucking meant it.

"Welcome, family, friends and loved ones," Mason began. "We're gathered here today to celebrate the marriage of Ashtyn and Rhys. You've come here to share in this formal commitment they make to one another, to offer your love and support to this union, and to allow Ashtyn and Rhys to start their married life together surrounded by the people most important to them. Will you, Rhys, take this woman to be your wedded wife?"

"Absofuckinlutley." Everyone chuckled, and Mason glared at me. "I will, man. I fuckin' will."

He shook his head slightly and proceeded. "Will you, Ashtyn, take this man to be your wedded husband?"

She smiled and looked straight into my eyes. "I will."

I grinned back.

Mason continued. "Does anyone object to the union of this marriage between Rhys and Ashtyn? Speak now—"

"I fucking do!"

My gaze turned to the sound of the voice to see Corey standing at the end of the aisle pointing his gun at me.

Again.

CHAPTER THIRTY-ONE

Ashtyn

Some brides feared it would rain on their big day.

I now feared dying.

I also feared losing the love of my life before we could eventually start our lives together as man and wife. We were seconds away from it being official, and now I was seconds away from learning the fate of this game we were in.

"You've got to be fucking shitting me!" Rhys spat, pulling me to him.

I heard everyone around us scream, and chairs were being scooted across the floor as everyone scrambled to move out of the way. Then everything seemed to happen in slow motion as though I was watching an epic fight scene on TV. My dad, who was sitting in the front row, moved to us while Ethan, who was sitting in the second row, turned and pulled his gun.

"Put the weapon down!" Ethan ordered.

Corey looked haggard and almost strung out. His grin was evil. "No."

I didn't know how he got in with three security guards, but as I took in his clothes, I realized he'd been one of the people working the event. He was dressed in the same black slacks and white shirt as the rest of them.

"I said, drop your fucking weapon!" Ethan bellowed again.

"And I said, no. This asshole has stolen everything from me."

"If you don't drop your weapon, I will shoot you," Ethan stated.

"Do you know what it's like to be on track for a full ride, but then have someone come in and suddenly find yourself benched?"

"He's still harboring bad feelings from high school," Rhys stated.

What the hell? So this had nothing to do with me?

"Yes, I am. I could be in the pros right now instead of in hiding and couch surfing to avoid the cops."

"This is your final warning," Ethan stated.

"I don't give a fuck. It's time Rhys learns what it's like to lose everything."

Corey slightly turned the gun, and it faced me, but before he could shoot, one of the security guards knocked him to the ground. The gun Corey was holding skidded across the floor, and Ethan rushed to grab it.

Corey was now standing and restrained by two of the security guys, one on each side of him holding his arms, and Ethan was on the phone calling 911.

Anger boiled in my blood. I didn't want this man to think he'd ruined my day.

My day that had taken six months to plan.

My day that had taken me seven hours to get ready for.

My day when I was marrying my best friend.

It wasn't the day that Corey Pritchett was going to ruin no matter how hard he tried.

I pulled out of Rhys's arms and moved, running past my father who was holding onto my mother and the people who were still in their seats.

"Ashtyn!" I heard people yell.

I didn't stop as I hurried down the white linen carpet to Corey. His gaze met mine and he smirked. He actually smiled. That only caused me to become angrier. Arms tried to grab me, but I shrugged them off. I faintly heard Ethan call my name too. Nothing and no one was going to stop me. I was the bride, and this was my day.

I pushed hard at Corey's chest and yelled, "I'm going to kill you!" Arms wrapped around my waist, but I continued to hit Corey's chest. "Who are you to show up here? You shoot Rhys, go on the run and now you think you can show up here and what? Finish the job?"

"I planned to kill you, bitch."

"You two haven't seen each other except this year and now, all of a sudden, you have a vendetta against him?"

"Ashtyn," Rhys whispered, and I realized it was his arms trying to pull me back. I didn't budge. I wanted answers.

Corey didn't respond.

"Answer me!" I yelled and slapped him across the face.

"Fuck off."

I kicked him in his balls.

It felt good to see Corey in pain. He tried to double over, but the guards held him upright. Cops started to rush in, and finally I let Rhys pull me back.

"It's over, Cupcake. He's going to jail."

"So much for hiring security," I sighed. At least I could walk outside tonight and not have to worry Corey was going to show up out of nowhere ... again.

"I'll talk to the coordinator and find out how he started working for them."

"Do you still want to marry me?" I asked, looking up into Rhys's blue eyes, not wanting him to leave me.

He furrowed his brow in confusion. "Of course I do."

"What if we still do it now?"

"Are you serious?"

I was. Maybe shock hadn't set in yet, but I wasn't going to let this moment pass. "Yes."

"Okay."

Rhys took my hand, and we moved to where Mason was talking to our parents. "We're still getting married."

"Of course you will, honey." Claire smiled tightly.

"No." Rhys shook his head. "Now. We're getting married now."

They all balked at his words and Mason echoed, "Now?"

"Now," I affirmed.

"How?" Claire and my mother asked at the same time.

I looked around for Ethan. He was talking to the cops. "Let me ask Ethan."

I broke away from Rhys and walked to Ethan. "Can we still get married?"

"We need to get everyone's statement."

"I figured that, but can't something be done? This is my wedding." A tear started to roll down my cheek. Fuck, I couldn't cry. This was my wedding day … at least I hoped it was.

"Let me see what I can do."

I hugged him then I went back to Rhys and everyone. "He's going to call a guy who knows a guy," I joked.

Dad spoke up. "He'll just get the okay from the arresting officer."

And that was what he did. "Everyone will be interviewed on the way out after the wedding, or they can do it during the reception. During the ceremony, they are going to get the statements of the security guards you hired and staff."

"Thank you!" I hugged Ethan again.

"Okay," Mason said. "Let's get everyone seated and start again."

Rhys turned to our friend and family. "Everyone, if you could please take your seats again, I want to marry the love of my life now."

People hesitated for a split second, but then they moved back to the room that looked as though nothing had happened. Rhys walked me back down the aisle, and then we grabbed each other's hands and stared into the other's eyes. The girls and guys resumed their places on either side of Rhys and me.

Mason cleared his throat. "All right, where were we?"

"No one objects!" Kenny stated from beside Rhys.

I chuckled without sound, and Rhys grinned. At least we could laugh about the situation. We stayed silent as Mason continued.

"Let's just cut to the chase, shall we?" We nodded. "Will everyone please rise?" Everyone did. "Will you, who are present here today, surround Rhys and Ashtyn in love, offering them the joys of your friendship, and support them in their marriage?"

Everyone said, "We will," and Mason instructed them to sit back down.

"We've come to the point of your ceremony where you're going to say your vows to one another. But before you do, I ask you to remember that love will be the foundation of a long-lasting and deepening relationship. No other ties are more tender, no other vows more sacred than those you will now undertake. If you are able to keep the vows you take here today—"

"I thought we were cutting to the chase?" Rhys asked, cutting Mason off.

I chuckled because I was thinking the same thing. This ceremony was probably longer than a Catholic ceremony.

"Okay, then say your vows." Mason shook his head and smiled.

Rhys grinned at me, and I instantly became nervous because I never knew what was going to come out of his mouth. And I was right.

He started to sing.

"You came in like a wrecking ball …"

Everyone started to laugh, and I rolled my eyes, but he continued. "Kidding! But seriously, Cupcake. I could sing you every love song written and none of them would ever tell you how much I love you. You're my slice of heaven, my infinity, my universe, and nothing will ever change that. No crazy ex," he waved in the direction of where Corey had made his grand entrance, "no stalkers. No one. No one will ever take you away from me. Today, tomorrow, when we're eighty years old, I'll still be loving you. And I vow to you that when I'm six feet under, I'll still be loving you because you, Ashtyn Valor, are my life and nothing will change that."

Tears started to stream down my face at how real his words really were. Three times he was put in a situation that could have ended with him six feet deep, and just the memory was enough to close my throat and prevent me from speaking.

"Ashtyn?" Mason said after a few seconds.

I swallowed, and Rhys wiped the tears from both of my cheeks, and just his touch was enough to remind me that he wasn't taken from me and he was there standing in front of me confessing his heart out.

"Today and every day, I think about how lucky I am that last year we both thought alcohol was the answer. But looking back, the answer wasn't drowning our sorrows. The answer was finding each other. You brought the light that I needed to see my future, and here we are, about to officially be husband and wife, and all I can think is that nothing can change it because this is how it was meant to be."

I took a breath and wiped the tears that continued to fall. "Forever will never be long enough because as long as there are stars in the sky, I will love you. You may be six feet under still loving me, but I will be right beside you. Without you, I wouldn't be whole, and I vow I'll need you for as long as I'm breathing."

"May we get the rings?" Mason asked.

Kenny and Jaime handed us each the proper rings, and then we repeated after Mason about the rings being a reminder of each other's love and then we slipped the band on each other's left hand.

"By the power of your love and commitment, and the power vested in me, I now pronounce you husband and wife. You may kiss each other!"

Rhys took a step forward, cupped my face with both hands and kissed the ever-loving shit out of me. Then we partied as though nothing had ever happened with Corey. Our cake was made out of cupcakes, of course, and even though it was a crazy night, I was finally Mrs. Ashtyn Cole.

Exactly where the game ended.

EPILOGUE

Rhys

Three Years Later

"I'm going to get you!" I warned, chasing the screaming toddler in a circle that went from our dining room, through the kitchen, into the living room, the entryway and then back into the dining room.

Dylan screamed and laughed his response.

"You better go," I warned again.

"Daddy!" Dylan laughed again. "No!"

I was trying to wear the ball of energy down because Ashtyn and I had a wedding to go to and my mother was coming over to watch him for the night.

Kenny and Abby were taking the plunge. It took Kenny two years to propose, and I was surprised he didn't do it sooner, but they weren't on the high-speed roller coaster Ashtyn and I were on. I don't think anyone was on the ride with us, but I wouldn't change it.

Corey went to prison and got thirty-seven years for trying to kill me. Ashtyn is now the lead anchor for the evening news, and yours truly has eight Emmys now. Ashtyn has ten, but who's counting? We got hitched, and then two months later we were pregnant with Dylan. We're now expecting another. I was hoping for a girl because Romi wasn't planning on having any more kids. Ethan and Carter only had boys, and both my mother and Ashtyn's mom begged us over and over to birth a girl as though I could talk to my sperm and tell them they'd better produce a baby with a vagina or else.

"All right, stinker. It's time to take a nap so I can shower with Mommy."

"Shower. Mommy?"

I picked him up and started to walk upstairs. "We're saving water, buddy, because you're trying to eat us out of house and home. You need to get a job."

Dylan laughed.

"I know. Your old man is funny."

"Funny!" he agreed.

I placed Dylan in his crib. "Be a good boy and go night-night, okay?"

He stared up at me and then started to sit up.

"No, no. Close your eyes and when you open them after you wake up, Grammy will be here."

"Grammy?"

"Yeah, buddy. Uncle Kenny and Auntie Abby are making it official, and I need to make sure he doesn't chicken out."

"Chicken nuggets."

I laughed. "Grammy will make you some for dinner. Take a little nappy, okay?" I gave him his brown teddy bear. "Boo Bear is sleepy. Take a nap with him."

Dylan snuggled closer to Boo Bear and then closed his eyes. I wasn't sure if it was my words, the fucking bear, or the fact that I'd chased him around the house for ten minutes. Whatever it was, meant it was go time to save water.

"We need to hurry," I informed Ashtyn, slipping into the shower behind her.

"I'm ready," she replied and pushed me until I was sitting on the built-in shower seat. "But you're not."

We both looked down at my crotch. "Nothing your mouth can't fix."

Ashtyn smirked and without another word got on her knees and then grabbed my dick. It started to harden right away. She sucked. She licked. She did some flicks with her tongue over the tip, and sure enough, I was now rock hard.

"We're not saving water," I pointed out.

"What?" she asked, my cock popping out of her mouth.

"Nothing. Suck, baby. Suck."

Ashtyn returned to her task, running her tongue along the underside of my shaft. She added her hand, stroking me in sync with her bobbing head.

"Fuck," I groaned and leaned my head back against the tiled wall.

"Mmmm," she moaned, sending a vibration down my entire dick and straight to my balls. Ashtyn cupped my sack and started to massage. I was getting closer and closer to coming, but then she stopped. Without a word, she stood, straddled my hips and then guided herself down and around my cock.

Bareback.

Fucking best feeling in the entire world.

The first time Ashtyn let me go without a condom was on our honeymoon. She'd asked me what I thought about making our fourth bedroom a nursery, and I was all for it. That afternoon—and the rest of our honeymoon in Hawaii, was spent trying to make Dylan. We didn't conceive him on that trip, but two months of trying led to me getting to go another nine months without a rubber. After Ashtyn had Dylan, she got on the pill, and just five months ago we decided to try to have another.

Once you go bareback, you never go back.

Now, as I look down at our adjoining hips, her little belly was sticking out, and pride started to swell in my chest. I'm not much of a crier—didn't shed a tear when I was shot, but the day Dylan was born, I cried like a fucking baby.

"Yeah, baby," I encouraged.

Ashtyn was rocking back and forth making my cock go as deep as it could. Her breasts were bouncing in my face, and I latched onto one of them, needing to taste her. Any part of her. Didn't fucking matter. I loved every inch of this woman.

"I'm close," she panted.

"Me too," I replied and grabbed her ass, spreading her wider.

She moaned against my neck and came as she bowed into me. I was right behind her, spilling into her pussy like cream being piped into a cupcake. To this day, I can't look at a cupcake and not think of Ashtyn Cole, my wife, my soulmate.

Abby was officially Mrs. Kenny Blackwell.

No one had objected to their union, and now after dinner was served, Ashtyn and I were dancing on the dance floor before we needed to head home. The DJ started to play When A Man Loves a Woman by Percy Sledge, and as Percy sang the words that I felt to my core about Ashtyn, we swayed our hips that were pressed together.

"Remember what I told you the night we met?" I asked into her ear.

She pulled her head off my shoulder. "You asked me a lot of questions, but what are you referring to?"

I smiled warmly. Ain't it funny how life changes? One minute you want to drawn your anger away with alcohol, and the next you meet the one person who's your reason for breathing. The person who is the center of your universe.

"I told you that you were going to make some guy really happy one day. And you know what?"

"What?"

"You have."

The End.

*Keep reading for a sneak peek of *By Invitation Only* by Kimberly!

NOTE FROM THE AUTHOR

Dear Readers,

I hope you've enjoyed *Use Me*. If you would be so kind to leave a review where you'd purchased this book as well as Goodreads, I would greatly appreciate it. Honest reviews help other readers find my books and your support means the world to me.

Please subscribe to either my blog, newsletter or both to stay up-to-date on all of my releases. You can find the links on my website at WWW.AUTHORKIMBERLYKNIGHT.COM. You can also follow me on Facebook at WWW.FACEBOOK.COM/AUTHORKKNIGHT.

Until we meet again, friends.

Kimberly

ACKNOWLEDGMENTS

I always start with my husband because he's the one that has supported me through this journey. This past year you've worked your butt off so I could continue to live my dream. I'm thankful each day that eHarmony matched us all those years ago. I love you, you know?

To my editor, Jennifer Roberts-Hall: You're the best! I know that was short and sweet, but it's true! You just know how to make me better.

To my best friend, Lea Cabalar: Thank you for doing my grunt work so I have time to write! I miss you! Girl's trip soon?

To Cristiane Saavedra: Thank you so much from the bottom of my heart everything you do for me. You truly are a friend and so happy that a fictional character brought us together. Can't wait to meet you in person in June.

To my alpha betas, Carrie Waltenbaugh, Kerri McLaughlin, Kristin Jones, Stacy Nickelson and Stephanie Brown: Thank you so much for all the hours you put into making this story the best possible story and telling me my ideas suck when they did. Truly, I couldn't have written this book without you all.

To my betas, Jill and Keri: Thank you for making sure the story made sense. I appreciate the time it took you and the feedback!

To all the bloggers who participated in my cover reveal, release day blitz and review tour, thank you! Without bloggers, I have no idea where I would be. You've all taken a chance on me and my books time and time again, and I can't tell you how much I appreciate it.

To Richard Allen, Veronica Eichman and Lindsey Wheeler: Thank you for letting my pick your brains to get the story as close to reality as possible.

To Jeremy Roenick: I hope you don't mind me using you in my book. You'll probably never read it, but just know that I'm thankful to have seen you play.

And finally, to my readers: Thank you for believing in me and taking a chance on my books again and again. Without you guys, I wouldn't still be writing and living my dream.

BOOKS BY KIMBERLY KNIGHT

Club 24 Series – Romantic Suspense

Perfect Together – The Club 24 Series Box Set (Books #1-6)

Halo Series – Contemporary Romance

Saddles & Racks Series – Romantic Suspense

By Invitation Only – Erotic Romance Standalone

Use Me – Romantic Suspense Standalone

And more …

ABOUT THE AUTHOR

Kimberly Knight is a USA Today Bestselling Author who lives in the mountains near a lake with her loving husband and spoiled cat, Precious. In her spare time, she enjoys watching her favorite reality TV shows, watching the San Francisco Giants win World Series and the San Jose Sharks kick butt. She's also a two time desmoid tumor/ cancer fighter that's made her stronger and an inspiration to her fans. Now that she lives near a lake, she's working on her tan and doing more outdoor stuff like watching hot guys waterski. However, the bulk of her time is dedicated to writing and reading romance and erotic fiction.

WWW.AUTHORKIMBERLYKNIGHT.COM

WWW.FACEBOOK.COM/AUTHORKKNIGHT

TWITTER.COM/AUTHOR_KKNIGHT

PINTEREST.COM/AUTHORKKNIGHT

Follow her on Instagram: **KIMBRULEE10**

BY INVITATION ONLY

BY

Kimberly Knight

CHAPTER ONE

Peyton

"So, this bitch gets in my face and demands I tell her what the *fuck* I'm doing with her man. *Demands*! Who the fuck is she, thinking she can demand I tell her shit?"

"And let me guess. You need an attorney now?" I took a sip of my cosmo.

My best friend Lorelei, and I had gone to the bar down the street from our work that we frequented almost every Friday night and sometimes for happy hour during the week. Rick's was everything you would expect from a bar in Beverly Hills. The food was great, the atmosphere was on point, and the drinks were always perfect and made with the best liquors. But what set Rick's apart from other bars in the area, and what kept Lorelei and I coming back, was the vodka tasting room.

It wasn't just a room. It was a walk-in glass freezer designed solely for vodka in its purest form. They gave out faux fur coats to wear in the twenty-eight degree box, and a vodka expert spent around fifteen minutes giving tastings and information regarding the hundred or so different vodkas that were lined along white leathered shelves. It was a neat experience. Lore and I had only done it once, but since it was a glass case, we watched people do it all the time.

Lorelei waved me off. "No, I don't need an attorney. Before I could do anything, Tom got in her face and told her to back the fuck up."

"Oh. Does *he* need a lawyer now?"

"No." She rolled her chocolate brown eyes. "You don't even practice criminal defense."

"Fine," I agreed. "Continue."

"This chick burst into tears. *Tears*! In the middle of the club."

"Wow …" I breathed, flipping my long, dark hair over my shoulder. "Why did she cry?"

Lore shrugged. "I guess they recently broke up and she's still in love with him. Funny thing, I don't care. I'm never going out with that dude again. I don't need that shit in my life."

I chuckled. "Gotta love online dating."

"Right?" She took a sip of her cosmo. "And what guy takes a girl to a club on their first date? I mean, I like to dance and drink as much as the next girl, but I'm not putting out unless they at least feed me."

"You're too much." I laughed.

"That's why you love me." She grinned and smoothed her hair down.

"I love you because you save my ass on a daily basis."

"I do save your ass daily," she agreed with a laugh.

We had been working for a family law firm in Beverly Hills for over five years. We met the day she was hired by Chandler & Patterson, LLP as my paralegal. She was my eyes to make sure I didn't screw up any pleadings, and my paper pusher, making sure my client files are in date order and pristine—among other things. And she's my best friend. Some firms frowned upon attorneys friending "lower" colleagues, but not C&P. When an assistant worked well with the person they were assisting, it was like a well-oiled machine.

Chandler and Patterson was a high-profile law firm that represented well-known famous actors/actresses, directors, musicians or other people in the limelight getting divorced and/or had custody issues. Given our clientele, we also specialized in prenuptial agreements and tried to do mediation when we could. Most of our clients didn't want the public to know what was going on in their marital lives.

I got into law because of my father. Before he retired, he was a criminal defense attorney for twenty plus years, and then a judge in Los Angeles. I wanted to follow in his footsteps, and while I didn't practice criminal defense, my ultimate goal was to become a family law judge one day.

"So, did the chick leave or what?" I was interested in hearing the end of the story since my dating life was shit. Shit meaning I went on dates that never led anywhere. I either didn't like the dude, or once he found out what I did for a living, it turned him off because he assumed I'd take him for all he was worth if we ever got a divorce in the end. Sure I knew what to do and what not to do when it came to the financial aspects of a marriage, but not all marriages ended in divorce. Needless to say, those guys weren't the right ones for me.

Lorelei snorted. "I don't know. She ran off crying, and I didn't see where she went. Tom bought me a few more drinks, we danced, and then I went home."

"Alone?" I smirked.

She furrowed her eyebrows. "Yes, *alone.* The guy had no potential. He was cute and all, but I don't have time for girlfriend drama. I'm too old for that shit." I was two years older than her thirty, so I was too old for that shit too.

"At least you have men interested in you."

"Pey," Lorelei leaned forward and grabbed my hand, "you have men interested in you. You're just not interested in them."

It was my turn for my eyebrows to raise. "No, I don't." I knew that wasn't exactly true. I was picky.

She blinked slowly, shaking her head as if she couldn't believe what I'd said. "See that guy over there?" She nudged her head at the bar.

I turned and saw a guy with a buzzed head of brunette hair, dressed in jeans and a button-down blue shirt, looking our way. "Yeah?"

"He's been staring at you for the last twenty minutes."

"He's staring at you," I argued.

"Um, no."

I looked at the guy again, and he raised his tumbler. I turned back to Lorelei. "Okay, so maybe he *is* looking at me, but only because it's a Friday night and he wants to get laid."

"And?" She chuckled.

"I'm not into that kinda thing. I want to be fed, too."

We both started laughing, and I turned to look at the guy again to see if he was still looking at me. He was, but he scowled then looked away.

"Aw, he thinks we're laughing at him."

I shrugged. "Good, he'll stop staring."

"We're fucking bitches."

I nodded. "We are. But I came to have a drink with my friend after work. I didn't come here to have a one-night stand."

"Maybe you need one."

I turned my head slightly and narrowed my eyes. "What?"

"You're so wound up because of work. I get it, it's stressful, but that's more of a reason to get laid."

"Well, not with *that* guy." I waved my hand in the direction of the poor dude.

A smile spread across her ruby lips. "Well, let's find you one."

My Uber driver dropped me off at the front door of my building, and after taking the elevator up to my floor, I stumbled out three sheets to the wind. Lorelei and I had drunk one too many cosmos—*five if I remember correctly.* And because we were in our own world, gossiping and people watching, we didn't find me a guy to go home with. That wasn't really my thing, though. Plus a lot of the men who frequented Rick's were lawyers, and I didn't want to get involved with someone I had cases against. That could get messy, and it was unethical. If attorneys did get involved with each other, they needed to inform their clients, and then one of the attorneys would need to withdraw from the case so it wasn't a conflict. Who wanted to do that for a one-night stand? Not me.

As I passed my neighbor's place, I placed my hand on the door wishing he'd open it, pull me in and fuck me. *If* I were to have a one-night stand, I wanted it to be with my sexy neighbor. Apparently, a lot of women had lived out that fantasy. I heard him all the time enjoying the company of those women, and each of them sounded different. I giggled to myself as I stood outside his door, remembering some of the things I'd heard.

"Did you get that lamp at Target?" one woman had asked between moans. "I'm gonna fuck you hard!" another woman had shouted. At first, I'd thought it was Sam shouting because it sounded like Batman's deep growl. And another that had me laughing so hard was, "You like that, you saucy biscuit?" Where Sam found these women was beyond me. And the ones who moaned over and over *and over* annoyed the fuck out of me. I wasn't sure if it was because he was that good in bed or they thought their screams were sexy.

And every time I wished it were me.

Since I was buzzed, I wanted more than just a quickie with my vibrator tonight, but my neighbor didn't open his door, so I carried my drunk self to my condo. Thinking about it, I should have had that guy with the shaved head at Rick's buy me my drinks and take me home. At least I wouldn't be pining over my neighbor, who didn't even know I existed.

That wasn't true.

Sam knew I existed, but only that I was the girl next door. We'd never said more than two words to each other in the three years that we'd been neighbors. Maybe he had a rule about not eating where he shits or, in this case, fucking his neighbors. Maybe he thought I had a man. Or maybe he thought I was ugly. I never saw the women he brought home (only heard them), so maybe he only screwed supermodels who talked like superheroes or had a thing for comfort food.

After stripping my clothes and leaving a trail back to the door, I stood in front of the floor-length mirror in my bedroom. No, I definitely wasn't a supermodel. For one, I wasn't tall and all legs. I was five-five, and I only had normal-sized breasts. Not the ones that spilled over the cups of bras or the ones that needed a push-up bra to even look like boobs. I'd heard the saying that a man really only needed a handful. I had that covered, but no more than that. I wasn't fat, but I wasn't runway material either. I was *normal.* I weighed what was right for my frame.

My desire to be with Sam started to fizzle out as I continued to stare at myself, thinking of all the reasons why he never gave me a second look. And then it happened …

"Yes!" the woman screamed. "Yes! Right there!"

I knew what she was referring to behind my bedroom wall. I'd never seen it, but if the banging was any indication, I knew he was fucking her hard because his headboard was hitting the wall next to mine.

Bam.

Bam.

"Yes! Fuck yes!"

Bam.

Bam.

"Well, son of a bitch," I muttered to myself. My buzz was definitely wearing off, and my hatred for Sam was rising. "You've got to be kidding me!"

"You like that, Nikki?"

"Yes!" Nikki screamed *again.*

I rolled my eyes. *Well, I could have answered that question.*

Sam started to groan, Nikki started to moan, and I'd had it. Before I knew what I was doing, my butt-ass-naked-self was banging on the wall between our condos. "Stop!" I shouted. "Some of us are trying to sleep!"

I was such a loser. Sure it was late, but it was a Friday night, and I'd just let my hot ass neighbor know I had no life because I was "sleeping" at three in the morning and not getting my brains fucked out like Nikki.

The banging of the headboard stopped, and I sighed. It worked. If only I'd done that years ago, Sam might have realized I could hear him and maybe he'd pick a different place to screw them. Like the couch or the kitchen counter. Hell, maybe even the floor.

I started to walk toward my attached bathroom when there was a knock on my front door. I stopped mid-step and didn't move hoping *he'd* leave. There was only one person it could be, and apparently, I'd pissed him off. More knocks came, and I held my breath. If he couldn't hear me breathing, he'd assume I was sleeping.

And more knocks.

"Open the door, Peyton."

He knew my name? I mean, I knew his name because I was a woman and we did that shit. As soon as I'd seen him when he moved in, I wanted to know his name, but of course, I couldn't ask him. That would be crazy.

I wasn't shy. I had to present cases in a courtroom, and all eyes would be on me as I spoke. I also met with strangers every day, from new clients to attorneys I'd never worked with before. But this was different. This was Sam. This was the hot neighbor whose name I knew only because I'd heard a chick screaming it. Of course, that was when I had a glass to the wall and my ear pressed against it, trying to hear what was happening in his bedroom. *Little had I known I didn't need the glass.* But I had no idea he knew my name.

"Peyton, open the door."

I sighed and closed my eyes. Sam had said more than two words to me now. Granted it wasn't face-to-face, but if I opened the door, it would be more than the eight he'd already said.

"I'm not going away until you answer the door."

I wasn't sure how our neighbors were feeling about Sam yelling at my door. It was late—or early. However you wanted to look at it.

Sam knocked again. "Damn it, Peyton. Open the fucking door."

Before he caused more of a scene, I snagged my robe from the back of my bathroom door and threw it on as I made my way to the front door. Thankfully I wasn't sleeping. My hair and make-up were still intact and gave me a little more confidence when I swung the door open.

"What?" I hissed.

He opened his mouth to speak, and then I watched as his eyes traveled down my body and then back up. "I thought you were sleeping?"

"I said I was trying to," I clarified.

"You sleep in full makeup?"

I scowled. *Who was this guy?* "No, I just got home and was getting ready for bed until I heard you—"

"Do you want to join us?"

I opened my mouth to speak, but no words came out. Sam smiled, and then I remembered why I was infatuated with him. He was tall, dark and handsome: the perfect combination. His white teeth shined against his olive skin, and I swallowed. My gaze then traveled down his bare torso, and my eyes widened. I'd never seen him shirtless, *and fuck me*, he was perfect. Washboard abs, a trim waist that connected to that V that drove women crazy, and not a lick of hair on his chest. His lower stomach was a different story, and I knew exactly where the light dusting of hair went.

"Do you want to join us?" he asked again.

"How do you know my name?" I blurted.

"What?" He chuckled.

"How do you know my name?" I repeated.

"Because we've lived side-by-side for three years."

I crossed my arms over my chest. "But we've never said more than hello to each other."

"Do you know mine?" he asked.

I snorted. "Kinda hard not to when the women scream it nightly."

"Does it turn you on?"

"I … What is this?" I asked, moving my hand back and forth between us.

Sam placed a hand on the doorjamb then moved in closer as he whispered, "You weren't sleeping, and are dressed only in a black robe, which leads me to believe hearing me fucking a chick was turning you on. So I want to know if you want to join us."

"But when you came over here, you didn't know I was only in a robe and *not* sleeping," I corrected.

With his free hand, he ran his fingers along the silk collar of my robe. "I've seen how your eyes drop when you see me, and a tint of red spreads across your cheeks. I know you want me, and I figured hearing me turns you on. I want to get you in my bed."

I stepped back, and his hand fell away from my clothes. "You think that I'd want to share you?"

Sam cracked another smile. "Have you ever had a threesome?"

"That's none of your business."

"That's a no. In that case, I'll kick Nikki out and it can just be us."

What the hell was happening? "I'll pass," I stated, and reached for my door to close it.

Sam grabbed it. "You sure?"

I was starting to realize that my fantasy with this jerk was only that—a *fantasy*. He wasn't who I thought he was. I mean, he did sleep with a lot of women, but I just thought...

I thought he'd one day realize the girl he wanted lived next door to him.

I was totally a loser.

"I'm not into that."

He smiled again. "Into what?"

I waved my hand in the direction of his condo. "Being another notch on your bedpost."

He laughed. "Peyton, we've been neighbors for a while. I *know* you want to be another notch, and I'm giving you the chance."

"You're such an asshole."

"But you've thought about it, right?" he asked, totally ignoring the fact I was pissed and had just called him an asshole.

Not wanting to give him even more of a bigger head, I said, "I thought that you were a nice guy."

"I am a nice guy. When I want something, I go after it. Doesn't mean I'm an asshole."

I crossed my arms over my chest again. "Why now? Why are you willing to kick that poor girl out?"

"When you banged on my wall, I realized that I could be fucking *you*, so I came over here to get you. Nikki is down for whatever. If I can only have you alone, then I'll kick her out."

"Have you ever heard the saying too little too late?"

"Don't be like this, Peyton. You know we both want each other.

I'm sorry I waited until now."

I rolled my eyes. "Wanted."

"What?" He tilted his head.

"I'll admit that I thought you were cute. But now I know you're a sleazeball, and I don't want to catch anything. Have a good night." I pushed him back and closed the door in his face. I was definitely no longer drunk or horny. In fact, I wanted to move right then and there. *What had I'd been thinking?* He'd been with countless women. *Countless!*

I picked up my discarded jeans and blouse as I walked back to my room and went to take a shower. I felt dirty just being in the same space as Sam. When I got out of the shower, it sounded as though he was literally screwing Nikki against the wall. I heard what I assumed was her body moving up and down the wall as he thrust into her. Sam was trying to torture me.

There was no way I'd be able to sleep with my head next to all the moaning. Therefore, I grabbed a pillow off my bed and went and slept on my couch.

Enjoyed what you just read? One-click *By Invitation Only* now to read the rest!

Made in the USA
Columbia, SC
05 August 2018